Love at Last Sight

Vedrana Rudan

LOVE AT LAST SIGHT

Translated from the Croatian by Ellen Elias-Bursac

DALKEY ARCHIVE PRESS

Originally published in Croatian by Biblioteka Azbest
as *Ljubav na posljedni pogled* in 2003.

Copyright © 2003 by Vedrana Rudan
Translation copyright © 2017 by Ellen Elias-Bursac
First Dalkey Archive edition, 2017.

Library of Congress Cataloging-in-Publication Data
Names: Rudan, Vedrana, 1949- author. | Elias-Bursaâc, Ellen, translator.
Title: Love at last sight / Vedrana Rudan ; translated by Ellen Elias-Bursaâc.
Other titles: Ljubav na posljednji pogled. English
Description: First Dalkey Archive edition. | Victoria, TX : Dalkey Archive
Press, 2017.
Identifiers: LCCN 2016047682 | ISBN 9781628971668 (pbk. : acid-free
paper)
Subjects: LCSH: Marital violence--Fiction. | Abused women--Fiction.
Classification: LCC PG1620.28.U3 L5913 2017 | DDC 891.8/236--dc23
LC record available at https://lccn.loc.gov/2016047682

ILLINOIS
ARTS
COUNCIL
AGENCY

Partially funded by a grant by the Illinois Arts Council, a state agency.

www.dalkeyarchive.com
Victoria, TX / McLean, IL / Dublin

Dalkey Archive Press publications are, in part, made possible through the
support of the University of Houston-Victoria and its programs in creative
writing, publishing, and translation.

Printed on permanent/durable acid-free paper

1

I'M RIDING ASTRIDE A bucking cloud and lurching about like a drunken slut in a western. Nobody's after me, nobody's shooting, not a saloon in sight, no customers, drinking buddies, cactuses, sun. I really am lurching, though. I feel like puking, gut in mouth, left, right, up, down. The sky is blue. Off in the distance I see a long, thick, red-plastic clothesline. On it white laundry that's been hung out to dry, the wind whipping it along. There's a pair of white feathery wings drying on the line too. Jesus! This is an ad for laundry detergent! I watch it on TV every night. White laundry and white wings drying in the heavens. They were bleached with Mava so they're pure, pure white. The angels use Mava as well. I'm in heaven! I'm gallivanting about in an ad! Riding in an ad?! **Being** in an ad?! Uh oh, now I see! This must be hell! I'm a hell's angel! I'll ride on like this forever and repent my grievous earthly sins?! And what about my defense? Well? Have I been tried? No, I haven't! I'm out in the waiting room! While I wait, instead of sitting on a wooden bench I'm riding this billowy horse. This is a heavenly judgment, I shouldn't be comparing it to earthly court. I'll wait for their summons. And when they call me I'll walk into the courtroom and declare, not guilty, not guilty, not guilty! How did this happen? Your honors, it was like this.

The alarm clock rang at two in the morning. Yes, this is key, I need to clarify that the alarm clock rang at 2:00 a.m. Your honors, in case you don't know, one leaves for the hunt at the crack of dawn. You need to be out in the woods before the woodlands stir. It's too late to go hunting once the birds are up. It was 2:00 a.m. when the alarm went off. He was in the bathroom. I heard him hawking phlegm into the sink. Hrk, hrrrrk.

I'll tell you something about the apartment we were in, him in the bathroom, me in our bedroom. This is a two-bedroom place, all poured concrete. We bought it, I can't remember the year, with a fixed-rate loan, three percent, those were the days, no foreign-currency clause. After a few years the bank wrote off the loan, inflation had devoured it. I remember us going off to the building site to watch our cozy little concrete nest rise. This is a gorgeous feeling, when your home is rising up out of nothing! Ah yes! When the building was finished it had to be cleaned. We ventured into our apartment and watched a worker, a man about our age, polishing the iron balcony railing.

A Bosnian guy. I gazed at the brownish nape of his neck, he was kneeling on the tiles, I committed his accent to memory, he didn't look at us, said only a word or two. You'll never, I thought while I watched him strip the rust from the iron balusters, move into a place like this! Every month you'll send your little remittances to Bosnia, after thirty years or so you'll go back to the godforsaken place you came from and spend the rest of your days there with your wife who never saw the city where you left your life. I hadn't figured in the war. It must've all played out so much the faster for him. How clearly I can see him! He's kneeling on our balcony and with his gestures, as if jerking off, he sands the balusters with steel wool, up, down, up, down. I was feeling terrific, leaning on my husband's stony shoulder. The Bosnian guy rubs away at a prick that isn't a prick and watches us out of the corner of his eye! Ha! Maybe I should say something, explain why I felt so great watching the poor fellow kneeling and scrubbing the railing on my balcony? Damned if I know. See, maybe that matters. It probably says something about me, about me as a person who observes the suffering, the misfortune of others, and relishes it. Oh well, your honors, forget what I said about the Bosnian, erase it from the tape as inconsequential, I killed my husband, what could the poor Bosnian man possibly have to do with that?

On weekdays I had to wake him, shake him gently, my husband I mean, and say to him, "The alarm went off, please, it's six, it's seven, it's eight, please ..." He had trouble waking. He'd harrumph, rise, spit, take a leak, dress, and go. You notice a nervous tremor in my voice? We all piss, we all hawk phlegm into the sink, but that doesn't define us. I'm deliberately focusing on his hawking and the sound of his thick, dark-yellow, rank stream of urine. I want you to form the worst possible picture of him. I want to conjure for you the figure of a vulgar male specimen who may not have fully shaken all the piss off his prick when he shoved it back into his shorts in the morning and vanished out the front door. I'm doing this deliberately.

I killed him. Like all killers I have the feeling that my crime will be less heinous if the victim spits, burps, and neglects to wash his privates. Hey, all killers are the same. They want forgiveness for the unforgiveable. I know you're shrewd so I don't say these words in calculation, I speak frankly, which doesn't mean I won't mislead, lie, tell the truth so it sounds like a lie, and lie so it sounds like the truth. That's as it should be. At least so I think. Each of us is doing our job, you judge me, I defend myself. All by my lonesome, may I add, I'm defending myself alone, obviously there aren't attorneys cavorting around up here in heaven. Yes, I must be concise, brief, clear, with no major digressions, your attention will stray, you'll dole out a worse punishment to me than I deserve, tiresome murderers get shafted because they prattle on for too long. Judges never have the time, they work to a norm, they don't care about the picky details. But murderers like me, for example, I, for one, think the details matter most. If it hadn't been for the picky details, speaking of myself here, I'd never have killed him. It was the picky things that pushed me over the edge. So there you see, right at the start, trouble! I'll keep to topic, I'll be clear. My husband, my late husband, liked to sleep in and when he was supposed to go to work I had to wake him. My husband, my late husband, adored hunting. When he went off for a hunt, he woke me. There you have it.

I hated rising early, I've said as much. I got out of bed, smeared a smelly lotion all over my body to repel the mosquitoes and ticks and waited, naked, for him to come out of the bathroom into the bedroom. Out he came and in he came. "Would you like me to make coffee?" "Yes," I said, it pleased me when he was well mannered. I went into the bathroom, peed, my stream of urine was thinner, quieter, and lighter in hue. I didn't hawk my phlegm into the sink, no, I brushed my teeth, looked in the mirror. A white face, high cheekbones, blue eyes, light hair. I bared my teeth, my teeth were neat, a long, slender neck, the rest was wall. I went back, naked, into the room. He looked at me the way a husband looks at his wife when he doesn't want to fuck her or upbraid her. I mean he looked at me, but didn't say, "Your tits are sagging, you should be exercising, you're too skinny," right?

He looked at me with no particular design in mind, I was there in the room, naked, I was supposed to put clothes on and go off with him to the hunt that he cared so much about, with me, from the bottom of my soul, hating … the hunt, I'm speaking of the hunt. At those moments my husband, my late husband that is, was invariably polite. I pulled on cotton long johns, a long-sleeved undershirt, a dark green shirt, dark green pants, thick knee socks, and padded—shoeless—into the kitchen. I sat at the table. He came in after me, made the coffee, looked me in the eye. A smile, lips wide, beautiful dark-gray eyes, handsome. We put our shoes on in the hallway, took our jackets, knapsacks and guns, softly, softly. We went out, got into the car, left. We drove and drove, some sixty kilometers. There were no cars or trucks on the road. We went off the road and took a dirt road another ten kilometers, parked, got out of the car, spread a blanket, sat.

"Listen to the woods," he said, "listen." I sat on the blanket, leaning on the car, I sat very still, I knew I must be quiet, "Listen to the woods" doesn't mean I'm allowed to say, "I'm listening, I don't hear a thing even though I'm all ears, I'm sleepy, I don't like the woods." No, no, there I sat and listened, I closed my eyes, like, I'm listening to the woods. Leaves may have rustled, branches may have snapped, an owl probably hooted, that's its job at 3:00 a.m., it was munching on some poor mouse. That I didn't hear. I sat there quietly and made a superhuman effort to keep from dozing off. Once I did doze off, I didn't want that to happen again.

"You fell asleep," he said that time. When I closed my eyes it was night, when I opened them, day. I couldn't claim I hadn't been dozing. "Why do you come out for the hunt if you don't like it?" "I like it fine," I said. "I like it so much, I was probably sleepy or it was quiet," I said. "The woods are never quiet," he said, "the woods are alive, the woods have a life of their own, a person must love the woods to be able to listen properly, there are people who don't care for the woods." "I love the woods," I said quickly, I got fidgety when we parsed my wrong moves. "Do you want us to go back?" "No," I said, "no, no, it's day now, let's go ..." We got up, I think, that morning when I'd dozed off in the woods, climbed a tree and waited for wild boars and waited for wild boars and waited … Or does it just seem it was boars we were waiting for? They didn't come, yet they were supposed to be there, we knew they'd been rooting around there for acorns. It was probably an oak we were sitting in, I'm thinking of the morning I dozed off in the woods, acorns grow on oaks. He was holding a hunting rifle called a bokerica, a bokerica is an expensive, nasty gun. If boars had come they wouldn't have stood a chance. He'd kill one, we'd load it onto the roof rack on the car, the boar's little eyes would still be open. We'd take it to the hunting lodge, other hunters would be there, one of them would be skinning animals, the others smoking, drinking, watching. One of them would use a big knife to saw the head off our wild boar, sop up the blood, and hand it to the hunter murderer. He'd take it later to a taxidermist, the head would be in a plastic, blood-smeared bag in the knapsack. Once the taxidermist had done his job the hunter would set the head gingerly on the back seat of his car, drive it home and, using hefty hooks, mount it on the living room wall. And whenever anyone came into the living room—neighbors or guests—the hunter would ask, have I ever told you how this little piggy met its end?

The murderer was given the finest cuts of meat. The rest was sold to the other hunters at a very, very low price. The murderer was also given the prosciutto. Prosciutto from a wild boar is one of the finest delicacies a person can savor, if that person isn't disturbed by the process of turning a live boar into a cured prosciutto. While they lick their slice of prosciutto, some of them are imagining the grunter under the feet of the valiant hunter on watch on his big fat branch; some have problems with cured prosciutto. I for one. Yes, I see how I'm fashioning an image of myself, the sensitive outsider forced to sit on a branch. Forced?

We spent hours up in that tree, I think, the morning I dozed off in the woods. The wild boars didn't show. He went to the car to fetch a second gun. I waited for him on the branch. He sat. He took aim. Bam, bam, bam, bam. The woods reverberated, birds screeched, frightened, alarmed. Jays dropped from the tree branches. They're exquisite birds, they caw, "Craaaw, craaaaw," their feathers are dark blue, black, indigo. Bright-tails. We clambered down. I gathered up the dead birds and dropped them into his knapsack. The dead birds weren't edible, nor were they much of a trophy, he killed them for practice and then he always tossed them into the recycling bin, the one for glass, plastic, old paper. He'd flash his teeth at me each time. He was picturing the expressions on the faces of the recyclers when they saw there, among the plastic Coca-Cola bottles, the shriveled, gray, feathered corpses of the little birds. He always chuckled when he thought of it. And I'd smile at him when I felt him picturing them. To turn those dead jays into a head-on collision was something I didn't need.

When we came down out of the big tree, that being the day I dozed off during the hunt, he looked at me with reproach and I felt a stab of guilt. Had I not fallen asleep, had I climbed up into the tree in time, everything would've been different. We came home and smeared the ticks on our bellies and backs with oil. A tick breathes through its ass and if you coat them in oil they smother and you can pluck them out easily with tweezers. I'm disgusted by ticks, I can't express in words just how disgusting I find ticks! When you love a hunter, you must oil ticks' butts. If someone had said to me, "Hey, you have the right to say, 'I'm not going into the woods,'" I would never have said, "I'm not going into the woods." So he'd go alone?!

I really liked how he knew what he wanted. I didn't want to let him go off alone into the woods. I was afraid that while he was there, waiting for the wild boars and staring down the barrel at songbirds, he might think, "Hey, my girlfriend doesn't like the woods! Who wants a girlfriend who doesn't like the woods? Fuck life with a woman who doesn't adore dead songbirds!" It was unthinkable to be left without a boar hunter! To be left without a songbird murderer was to be all alone. With no man, no partner, no male specimen, no future father for my children. Not going into the woods would mean venturing out again on my own hunt. This hadn't been my first. I'd grown a little hunt-weary. A hunter at twenty-seven, and then to start again from scratch? What to stalk, whom to snare, where were the best hunting grounds, which rifle to balance on my shoulder, how to love so that the next quarry would always love you back?

This one likes hunting. Not everyone does. I barely got used to getting up at 3:00 a.m. and lugging a rifle around on my shoulder. What if the next quarry wanted to go fishing on choppy seas?

I can't stomach it, I can't stomach it, I hate the sea! I so hate the sea. No matter whether there are peaceful swells, a south wind blowing, a gentle mistral breeze. I hate the sea on TV, in the movies. I also don't like a black sea that roils and glowers at me, the sea between the boats and the boardwalk. I hate the sea! I also hate fishermen! I know there are men who sit at home, watch soccer, read, listen to music. Those are the men I prefer. But, I thought, chances are they drink beer. Beer disgusts me. I had to catch me a male specimen! A hunter? A fisherman? A beer drinker? Which is why I opted for the hunt. I wasn't overly sorry for myself. What did it matter that I didn't like getting up early, going into the woods, hunting? This would be no more than a passing phase in my long life. If it became my only life, over the years I'd come to love the ticks, those disgusting, oh such disgusting creatures, and the hunter would always be at my side.

Love means being able to adapt until your hunter finally strokes your bare behind and says, all done, no more!

When we came back from the woods, if I'd managed to tiptoe silently over the leaves, if I hadn't trod too noisily, he'd treat me to his prick. This was a splendid feeling. I was a good dog, I got my bone. How is it, being a dog? This isn't a question for philosophy. If you love someone you're the dog, if you don't love them, you're the master. How to stop being the dog and start being the master? The question makes sense if the dog longs to be the master and the master the dog. This is unlikely. How to be the master and yet love? How to be the dog and not love? Can two masters cohabit? Two dogs? What kind of crazy connection would that be?! Both dogs love fetching a stick. Who's going to throw the stick? So many weird questions! There has to be someone to throw the stick! For a relationship you need both dog and master. That's how it seemed to me until I figured out I wasn't up to chasing sticks. I didn't want to be a mistress. I wanted to break free of that story. Break free, simple as that. The story of my life is a story of breaking free.

Years matter, but from a celestial perspective, while I'm riding astride this foul billow I can't think in earthly terms. When, how, why, who, justice, guilt, sin, crime, innocence. The dead have the right to their truth. This may be the alibi of a foxy dead slut who even in the sky feels an earthly need to lie and portray herself in a favorable light. Dear god, can the dead stop being human? If I were different, if I weren't what I was on earth, this story would be more objective. Somehow I feel I'm myself in the sky while I'm riding here astride the cloud and preparing for judgment, I'm the old me, the earthly me, and not altogether credible. How terrible is that, what a nasty feeling when you're dead and still you feel you ought to be making a good impression! If we feel the need to lie even after death, what is life? I'd thought death was all about vanishing and silence. It's not, I seem to be talking, talking, speaking, speaking, the endless blue universe resounds, the white wings flutter on the clothesline, the laundry ripples. I'm restless and anxious, your honors! I await your summons, I'm scared.

In the kitchen we sponged our armpits, crotches, feet. I'm talking about when we came home from hunting, I'm talking about the time when we were still tenants. My stories are starting to overlap, I should be clearer. I'll try. Once, while we were young and still renting, we went on a hunt. That's when I dozed off. We were living in a concrete row house. Workers' housing. The houses were for workers employed in shipbuilding, housed there with their wives. While the husbands were welding metal plates onto huge hulls, blasting them with light-blue flames, their wives were at home screwing strangers. To me, at least, they were strangers; the women knew them. I relished that, I think, I was glad the women were screwing like that, so I could savor telling my boyfriend about it and entertain the feeling that I was a saint among sluts. All women are sluts, said my boyfriend then, and never, never once did he add, except for you, my mother, my sister. So now I'm talking about us in that little house. I'll repeat, we'd come back from hunting, I'd dozed off in the woods. With a wet washcloth we wiped away the foam, dried with a big towel. We were allowed showers only on Saturdays, in the early afternoon, in the second-floor bathroom.

We often came back from hunting too late for that. After sponging off we'd fuck. My master had this little prick, most of the time he was in a hurry, my movements had to be firm and sharp, I think, when I cradled him in my hand. All of this took some ten minutes, maybe less. It's not that I feel it should have taken a whole half hour, what I mean to say is that I felt his and my quick strokes were maybe not crazy love. Oh blah blah blah. Masturbating?! Those sharp strokes weren't love? I felt the rapid strokes weren't love? Who am I speaking to? Who am I addressing with this shit? Judges I can't see but before whom I'll stand? Your honors who are waiting for me behind a violet cloud? God? He's not around but he'll show up and judge me later? And why wouldn't he show? I'm in heaven, his bailiwick. He also judges people here who don't believe in him! Meaning what, those movements weren't love? Meaning I'm bullshitting, now as I'm going cold.

I loved him, I was wild about him, I could hardly wait for him to reach for me, I'd come at his slightest touch. Now I can lie and say that walking by the side of a tall, handsome man with broad shoulders and big hands was a feeling that was nice, but no better than that! What about my little hand in his big hand? And my head on his chest? And the jealous glances of other women when I strolled next to my male specimen along the streets of our city? And my hand receiving from his the large stem of a violet orchid? And kisses on the nape of the neck while you tie your shoelaces? And talking for hours on the phone? And the tears when he went to Bern for a month? And when he bought me a dark-blue cashmere shawl? And the thick silver necklace at my slender throat? And when I sat at the bar in a hotel, surrounded by men, wearing a barebacked evening gown and he came over and the other men all disappeared when he planted a kiss right on my décolleté? Yes, yes, oh, yes, yes, I can say this wasn't love. Who'll stop me? If this wasn't love, what is? Love is to fall for Mr. Right and live with him until death do us part? Brilliant, yes, that's my story, I was with Mr. Right until death did us part. Why does my helping along the death a little matter? Does it mean our love wasn't true? Now, after so many years, it's fifteen years since we first met, it so happens, or rather so happened … if this ride is the ride of a dead woman, if I'm no longer alive, I must get used to speaking in the past tense …

What a load of bullshit, I know I'm alive! There's no heaven or hell except in the tales of lying priests! But if there's no heaven or hell, if I'm alive, if this is life and not death, why can't I firmly squeeze the flanks of the cloud horse, which isn't a horse but a cloud, why can't I send it trotting into a stable and stop this bobbing and weaving?! I'd tie up the nasty nag right there or leave it to float away and then rest my head on something solid and vomit, vomit, spew till I die, if this is, indeed, life.

I know now that it was wrong to hunt him, snare, lure, cast the net, set the traps, suck his prick exactly the way he liked most, scratch his balls with my fake nails. He was my wild pig whose head I'd mount upon the wall! The neck, the rosy nape with no deep wrinkles, the gray eyes, blond hair, the substantial, tall build, firm hands, broad palms, smile, fine teeth, pure complexion, pale, high cheek bones, sharp chin, light muscular chest. Yes! He'd shine in my movie, sit there silently and gaze at me. I wasn't obsessed with him because he fucked well. No. Sex is technique, you sit in front of the mirror, spread your legs, find the zones, rub them a little, and you have forever resolved the question of sex. All you need for whoever comes along is to show them the points and the moves. Every man who watches what you show him carefully will be a perfect lover. Some prefer not to be shown. They think they **know**, that they know your cunt better than you do. You mustn't tell them, hey, nudge that finger a little to the left down there. Not in your wildest dreams! We women must be Pattons; if Patton was the legendary military leader we have to be Ms. Pattons, guiding his finger in such a way that he believes he's the Patton. And then we moan, don't we, so wonderstruck by his tactics and techniques. Oof! We encounter the masters and military leaders, but what we really need are handymen we can tell, "Lay the pipe right here, boys!" Look, I'm riding on a cloud that keeps bobbing and weaving, but now

I know what kind of a man I need, now when I no longer need one; what I need is someone who'll hear me out, judge me, and get me down off this fucking, celestial horse.

I'm lying! I need a man! This minute! At once! Hear me?! A real man! A Marlboro man! The Marlboro man from before he had lung cancer! I need a cowboy to rein in this heaving stallion! Yes, while I walked the Earth I was a strange woman. I didn't go blithely out seeking boys, handymen who'd ask me, "Hey, toots, do you want this shelf a little to the left or right, up or down, crooked or straight?" Those cheery guys interested me not at all. I needed a walking stick! Quick! Catch! Carry! Run! Come! Crawl! Shut up! Shshshshshshshshsh!

2

WE SAT, I THINK, leaning against the car that day when I didn't doze off during the hunt. By then I was already a seasoned hunter. I'd been traipsing over hill and dale, woods and woodlands with him for fifteen years. We'd come too early, he was breathing there beside me, we were yet again on a special, secret mission whose purpose only he knew, I didn't. In my opinion we were there at least two hours too early. If a fifteen-foot eighteen-point buck had shown up we wouldn't have seen it. He listened to the woods but the woods were asleep. We waited for morning to inch toward us. I didn't dare doze off, not for the second time in fifteen years, nor did I dare lean on him, he would've flinched. At these moments he loathed physical contact. "Hey, scooch over, we're in the woods." Day came closer. The birds stirred, a breeze picked up, chirp, cheep, cheep chirrup, chirp. I expected we'd climb a tree. I'd sit there and hold the gun, I wouldn't know what to do with it, but better have it than not. Maybe I already said so, maybe I didn't, but in the hallway he handed me the gun with the safety off. He looked me in the eye, every bit as solemn as a general handing a folded flag over to the little son of a great, fallen hero. I carried the gun to the car, stowed it in the bunker, we stopped by the edge of the woods. And here we go again from square one, the hymn is played, the cannons fire, the Marines stare straight ahead, people around them sniffle, I'm the son in the little uniform, the general bends over and hands me the folded flag ... But I, I'll have to tell you about this, it's important. When I was young I, I wasn't the little son of a fallen Marine, when I was young I ...

I'm little, little, a wisp of a thing. The square is big, paved with fresh asphalt. The square has been paved for the first time. Cows will no longer ramble through it with the ungainly geese and plump chickens. They're banned by law. Whoever had live-stock either had it slaughtered or moved it farther from the square. We'd already moved our sow, Mara. Mara knew how to drink water from a rubber hose, she grunted, she often licked her lips, I thought Mara was laughing. This wasn't true, pigs don't laugh, nor do dolphins, it's just that their mouths curve up in a grin, an upside-down frown. "Turn that frown upside down," my nonna would say when I cried.

The turkey in the doctor's garden said, "Blblblblblb, blblblblbl." It'd puff up, I'd listen to it and watch it till Nonna grabbed my little hand and dragged me home. And then it was gone. "We roasted it," said Auntie Maja, the doctor's wife, "with potatoes." I wailed. "Turn that frown upside down," said Nonna, "a turkey is just a critter."

St. Marina is the town's patron saint and St. Marina's day is a fête. There are a lot of wooden stalls on the square and behind the stalls stand swarthy, fat gypsy men and swarthy, fat gypsy ladies. We, the children, skip from stall to stall. They sell plaster cats, brown with white spots, dogs and horses rearing on their hind legs, piggy banks with no plug. You had to smash the piggy to extract your savings. Pink gloves, headbands, little boxes with soapy liquid, puff, puff, and bubbles float into the air in rainbow hues. A ball of sawdust wrapped in crêpe paper dangles on a thin, ever so slender elastic thread. It bounces up, down, from hand to hand, until the elastic snaps. Then you cup it in your little hand. All the fishermen from town and men from the surrounding villages wear white shirts and roll up their sleeves. These white shirts are for church-going, for funerals, and for St. Marina's. They're seldom washed. When they're taken off the damp backs and moist necks on which there are still snippets of hair left from the haircut the day before, the shirts are stowed away in the closet till next year or next Sunday. Around the collar is a yellow ring. There were no washing machines back then. Women washed their laundry at home. They drew it up out of the hot, soapy water in a wooden trough, scrubbed it on a washboard, piled it into a tin washbasin, and took it to rinse in the village spring. At a special spot by the spring with a roof over it, boxed with concrete walls, there were flat stones to kneel on. You knelt, dipped your washing into the freezing cold water, it floated on the bubbling, gurgling surface. On St. Marina's day the spring wasn't used for rinsing laundry, on that day—only—the men waded into the spring and pissed into the freezing cold water.

I'm here on the square, a small girl, very small. I skip among the stalls, I've already had a coffee-ice-cream cone, one scoop. The shack where the ice cream is sold is right by the sea, and the lady who sells the ice cream has a soda factory, her name's Ana. When she's at the soda factory she wears black rubber boots because the stone floor sloshes in water. The bottles for the soda are thick glass, clear, or Parisian blue, heavy. "Bring me a bottle of soda," says Papa, so I go to the factory. Auntie Ana gives me an orange drink in a little glass bottle that isn't smooth, "Have it while I fetch the soda." On St. Marina's, Auntie Ana sells ice cream at the shack and doesn't wear the big, black boots. I ate the scoop of coffee ice cream early in the morning, many hours ago, it's all gone, but if I try, I can burp it up and taste the flavor of the coffee and the ice cream cone. Papa sits out in front of a bar that has no name, it's called The Bar. He sits there with his fishermen chums, all in their white shirts, their shirtsleeves rolled up, they drink wine and laugh. I jump into Papa's lap, "Please, please, please, one more ice cream cone, just one more." Papa swings me up in the air and then sets me down on the pavement, the pavement smells like fresh asphalt, this is a new smell in my life. "Enough," says Papa, "no more, go play, quiet now, enough." I say, "Please, please," I flash my small, white teeth, "Gimme …" Then I go slowly over toward the stalls, watch the gypsies and the soap bubbles that float up into the sky with a hundred colors on them. Keti's thin elastic snaps so she's cupping her ball. On the steps to her house her sister is playing with a real kitchen, she got it from her nonna in Italy. Keti's sister even has a little stove and little plates and tiny coffee cups and tableware and glasses, she has everything. I'm not allowed to touch it, neither is Keti. Only her sister. I look around everywhere, left, right. I try to burp up the ice cream and the cone. Nothing, nothing.

I'm sitting on a little chair by the stove, it's hot, my favorite tomcat, Sweet Grapes, is purring in my lap, I'm in first grade, I'm reading a little book about a frog, the book has several thick pages, it's more a picture book than a proper story, there's one sentence printed in big letters on every page, the book's called "Who is Hopping?" About a frog. I already read a book about Puss-in-Boots and dwarves dwelling in colorful mushrooms. Papa comes into the kitchen, his eyes are bloodshot, he sits in a corner of the kitchen, looks at me sideways, I look at him sideways, Sweet Grapes purrs. "What's up?" asks Papa. "Nothing," I say. "What are you reading?" asks Papa. "About a frog," I say. "And your handiwork?!" "Only a little is left," I say, "one more rose and a little leaf." I don't look at him anymore, I stroke Sweet Grapes who purrs. The big tablecloth with a bouquet of roses in every corner and a huge heap of roses in the middle I crammed into the basket in my room, the school handiwork exhibit is three weeks away, I don't much like handiwork. Papa stands up, grabs me by the hair, drags me up the stairs. "Where's the tablecloth," he barks. I kneel down in the room, take the tablecloth out of the basket. "You cow," says Papa, "you lazy cow," says Papa, "you can't live from reading," shouts Papa. "Do something, cow!" He grabs me by the hair, lifts me up off the floor, shoves me down the stairs, I fall, get up, then sit on the little chair. Papa sits in the corner. I'm on the little chair, I spread the tablecloth over my knees, I poke the needle into the leaf sketched on the rose stem. Sweet Grapes lies down next to me on the tiles because the tablecloth's in my lap. There's green floss in the needle, I prick, I prick the little leaf.

Keti and I are lying in the grass. White cherry boughs bend clear down to our noses, white cherries are watery so the worms like them. We don't pit them, we swallow them whole. How old could we be? Ten?

"I'd like a boyfriend," says Keti. "Me, I want a bike so I can ride everywhere and go find my mama and papa." "Silly girl," says Keti, "what mama and papa? You've already got them." "Not them," I say, "the real ones, those aren't my mama and my papa." "Come on," says Keti, "you're so cuckoo, how come? I wouldn't want a different mama or anything, I want a bike, too." "You've got a bike," that's me speaking. "Yes," says Keti, "but it's the one bike for me and my sister, I want my very own." I split open a cherry. "Look, Keti," I say. There's a worm in the white flesh. "See?" "Yucky," says Keti and spits out the cherry, "yucky, yucky, let's go home." My papa's on the square. Who knows what time this is in the afternoon? Five, four, six, a nice day. "Where've you been?" says my papa. He's wearing an everyday colored shirt and ordinary, broad pants. He stands next to me, I see his eyes, they're bloodshot around the edges, he smells like garlic and something else. "Keti and I were eating white cherries and they have worms, we were so surprised, Keti ..." He cuffs me across my left ear with a whack. "You pig, you pig ... Go home, you lazy pig, get to work!" Under the mulberry tree there are fishermen sitting, they watch us. I cry and run home. I'm home. Mama's on the second floor in the toilet. She comes down to the kitchen, I know she was smoking, I can tell by the smell. She always smokes in the toilet, cigarettes called Fifty-Sevens, only a half, she tucks the other half in her apron pocket for later. Papa wasn't supposed to know she smoked, but all of us knew, he, Nonna, me. "What's wrong," asks Mama. "I was with Keti under the cherry tree, Papa slapped me, my left ear's ringing, I can't hear a thing on that side, it hurts so bad, I want to see the doctor." "Go tomorrow, you'll be fine, what were you doing walking through the square any-way when there are other ways to go, you could have walked by Auntie Anica's house, if you'd gone that way everything would've been fine. It's always trouble with you." "I did nothing wrong," I say and cry, my ear hurts, "I can't wait, I can't wait," I scream and dash up the stairs to my room. Mama doesn't ask, "What is it you can't wait for, darling girl?" If she had, I'd have told her, "I can't wait for my real papa and real mama to come and fetch me so I never see you again, never, never, never, never, never! So I never set eyes on you again, ever, ever, ever! Aaaaah ..."

I'd take Nonna along with me to my real papa and real mama. Nonna loves me. Whenever Papa beats me or Mama, she unbraids her long, thin, gray braid, skinny as a mouse's tail and then she wails, yooooy, uuuuuy, yoooooy. This is how Papa whupped Mama, he threw her down onto the kitchen floor, on the dark-yellow tiles, and then he stomped on her and red bubbles came out her mouth, puff, puff. There was no phone in town, Uncle Toni was our telephone operator. To call the police he had to climb up on a wooden pole using big hooks.

The police would come. "You'll have to go with us, comrade!" With them he'd go.

I sneak, I peek. I'm in the bedroom. Papa's and Mama's. Papa was going from house to house collecting dues for the Red Cross. In a big notebook with a thick cover are the first and last names and all the amounts. The money is in the notebook, too. Auntie Maria has a little shop, she sells caramels, newspapers, cigarettes, pencils, notebooks, and tin hair curlers. Every day I slip bills out from the fat notebook and buy five caramels, some days even fifteen. Uncle Mario's in the shop each morning. He has this big hernia, bulging, between his legs. "Where are you going, Mario, with that hernia," asks Auntie Zora, his wife. "What do you care," says Uncle Mario. "I know, I know you're going to the beach where the naked ladies are, how can you strut that hernia?" "Oh I can, what do the foreigners know what's inside my shorts, heeheeheehee," laughs Uncle Mario. And Auntie Maria laughs. I wait for my candy. Every morning Uncle Mario consoles Auntie Maria who's in love with Mirko the Policeman. Uncle Mario's also in love with Auntie Maria, but there's nothing for it. He has a wife and kids and the policeman is a member of the Party. He doesn't dare get divorced, the Party would forbid him and so would the president, Uncle Božo. Auntie Maria's divorced, she has a daughter. Uncle Božo said, "Let's give little Meri to her father, a divorced woman who's not in the Party shouldn't be raising a child." Her father didn't take little Meri because his wife didn't want him to, or so my nonna said. "Who gives you all this money, you're here every day," that's Auntie Maria asking me. "Uncle Lovre," that's my squeaky voice. Uncle Lovre's my grandad's brother. He came back from America to die at home, said my nonna. He slept at our house in the little room, he had dollars in a bank in Opatija, he ate fish with all the bones, and never did one stick in his throat. Never once. He kept dollars under his pillow, Oh, Mama would never have taken his dollars from under the pillow when he was sleeping drunk. "We're honest folk," said my mama. Then he moved over to my aunt's and she robbed him. "So that's our thanks," said my mama, "for all we did for him, the cooking, the washing, the ironing."

I wanted to throw the big notebook into the sea, let the water sweep it off, let Papa wonder, where's that notebook, where's that damned notebook, "Have you seen my notebook somewhere," that's him asking Mama. "What notebook?" Mama would say. "Where's the notebook? It's gone."

Too late. Papa spotted me on the square. He chased me. How did I run?! Oh how I ran, I ran! Like an arrow, like a tiger, like a leopard, like a gazelle, like an antelope, like a rocket, like my uncle Antonio's motor scooter. How fiercely, fiercely I ran! Uh, uh, uh, uh! I felt his breath on my back. I'll never forget his breath! Uh, uh, uh, uh, uh! Garlic and white wine. Ooh, ooh, ooh, ooh, ooh. I'm racing! The first stairs. Up them! And Papa after me! Ooh, ooh, ooh, ooh, ooh … I want to stop! I want to stop and cry and say, "Papa, don't, there's no point, I ate the caramels, let's stop, talk, everything hurts, I can't run anymore like this, ooh and ooh, don't hit me, how come, let's stop!" I don't stop. I run up a second set of stairs and to Auntie Mitzi's door, then through the door. Auntie Mitzi locks the door, Papa bangs, bam, bam, bam! Pound, pound, pound, bam, bam, bam. In vain! I pant, I quake.

"Sit down," says Auntie Mitzi. I sit on the sofa. Auntie Mitzi sometimes tells me stories and I dip my little hands into her beads. She has so many beads in dishes, violet, green, gold, pink, pale green, tons and tons of them. She tells me how it was when she was young. Our town wasn't obliged to pay customs so everything, coffee beans, and sugar, and gasoline, was cheaper here. Auntie Mitzi and the other young women smuggled coffee and sugar and gasoline under their long skirts. The customs offi-cers were in a little wooden shed. Sometimes they'd let Auntie Mitzi pass, sometimes they pulled her into the shed. Auntie Mitzi had to lean over and they'd take turns one by one. They fucked Auntie Mitzi even though she had a hunchback. But she had white skin and big, white tits. That's why they liked her and they said her hunchback brought good luck. Some of the girls had babies. The little boys were called Đanfranko, Đorđo, Marjeto. The little girls were called Anabela, Klaudia, Maria. When the war was over, the women would search for the fathers of their children through the Red Cross. If the Red Cross found them, the Marjetos would get liras. Some of the customs officers mar-ried the mamas of the little Marias and Klaudias, and then, when the war ended, fled to Italy. But the Red Cross would find them and said, oh ho, sir, you have two wives, and the customs officer would go to jail. Marjeto's papa was in jail and his mama cleaned our school.

Auntie Mitzi gives me two eggs. I stir sugar and the yolks, she beats the whites with a big fork. With a wooden spoon I stir and stir and stir the sugar and the egg yolks. The egg whites are stiff, when the plate is tipped the egg whites stay firm. Auntie Mitzi lets the egg whites slip into a big porcelain bowl. In they slip, I mix it all up, I lick the wooden spoon, lick my little lips. Aunti Mitzi goes off to Papa, she comes back and says, you're safe, he won't harm you, you're just a child, he promised, he won't hurt you, the two of you will patch this up. I go home, feet dragging, I stare at my black rubber shoes. Uncle Berto made them for me, he has all these naked ladies in his workshop, they have big titties and skimpy panties and they laugh from the wall. Uncle Berto's wife has a gray bun and she brings Uncle Berto tea, coffee, chicken soup, a clean handkerchief. Uncle Berto sweats buckets, he jabs a tire with a spike, drips slop from his forehead on to the tire, drip, drip, drip. Our house is close by, trudge, trudge, trudge. I walk slowly. It's already dark, I go into the kitchen, Papa takes me by my little hand, "Come," he says. We go up the stairs, me first, Papa behind. The stairs are narrow, wooden. And now we're in my room. Papa undresses me, slowly. And now I'm naked. He rips up a sheet. I stand and watch. The door is closed. He ties me to my bed. I'm bound. Papa pulls the belt out of his pants. He beats me with the belt, he beats me with a belt that has a big buckle. On my back, legs, arms, neck, head. He beats, beats, beats. I scream in a squeaky voice, "Help me, Maaamaaa, Nonnaaaaa …" Nonna's in the kitchen. She's probably unbraiding her thin, long, gray, mouse-tail hair. I hear her calling out, "Help, people, ayoooooooy, ayoooooooooy." Mama's probably smoking in the toilet and going smack, smack, with her lips, staring into the smoke and flapping her hands, chasing the smoke out the window, tucking half of the cigarette into her apron pocket, for later. "Slut, slut, slut," shouts Papa. "Nonnnaaaa," that's me shouting, "Noooonnaaaaaa," that's me shouting, "Nooooonnnnaaaa," that's my squeaky voice. "'Papa dear,' 'Papa dear,' 'Papa dear,' you're all 'Papa dear,'" roars Papa. "Nonnaaaa," that's me shouting. Nonna screams, "Ayooooy," Mama waves her hand so the smoke goes out the narrow window. "Ayooooo, ayoooooooooy," and then I'm out cold. Now I'm awake and wet from the cold water and I'm untied. Nonna's smearing olive oil all over me, the olive oil is dark green and smelly.

Now it's summer. I'm maybe twelve, thirteen. I'm on the waterfront. I'm skipping happily, I caught a gray mullet! Gray mullets are so hard to catch. They have thick, fat lips, they writhe around on the lure, they fumble with their lips, they wriggle free of the lure, you don't see how, suddenly the lure is bare, I caught me a gray mullet! The fishermen are sitting under the mulberry tree, they watch me and laugh, they say something to Papa, Papa comes over, "Go home, put clothes on, cow, no colony this year, cow!" I drop the gray mullet on the waterfront and race home. I cry, cry, cry, cry. "Aaaaaaaaaa." Mama's sitting in the kitchen, she's silent, she stares at a point that's everywhere and nowhere. "I have to put on another shirt," I cry, "Papa won't let me go to the colony because my titties have grown, ayoooooy, ayoooooyoooooy." I'm wet with tears, I pull another shirt over my shirt. "I won't be going to the colony ... ayooooooooy ..." The colony is in Slovenia, we take a train to get there, our mothers wave goodbye. Then we take a bus to this big manor house, we sleep in big rooms with big windows, the air smells nice, we're all skinny, we're supposed to fatten up, really fat, after three weeks. They feed us five times a day, over our shoulders we toss tin cups full of raspberries or blueberries. For us they bake loaves of bread, big ones, and we play Red Rover with Slovenian girls who are bigger and stronger than us. We travel by bus all over Slovenia, we dance around a camp fire at night, we don't wash at all, we weigh ourselves once a week, if you lose a little weight—that'd be me—they shut you in a room, keep you quiet, fatten you up. Then I look out the big window. This old Slovene guy keeps a transistor radio on a hay stack, music blaring, he scratches a cow that has flies on its eyes. On his ear is an earrrrring! I am too going to the colony, aaaaaaaaaa! "Don't shout," my mama tells me. Nonna isn't there. I'm wearing two shirts, I pull on a third. My titties don't show, the fishermen won't laugh at me anymore, they won't say things Papa, Papa won't come over and say ... With my upper arm I wipe my runny nose.

At the hotel on the square they'll be celebrating New Year's. Just steps from our house. "Please, Papa, please, I'm asking, please, I want to go to the New Year's party, please please, I'm praying to you as if you're god, please." Papa isn't saying anything, he sits in the kitchen corner. Mama's smoking her Fifty-Sevens up in the toilet, we smell the smoke but it's as if we don't. Nonna's talking to Papa, "Let her go, all the kids are going, let her go." Papa isn't saying anything in the kitchen corner, a fire burns in the stove, the water in the water pot is hot, the cat's lying by the stove and farts softly. Stink spreads through the kitchen but it's as if it doesn't. Sweet Grapes is always farting, we're used to it, no one asks: What smells so bad? anymore because we know Sweet Grapes is always farting, there's fish to eat every day. When there's a full moon who knows what Sweet Grapes eats. Mama comes down from the toilet. "I'm pleading, I'm praying to you as if you're god," that's me speaking. "Dear god, what could happen to me, nothing, I'm no slut that things happen to me, it's local people who'll be there, no foreigners, just from around here, I'm pleading with you, dear god." Papa's silent. "Let her go," says Nonna, "it's right next door, steps away." Mama's silent, she sits by the stove, her mouth works, smack, smack. You can hear the water boiling, it's hot, the cat purrs, it's really hot, Papa sits in the corner, saying nothing. "Please oh please," that's me speaking, that's my voice, "Keti, you know Keti, how strict Keti's papa is, when he said, 'go Keti,' then what can I say, he said, 'go, Keti, just you go, Keti, it's right here, two steps away, what can happen to you, little Keti,' that's what her papa said to Keti." "I mean it, let her go," says Nonna, "there's no point to this, do you hear." Nonna's voice rises. Papa walks out of the kitchen into the dark and gloomy cold night.

Nonna says to me, "It's OK, go." Mama's sitting by the stove, silent. The cat farts softly, so softly. I put on a black skirt and a white blouse, I put on my patent-leather shoes, I have no coat but it's close to home, two steps. And now we're in the hotel hall. The table is vast, several tables lined up under white tablecloths in the shape of a letter L. There's a big holiday tree in the corner decorated with balls that break into a thousand bits if they fall.

At the top of the tree is a pointy ball, it's silver-white and dark red in the center. Through the glass wall of the hall the old men and women watch us, they stand on the square, we dance and eat and sing. They wave to us, they smile. There's Uncle Mario, dressed up, you can't see his hernia but we all know it's there. There's Auntie Zora, tall, she has beautiful, big teeth. There's Auntie Mitzi with a shawl around her shoulders, you can't see her hunchback but we all know it's there. Here's Auntie Maria who watches Uncle Mirko dancing … He dances with his wife whom he mustn't divorce because he's in the Party. We all know about that, too. They wave to us from out there on the square and we smile and dance and we dance and dance. It's exactly 11:45. Papa comes into the hall. Broad, grimy pants, the dark-blue wool cap he wears fishing, he's filthy with fish scales, I can't see them but I know they're there. A dirty jacket. Rubber boots. Papa stinks of fish. Pančo, our German shepherd, Pančo bounds up onto the table. We scream. "Cow," says my papa, grabs me by the hair, "No one's smooching with you, slut! No one!" Pančo barks, knocks the glasses and the bottles off, Papa yanks me by the hair. Everyone's quiet and they all watch. I can't look at them, my head is twisted, I feel them watching us, I can't hear the music.

We're on the square. My hair hurts, Papa's dragging me across the square. Pančo's bounding around and barking cheerfully, bow wow wow wow bowowowo. I'm crying and crying, sobbing and sobbing, I can't say a word. "Lunatic," says Nonna. Mama's sleeping, she doesn't come down to the kitchen, I scream, "Looney, looney, looney!" I'm outraged, completely outraged! Why won't my parents come for me?! Why have they let this happen?! They're waiting, waiting! For what?! Nonna unbraids her thin, gray hair, she unbraids and unbraids the braid thin as a mouse's tail and gets ready to shriek yooooooooy, ayoooy, people, heeelllllp … Papa falls down onto his knees in front of me. He cries, "Aaaaaaaaaaa." He says, "Stay home, I'll buy you a record player." Snot drips from his nose, his eyes are wet, he stares at the tiles, groans, sniffles, his hands shake, huh, huh, that's what I hear. I sob, he goes off to his room, changes into a dark-blue suit, he's wearing a white shirt, he goes to the hotel. I'm in my room, I write in my diary, I cry till morning. After the holiday I get a record player.

I'm a big girl now, sixteen, I have a boyfriend. Every afternoon I go to the village spring where we rinse our laundry. At the spring, my boyfriend, this Slovene, follows me in, he doesn't know that men don't frequent this place. We're alone. "You promised, you promised, it's my birthday tomorrow, you promised." I'd promised I'd kiss him. I'm wishing I hadn't. He's tall, skinny, pimply, ugly, I don't like him but he attracts me because he likes me. He's the only one who hangs around with me. "Come out to Sveti Ivan tonight," that's him speaking. Sveti Ivan is the nicest beach, there are a lot of benches there and not much light. I'll come. I sit on the terrace. First Papa has to leave the house, then I will. I see people walk by, I hug my knees, press my face against them and wait for Papa to go out. He goes out. I feel him behind my back, I don't say a word to him, he says nothing to me either, I'm expected to go to bed. I sleep up on the second floor, he doesn't check to see if I'm in my room, I wait for him to go. In the summer he comes home from fishing in the early morning. If the moon is full, he's out at Sveti Ivan. Now I see him on the street, the street is below my crisscrossed legs. He's showered, shaved, and is wearing a checked shirt and pants with a crease sharp as a razor. He starts walking toward Sveti Ivan, I see it from our terrace. It's getting dark, my boyfriend's waiting for me by the monument. Our arms around each other, we walk toward Sveti Ivan. We sit on the last bench where there are no streetlights, the rest of the benches are feebly lit. My father comes along. He walks along at a jaunty clip, cuddling two Slovene women. They're on vacation at the Slovene vacation center. My father's a guard at the vacation center during the winter, he has a dog and a pistol. Father bangs Slovene ladies. They drink something, all three of them, from a small bottle. I hear a strange sound. Hahahahahahaha. My father laughing. This is the first time I've heard his laugh. I wouldn't have known it was his except he was the only man sitting on the bench and laughing. Many men are sitting on the benches, it's summer. They're quiet. And my boyfriend's quiet. Then they sing, the three of them, "Moj očka ma konjička dva," an old Slovenian chestnut. My father has a nice baritone, it's the first time I'm hearing it. My boyfriend, the Slovene, hisses in my ear, "You promised, you promised." I part my lips, for the first time in my life someone else's tongue is in my mouth. A ghastly feeling! I'm sickened, I'm about to puke. I spit out his tongue and say, "Happy birthday, we're done." My first boyfriend mumbles something. My father sips from the little bottle. I'd like to go over to the bench, take the bottle from his hand, lean over and drink down a long swig of alcohol to wash away the shit that the fat, fleshy, sluggish tongue left in my mouth. I don't. The bottle is held by my freshly washed father, my father in a clean shirt and pants ironed with a crease. He may be freshly washed, but still I smell his stink of garlic, white wine, and Papa.

3

AND NOW I SEE us again in the woods. We wait, we wait. Chirp, chirp, chirp, chirp. Morning's on its way slowly, slowly, but not here yet. Chirp, chirp, chirp, the birds twitter softly, they're not quite awake, they don't shriek frantic with joy at the breaking dawn, it hasn't yet broken, not altogether.

I used to be a teacher. Most teachers like their job. They step into the classroom full of the need to teach something to the little, or slightly bigger, tykes. They aren't bothered by the kids' smell, or the dreariness of their fellow teachers, or their malice, or the principal, who's principal only because he's the only man at the school. The boys, with their moves, smacking lips, glances and comments, I speak of the time when I was a teacher, showed me that their grimy little balls were brimming with yellow sperm all set to squirt my way. The girls saw me as competition. With my bare legs and cunning, which was, usually, greater than theirs, I showed them I was stronger. In the teachers' lounge the older women couldn't forgive me my firm thighs and bare legs. I pitied them, convinced they'd always been old and I'd always stay young. A nice feeling one loses with time. At the end of the school year I didn't flunk the kids, although Croatian was a tough subject. The older teachers said, you prefer to spend the summer doing nothing. I said, it isn't honest to assign failing grades to children who made an effort. Yes, they did make an effort! Even the prickheads who'd been held back, who didn't have a single book, and all they had of the school supplies was glue and a plastic bag. I was bold, young, brash, sure of myself and brave because I didn't care about the job. If they threw me out I'd have lost nothing. I didn't care who smoked in the lavatories, whose mother was a drunk, who was changing the grades in the classroom register, whether the principal was screwing only the geography teacher or the kid who was teaching chemistry as well. I couldn't believe that this man, who came to school every morning with a lock of hair brushed forward and fanned across his bald head, was screwing anyone. They call his hairdo a flag in the States because, when the wind blows, the big lock of hair flops around. If that gentleman is screwing, if there's any woman who has the stomach to fuck with him while his flag falls over his bulging eyes and his stout body groans as he orgasms, more power to them. What mattered to me was getting my salary at the end of each month. Because I was getting paid at the end of each month I could leave home. Nonna was gone, I was starting to forget her. High cheekbones, thin lips. Sometimes she'd smile at me in my dreams, cover me with a woolen blanket, smooth my hair. She was always taller than me in the dream. I grew tall early, while I was still a girl I was already a head and shoulders taller than Nonna.

I left home abruptly, there was no one to see me off to the bus. The suitcase wasn't made of cardboard, I had a bag, my father and mother saw me off in a cloud of dust, arms around each other. It was like this, your honors. I came home from school. I had on a black turtleneck and a long, black skirt, on my feet I wore black Doc Martens look-alikes, they weren't the real thing but that was the general idea. I hadn't thought about how Papa would take my darker image, I'd forgotten he always needed a little time to get on board with the latest trend. All my life my old man had been saying, "While you're under my roof, while you eat my bread, I make the rules." I was eating my own bread at that point and wearing my skirt. I came into the kitchen, the old man was sitting in the corner, the stove was hot. The silence could be sliced with a knife. My mother looked me over, frozen in fear that I might say something. There was no talking in our house when the old man sat in the corner, and he was always sitting in the corner. Only the shortest sentences were allowed to cut the air. "Soup!" "Bread!" "Salt!" "More salt!" "Cold soup." "Pass the wine!" "Sit up!" "No elbows on the table!" "Straighten your back!" "No talking with food in your mouth." We never sat at the table together. I'd dine alone when I got back from school. Father ate at one o'clock, alone. Mother ate at a different time every day, the dish on her knees, never at the table. I sat by the stove and leafed through the paper. "People are stopping me," he said. We said nothing. He wasn't drunk, just in a foul mood. His eyes were dark gray, glowering. "People are stopping me," he repeated. We said nothing. "People are laughing at me," he shouted and pounded the wooden table with his fist. It would've been funny if my father had been Mastroianni in some Italian movie. The paterfamilias raging for no reason, the two little women quaking with fear, the movie theater—with laughter. What did the younger woman do? Older women never do anything anyway, they just cringe their whole lives? I stared at the newspaper, poised like a gun at the ready, I already knew what a gun at the ready looked like. Mother wiped her hands with a kitchen towel. Wipe, wipe, wipe, wipe. "You look like a slut!" I stared him right in the red-rimmed, dark-gray eyes. I set the newspaper down in my lap. "Who looks like a slut?" "Stop," said mother, "stop, quiet, quiet, you're always starting things." "Who started, I didn't start! I'm sitting, reading the paper, minding my own business. Why don't you say anything to him?" "Talk to me slut!" "Fine, I'm talking to you, who's a slut, you ape?" He looks at me, caught a little off guard. I, too, was startled by the "ape." Mother cringed, clutched the towel with both hands, froze, and stared at the kitchen tiles, her back to Father, her side to me. "You look like a slut! People are laughing at me, they stop me on the street, 'Did a friend of your daughter die?' they ask, 'who's she mourning for in black to the floor?!' First you flaunt your cunt, now you're joining a monastery! Make up your mind, what are you, a slut or a nun?" "Monasteries are for monks," I said. "Nuns go to convents." "What will you be, a slut or a nun," he repeated. "A slut, I'll be a slut, like your sister who croaked of syphilis at the Trieste brothel, if you like. Long skirts are so much more enticing, a surefire boner for anyone who sees me," I stared straight at those bloodshot rims. He rose from the table, wordless, I got up too. He came over to me, we didn't often stand one next to the other, but I'd have picked out his stink of garlic and white wine from a thousand stinks. His breath hit me. He grabbed me by the chest. I felt his arms, hands, palms, fingers on my breasts. His mouth was open, wads of spittle along the lips. He lifted me into the air, carried me out to the hallway and smashed me into the glass cupboard doors. I was amazed at his strength. The glass came raining down onto my head, blood blinded me, glass all over my arms. And shoulders and head. This may sound pitiful, oh so pitiful, but everything went dark. Everything really did go dark. I might have thought I'd blacked out and that was why everything went dark. But I didn't, I knew I was conscious and the dark was my black consciousness. Beside, yet inside, myself. What's called "going dark" looks precisely like "going dark." You go into darkness, the dark goes, the rage remains. I shook off the glass. My mother looked at me. She was silent, wringing the dish towel. I went over to the stove, grabbed the huge pot by the handles in which water was boiling, I don't remember whether the handles were hot, I didn't feel a thing, I turned slowly toward Father and flung the pot at his head, intending to kill him. He moved his head, it jerked somehow. The pot hit him squarely in the face and pinned him to the chair by the wall. Then, like a character in a slow-motion film, he slid from the chair and slumped to the floor with bloody head, limp body. Mother screamed, "Stop! Stop!" I was completely cold, icy somehow. I bent down, lifted the pot from the floor, waited. I waited. The heavy pot was in my hands, empty but lethal. If he'd twitched the wrong way, lifted his head, I would've finished him off. I waited. Mother watched me. The dish towel was still in her hands. He lay limply, softly, as if asleep. I poked his head with the toe of my shoe. He didn't flinch. I jumped on his soft belly. I jumped and jumped and jumped. Jump, jump, jump! Nothing happened. If he'd been made of rubber perhaps air would have puffed out of one of his orifices? Or he would've burst, pop! I jumped and I jumped. When we were little, we shared our midmorning snack at the school playground. "Want a bite, want a bite?!" Some of us would nibble, break off a piece of roll, but seldom. It was polite to offer, not to nibble. I stepped off Father's belly and said to Mother, "Come on, have a jump, want a bite? Want a bite? Jump, jump, he's done for, have a nibble!" She stared at me, her eyes wide, and shook her head left, right.

I made up that part. It would've been better if I'd jumped that day on my father's belly, jumped and jumped and jumped until his guts started squeezing out through those bloodshot eyes. I didn't, in life I always jump either too early or too late. The guts of all my enemies are still inside them. I went up to my room, threw things into a bag, and left. I didn't ask Mother what happened later. When did the doctor come? Did the old man go to the hospital? How long was he on sick leave? Did I fracture anything? I knew my father couldn't be killed! He was indestructible! Eternal! A fucking Schwarzenegger! I didn't intend to stick around. Yet for the rest of my life I've felt him right beside me. He's waited for me behind every corner of every street, in the park behind trees, in front of movie theaters, school, the radio station, the entrance to the building where we lived, at the construction site of the home we built. He's standing this minute behind that cloud over there! He's waiting! He's hiding and peeking! That wasn't, that isn't a nice feeling! He threatens me from the shadows. Even invisible, he's made me restless. How strange is that, I was a middle-aged lady, forty is a respectable age, yet my papa always has his eyes on me no matter what?!

4

THIS, YOUR HONORS, is probably exactly what you were expecting. That when speaking of my crime I'd bring up my childhood. A person is determined by their childhood, especially criminals. If this is so, keep it in mind. Before you judge me, remember the small, small girl, and Papa who beat me and didn't give me ice cream, Mama who didn't defend me, was silent, the bitch, in the kitchen corner, and Nonna, the only person I loved, who was unable to defend me, she weighed barely forty kilos, if that isn't a sad tale I don't know what is. I could cry over myself for hours, I'm good at it, everyone is, but I haven't the time. It seems to me, if I hurry, if I tell everything extra fast, I'll be able to dismount. Any judgment is preferable to this lurching limbo, unless the ride on this heavenly horse is, itself, my judgment?! Don't! Don't do that to me! "Noooooooo!" echoes through the universe. Say something, speak up! You insensitive scoundrels, that's what you are. Though I may be being unjust. You sit at a table and wait for the story. You evade dialogue with me. You prefer me insecure this way. You think your questions might help me save my skin, is that why you're silent? I have no choice. I don't wish to defend myself with silence, silence is admission. Back I go to the woods.

Morning came. I looked around for the big tree. For years I'd been waiting for wild boars on the branches of that tree, me on one branch, him on another. "Where's the tree," I asked softly. "Pssssst!!" He got up. I got up. He began to move. I began to move. I needed to pee. I always needed to pee in the woods, I didn't dare say so, not in a million years! Peeing, including pulling down my pants, long johns, and the sound of the urine stream on the leaves underfoot. Peeing in the woods is like a siren in a city while planes buzz overhead toting big fat bombs. There'll be no peeing! We walked and walked, I floated. When a little branch snapped under my shoe, he'd glare at me. I'd freeze, then move again. We walked and walked. Bushes, bushes. Twigs scratched my face, I trod in his footsteps to conceal my footprints. From whom? Stupid question. A person in the woods is surrounded by enemies! Tap, tap, tap, let my foot slip into your footstep. We stopped. The meadow was vast. He signaled to me with his eyes. Closer! Even closer! I came over. He crouched. I didn't lean my head on his chest, we'd been together for fifteen years, my head had rested on his chest countless times, this was no longer a gesture that could make me quiver, make my hands sweat, we were in the woods, after all, hunting, surrounded by wild beasts and enemies. We'd make love, my hero and me, his wife, once we'd saved ourselves, when we'd vanquished the enemies. After the war-hunt I'd give him, the warrior, his respite and reward. Now I'm all ears, poised for his command. "The wind's blowing the other way," he whispered, "it won't sense us." He moved his mouth from my ear, straightened up, looked at me. I nodded. The wind is blowing the other way, that means it's blowing the right way, great, wind, we may yet be saved! He moved toward a large bush, I slunk after him. He kneeled, lay on his belly, pointed the gun into the distance. I did the same. I lay there on my belly, gun in hand, and waited, waited. I waited for the enemy. The opponent. Evil would rear its head and I would vanquish it.

That apartment, the one in the concrete row houses, in the workers' housing project where the wives of the shipbuilders screwed strangers, I found through an ad. Groceries were five kilometers away, no phone, no bus line. It was a studio, said the ad, in the landlord's future living room. Half the room, some fifteen square meters, was our future bedroom, the other half— the kitchen. The toilet was in the hallway, the bathroom on the second floor, baths allowed only once a week, and we accessed the toilet through the landlord's dining room. The walls were thin, when Franko was having sex at the start of the street, my boyfriend would get a hard-on where we lived at the end of the street. That's how shoddy those buildings were. It was all I could afford. I had my own key, at last my own key, my little birdcage, my own front door! At the age of thirty-two! He couldn't call me. I mean my boyfriend couldn't call me. Every day, after class— did I tell you I was a teacher?—I'd roam around streets he never frequented, linger in the park, gaze at the magnolias and camellias, come home late. I wanted to make him jealous, insecure, prove to him that I could live without him, that I didn't need him. I read somewhere that men are easiest to catch if you push them away. At this point I still was convinced I must catch me a man. That a husband and a baby carriage are what you need for happiness. I was certain, as I strolled by the side of my husband, no—my man, my **husband**, I'd feel safe and be a happy woman. Objectively happy. And not only would I feel happiness personally, no, everyone would know. People who saw me on the street would see I had the gait of a married woman, they'd know, she, there, that long lanky one, she has a husband, she has a child, she's one happy woman. I felt an awful, awful, hideous need to pound my happiness into the ground, to jump around it in big clodhoppers so I didn't teeter or fall. By the time I was thirty I was suffering because I hadn't managed to bind myself formally to a man. I experienced this as a defeat. It's not nice that I speak of myself so candidly.

Your honors, I realize I'm exposing my weaknesses to you, I should be hiding my vulnerability, packaging up my life story into something charming, romantic, this is so blasé, describing myself as on the prowl for a male specimen, and just a smidge unconvincing in this day and age. Women have changed, no one says happiness means pushing a baby carriage in tandem anymore. I know all this, but is it somehow easier for me to admit that he was the man I wanted no matter what? Why him? Good question. He wasn't the first man in my life, I had them, had . . . Can I say that? Had? I had them, if I did have them, if anyone can possess anyone, screwing suited me, I screwed several men before the last ... Last? A minor digression, the man I fought for and was determined to catch no matter what wasn't the last man in my life. Meaning? Yes, I'd had a few, but they didn't arouse me. No, I don't mean to say they were bad in bed, that I didn't come, not that. It's that they didn't arouse me. I distinguish sex from arousal. He did. I wanted to have him. Yes, **have**! And not give him to anyone. He could be my plaything, my favorite handbag I'd polish with special lotions, buff with a woolen cloth and store in a linen sack until the autumn. I wanted to **have** him! Sleep next to him, wake, hear his voice over the phone, slip my fingers into his big hand, tell him, "breathe on me," and then sniff his breath that smelled like a child's sore throat, I wanted, and—you won't believe this—to swallow him, hold him slumbering there inside me, shrink him down and tuck him into my bra, though I don't wear one, I wanted to walk down the street and bump into him unexpectedly, then go over, wrap my arms around his neck and slam my crotch into his, I wanted to walk by his side through town and shout, he's miiiiiiine! That's what I wanted! I think, I'm almost certain of it, I loved him something awful. I was sick with love. I thought, I know, I know, I know, your honors, you'll say, "you're such a cliché," I know this, but I'm telling the truth! I felt that if I didn't snatch him, if I didn't grab him, I'd die. I wouldn't survive if he and I walked through the world each on our own side of the street! Do you understand me? And then I killed him?! See, see what I'm like? I'm not a piece of trash who forgets everything that came at the beginning. You see, you see, I'm telling the truth, I'm not evading my responsibility. I'm not saying he seduced me. I'm not saying he tricked me, no. I wanted him, I nabbed him!

I admire you, your honors, your job is a vexing one. You listen to pointless stories from murderers who zip from one subject to another, you have to grope your way through a maze of useless information and produce a fair judgment. I'm of no help to you in this. Who knows whether to my detriment or benefit? I have the feeling you'll be more merciful if you hear the story in all its minutiae, but then too many details may obscure the essence. And the essence, no matter how you turn it and spin it, lies there in the corpse of my husband. Is his soul astride another cloud? Is he, too, waiting? Or maybe you've already heard his case?

Fine, I'll get back on track. So there I am, subletting in the row house, living alone, he's still at his folks, I come home late, he's waiting for me there because he has a key, I roam around, I want to make him jealous, make him marry me. Dear god! After two months he asks me if he could move in. Yes, yes yes! See, see?! So do I scream? Fling myself into his arms? Lick his eyes with my wet tongue? Weep, sniffle, let him blow my nose for me, smooth my hair? Thrust his hand down between my legs, see, see how wet I am? Howl and moan, hey, everyooooone, victory! Victory? He capitulated! The male specimen wants to live with me! Wave a V in the air like some crazy sports fan who notices the TV cameras or a fighter on a tank?! I do none of that, I don't want to scare him off. "Gee, I don't know," I said, "talk to my landlady, I haven't planned for this, who knows whether they'll agree, maybe they'll jack up the rent." What a sly fox I was, what a fox! "We both have salaries," he said, "the two of us will find it easier to pay the rent!" Oh, oh, oh! If I act cool enough, if I don't show my mind, if I'm a true hunter, he'll kneel down before me, hide a ring in a dish of ice cream, pass me the dish, say, "lick this a little, let's get married!" I'll be amazed, I'll falter, "I don't know, I hadn't planned on this, a wedding …" I'll pause long, oh so long . . . The pause will be as long as a thread of a spider's web … A long, too too long thread . . . I'll wait for him to repeat it … Oh, oh, oh! The landlady says, no problem, you're here all the time anyway, she doesn't jack up the rent.

All the women in the neighborhood were married. Schoolteachers, nursery school teachers, salesladies, workers, housewives, hairdressers. We'd socialize in one of our poured-concrete living rooms on a Saturday morning, a Saturday when he was off at work. Those were nice days. The bedding airing over the windowsill, curlers in our hair, doing our nails, pinching our coffee cups between our finger and thumb so as not to muss the nail polish. I wanted to ask them, hey, listen, hear this, just a minute, how did you get them to sign on the dotted line? I never asked. That would've raised an eyebrow. They were sick of their husbands, many of them wanted to leave, some were halfway there, they made no effort to hide that the gentleman who parked every morning in front of their entrance was no plumber. Their husbands were home most of the time, forever circling, never letting them breathe, fucking them daily. Lucky you, I thought, lucky you, lucky you, why does mine leave me by myself while he plays basketball, suggests we go out separately on Saturday night, comes home at 3:00 a.m., I find long, dark-brown hairs on his coat and I never say a word. I can't swallow water or sleep?! All of you are married, you fuckers, it's just me whose hand isn't being sought, languishing here ringless, soft, limp like a cat in winter under the warm hood of a car. They envied me my freedom that was choking me and I envied them their jail time that would've given me a rich sense of security. They'd married young, nabbed their male specimens in time, my time was running out. When we moved here we'd already been together five years. I'd thought my life would move faster. I was thirty-three, my prey was still a hunter. He strolled around distant, strange forests, sniffed, licked. As if I were no hunter I lay and waited for him to stab me with a knife! I was carrion, rotting on that vast meadow. A fox, a bear, a seagull, an eagle, a hawk, a vulture would amble right by me …

Hey! Up in the air! Pregnancy! Yes, pregnancy! Good old pregnancy! After sex, you're supposed to lift those legs up into the air so the sperm doesn't drain away, hold them there for minutes, ten at least. I straightened my back, "I need exercise, sex makes me hyperactive," I said. Or I'd wait for him to fall asleep, then up went the legs and I'd hold them in the air until he woke. Hallelujah, hallelujah, I sang when the gynecologist said, "Do you want to keep the pregnancy?" the nurse watching me out of the corner of her eye. "Of course," I said. "Congratulations, the nurse will explain to you how to care for yourself, you're a young mother now." A mother? Young?! I never actually intended to give birth, I never imagined a child would come out of me, I just wanted to be a married woman, not a mommy! And yet, I'd witnessed the scene so many times!

He's out in the garden. He holds a rubber hose and waters the garden, she arrives, steps out of the jeep, he glances over at her, distracted, taking care not to spray the golden retriever, the dog winds around his legs, she comes over, whispers in his ear, he gazes at her, the rubber hose drops from his hand, the dog suddenly leaps back, shakes its fur, water droplets in the air, he swings her up then slowly lets her down, she's pregnant, this woman with a flat belly, his eyes full of tears of joy, yes, yes, yes! I should've gone to my man, gone home to the row house that wasn't mine, still under construction, we had no bathroom, except once a week, we washed in the kitchen, we had our own toilet, sometimes the landlord used it for a shit because he doesn't feel like going upstairs, we mainly peed in the kitchen sink, we had no dog, the houses in our neighborhood had a postage-stamp garden, the local dogs and cats were always ending up under the wheels of cars, no one watered the flowers with a hose, there were no flowers, not a single woman drove a jeep, I had a drivers' license but I didn't know how to drive, I didn't dare whisper the joyous news in his ear, his ear wasn't poised to hear the news, and even if he were to toss me into the air who knows where I'd fall, there was a narrow street in front of the house with cars buzzing by, he couldn't stop the traffic to toss me into the air, the house had seven-foot ceilings, he could only lift me up warily, otherwise my head would knock against the ceiling, the couple in my film were married, I wasn't his wife, I wasn't his wife, I was nobody's wiiiiiiiife!

Our dialogues should be ringing in my ears. I answered many questions. "Why did you go off the pill?" "I didn't, I forgot to take it." "What's the point in having a child, we have no place of our own, who knows when we'll get one? Have you thought about an abortion?" "Yes, I have," I answered quickly, "the doctor told me it could be dangerous." "Everyone gets abortions these days and they manage, this isn't the Middle Ages." He looked at me, his eyes were a little lighter, gray, but a different gray nuance, pale gray. "I'm not getting an abortion," my voice was firm. "I don't think having my child has anything to do with you, giving birth is my choice, why are you trembling?" "I'm not trembling,

I'm a father, if, indeed, I am the father," he added. Is he mess-
ing with me or does he mean this? "If, indeed, I am the father,"
he repeated. "We're not talking about whether or not you're the
father, we're talking about abortion. I'm allowed to decide about
my own body!" "This isn't fair," he looked down at his hands,
"suddenly your bulging belly is yours alone and I have nothing to
do with it?" "You do, but you don't matter until you start insisting on an abortion." "I'm not insisting," he looked at me with
his light-gray eyes, "I'm suggesting." "Your suggestion is denied,"
I looked down at my own hands, "this is where this story ends.
If it doesn't suit you there are two doors. One goes to the garden
and out to the street, and the other into the yard and out to the
street. Sit in your car and drive away." I was amused by the new
woman I'd turned into who would've rather died than talk this
way before. "Well, well," he looked at me with those light eyes,
"you think it's easy going through life with a child born out of
wedlock, the world hasn't changed much." "Leave that to me.
This child happened to me, I didn't plan for it." I really shone.
"I won't flush it down the toilet just because you think that'd be
better for me, why are you so concerned about me all of a sudden?" "Better for both of us!" "You and I are not a we, you are
you and I am I, why think that the two of us are a we?" "We've
been together for years, we'll have a child ..." "I'll have a child,"
I interrupted him, "we aren't having anything. Don't you ever
treat me like something you created, I am I, distinct from you,
remember that?" I was speaking so well! So we got married. A
wedding! The day of my greatest victory! I don't remember anything! Why does a person remember only the battles lost? Oh,
you'll say, you, celestial judges, when they take me in to you, the
celestial cops, how boring a story this is, no plot, no sharp, pithy
repartee, pick things up a bit, ma'am! That's because, your honors, I'll say, because my gut is in my mouth, awful, I feel awful

while I lurch. If I could only throw up I'd be saved, I can't, may I dismount, gentlemen? I'm not a believer, your honors, I know there's no heaven or hell, but while I'm riding like this on this goddamn cloud, lurching and swaying, I'm not entirely certain there is no god, so may I dismount, gentlemen? I'll tell you everything, the truth and nothing but the truth. But you'll tell me, I'm sure, your honors, you'll tell me, dear sirs, that there's a crime, yet there are mitigating circumstances.

My belly grew and grew. I loved myself until the moment when it became obvious that my belly was a pregnant belly. At first I was flat but my breasts were huge. When my belly began to swell that wasn't quite as nice, meaning that I was beginning to disgust myself. I felt as if people were ogling me on the street and saying, "Look at her, she had herself a fuck." He began to avoid going out with me. Once I got an infection from ingrown toenails on the big toes of both feet. In November. The doctor had to pull off my toenails and bandage my toes. The only footwear I could manage were sandals. When I went for a follow-up examination wearing a winter coat and summer sandals, I happened to run into him. He was standing there in the company of young women and men out in front of the court. Our glances met, but it was as if they hadn't. He turned away. A strange feeling. Whenever we walked together he'd be either a step behind or a step ahead. It began to feel as if only women with flat stomachs were cruising around in our world on the streets where we walked. My life changed. I didn't go to work, no one came to the future living room of the concrete row house, he was always out, I was at home. This was all wrong! A pregnancy can't be aborted in the seventh month. Had such a thing been possible I'd have been first in line. So I went on playing the happy mother fast asleep at 3:00 a.m. when he slid into our bed. I breathed with the rhythm of someone sound asleep, the way a person who's imitating a deep, fast, peaceful sleep breathes. He'd drop right off and I'd keep watch, keep watch and say to myself, this'll pass. What a terrible mess! What was I expecting from life at this point? What was my plan? Grab a man, bind him to me by a steel cord! With a blowtorch that fuses flesh?

He was escaping me, I didn't own him. I longed to be a happy hunter with a dead bird between my rubber boots. Yet he'd come and go. I stayed. Between his comings and goings we didn't talk. I was pleased that I no longer had to interact with the smelly kids in the smelly classrooms. The landlady asked me to prep her young son for school. I refused. I could hear, there was only a glass door between our kitchen and their dining room, when she was saying, "Toni, now say a, a, a, a, boy, b, b, b, b, apple." The boy would repeat, "A, a, a, boy, b, b, b, apple." Then the landlady would catch the slip and she'd growl, "Toni, goddamn it, a, a, a, apple, b, b, b, boy." And poor little Toni would repeat "A, a, a, apple, b, b, b, boy."

I'd air the bedding on the windowsill, soak the dirty linens in a big, boiling pot on the stove—where did I get that pot?—rinse them out with cold water in the kitchen sink, hang them out on the clothesline in front of the house and sit there watching the white sheets on the line. Why did that feel good? I washed the kitchen cupboards until they gleamed, picked dandelions in the yard and put them in a glass. Whenever he left the house I'd sniff at the crotch of his dirty jeans, look for yellow stains, as if grown men come in their jeans and not in someone's cunt. You're a jealous, possessive cow who can't get used to your ultimate victory, I said to myself. What a feeling this is, snaring a husband! Only hunters get it! You lurk, you lurk, you lurk, the gun is in your hands, the birds chirp, you think, they'll scare off the prey grazing out there somewhere, a breeze blows, and it'll blow in the wrong direction, your sweat drips into your eyes, you'll blink aloud, and then, finally, you shoot, it echoes, the lion falls, its mane bloodied, the birds shriek in a cloudless sky, the monkeys chatter and clap, you get up, wipe your hands on your pants, oh, and the lion, dead, is waiting. Every hunter wants that dead lion, a roaring lion isn't what they crave. You never know whether it's yawning or about to swallow you whole. My lion was alive, his muzzle full of roars, I was waiting, gun in hand. If I shoot at the wrong moment the lion will go strolling off, its muzzle full of yawns and I'll be staring down the barrel of my gun, thinking how I'll have to take it apart, clean it and lubricate it, as if I'd killed, even when I hadn't. At home, with my gun clean, I'll be all **alone**! We didn't talk, we didn't talk. My belly swelled to gigantic proportions. I gave up on myself as a human being who would ever be womanly again. We didn't screw. He'd give it a try, I often pushed him away, I felt him reaching out for me in pity. I became accustomed to seeing the shadow of the shapeless elephant behind which paced a tiger, ignoring her.

I went to an obstetrics ward one day and gave birth. He didn't hold my hand. I'd never have agreed to such a thing. I didn't want him staring at my bloody cunt. While our daughter was coming out he was dancing on one of the Opatija terraces and screwing some babe. "Here," said the midwife, "here's a creature you'll love more than anything in all the world." Stupid bitch! She rested the child's head on my lips and I kissed it, as I was expected to, tears of joy trickled down my face and I was expected to do that, too. I only cry when I feel nothing. They took the child away somewhere. I waited for him. We talked. What did he say, what did he say? I remember, I do remember how he flashed his big smile at the prettiest new mama in the room. Her bed was next to mine. I saw her, before she gave birth, sunny, young, a lithe body. The doctors had thought the day before that she was there for an abortion. That's why they put her in the bed next to a dying woman. She was dying all night from complications of the kidneys, her face was sallow. In the morning they pulled her, dead, out of the bed and wheeled the younger woman off to the birthing room.

"I'm good," said the young woman, "I don't give a shit, just as long as we get out of here alive, holy cow, what a hellhole! My doctor told me I'd give birth painlessly, we practiced hypnosis for six months. Then I go into labor while he's off in Zagreb, the fucker! Hey mama, if we get out of here alive we'll get us drunk as dogs!" "I don't drink," I said. "Who cares, we'll roll a joint, this shit calls for a celebration. Know what my husband asked me? Whether I'd checked the baby's toes to see if the kid's toes were as big and ugly as his? Can you believe the creep?! I had this baby, you heard me, yelling blue murder, and now when my son's finally out I'm supposed to check the kid's toes?! Mama, this is my last run-in with the miracle of life, no way will I ever again let something come crawling alive out of my cunt, no way!"

He shut the door to our room, caught sight of her pretty face, flashed her his big, white teeth, and then dipped his eyes into mine. You can fuck who you want, grin at whoever you want, but only I have borne you a daughter! Soon it became clear to me that birthing a daughter wasn't a sure way into the world of safe love. Even with that I didn't earn the right to lifetime possession of the father of the child. Your honors, your honors, how astonished I was when, several years later, I realized I was the mother of a child whose father no longer attracted me?! This was a low blow!

All people's eyes are wet when they first set eyes on their child, I thought, when they first see their child in tandem. A husband and wife together, a father and mother together. When I first saw my daughter, right after she was born, my tears flowed because the people around me were expecting tears. Obstetricians and midwives are on the lookout for moist eyes because all new mothers cry. And when you see the new baby with its father, you simply must cry. You think he's thinking you must cry, the new mothers in the adjacent beds expect the tears because they cried when their husbands visited. You can't be the only one in the room, on the obstetrics ward, in Croatia, in the world, to remain dry-eyed when you're first with your child in the company of the child's father. A person must follow the rules, fuck the perverts! Oh, those first, epic moments! Patting the little head! Unwrapping the bunting to see those little toes! One, two, three, to ten, one only counts the toes! Ohoho, ohoho, ohoho, the crowing when the baby yawns! "Hello," you're supposed to say that when the little prick perks up and pees on Daddy's tearstained face … Yes, I never so much as looked at the little prick. Oops, guess I forgot!

Your honors, I'm not lying, please believe me, why would I lie, this is negligible after all, I forgot every sigh, every shout in that room, in the obstetrics unit, in the park around the ward, there's something different there today. Clean forgot! Sure, I know, they're always updating old buildings. Fine, I'll try. I'll jump past the smile and the glance he directed at the cutie in the bed next to mine. He stretched his big mouth and flashed us all his handsome, big, white teeth, sparkled with his gray eyes, turned to me, oh, I probably thought, oh, you're mine, mine. You're mine! He leaned over, kissed me on the forehead, I wanted him to kiss me right on the lips, he didn't, I disgusted him, all the blood and all the milk and all the smell of sweat and sanitary pads and shitty babies. What did he say to me? "She's gorgeous," surely he said that, they all do, "I spotted her straight away among the other babies, she has your eyes," maybe he said, "the nurses all adore her because she is prettiest," and he said that, too, but I don't remember a word! Not a word! I only remember what I was thinking. This is only the first step, I'll grab you, this is the first real step! If it's too short, I'll take the next step! I'll catch you! You'll be mine! You'll forget your afternoon adventures, the cunts and breasts of the other women, you'll fuck only me! Only me! Me only! Forever! I breast-fed my daughter, her name is Eka, changed her diapers, got up at night, took her temperature, watched her first tooth come in and fall out. But, but … I had only one plan. Reel him in! Tether him to the fence, let him graze on my meadow, let him be my horse and I'd be the mare who knew how to cherish him. I don't know why I thought horses are animals who fuck only a single mare their whole lives? Because I'm not big on animals. Now it seems to me that horses—the ones that graze alongside the mares—have no prick at all, I've heard something on the subject, and those who fuck aren't referred to as horses, they're studs and they don't mount the same withers their whole life long. The monogamous animals are … Pigeons? Pelicans? Reindeer? No clue. I imagined him the horse and me the mare. Some spiteful golden fish or other granted me my wish. When my horse was by my side he treated me in a horsey fashion. And later, much later, when I longed for him to act the horse, the biggest horse in the world, he played the stud. Those fucking golden fish! Either they disobey us deliberately or we've been wishing all wrong!

5

BACK WE GO TO the bushes. As a reminder, I was lying there on my stomach, rifle in hand, squinting through the sights. He signaled. With his eyes. How did I spot it while I was squinting through the sights? If you're married, your honors, you know. You feel your partner's eyes on you. In marriage one rarely sees, in marriage one feels. So, there I was squinting through the gun sights and I felt his eyes, I looked over, I saw his eyes, he signaled with his lids, I inched over. Softly, softly, ever so softly. Ear, lips. "Release the safety," he whispered. I released it. Click, it echoed, the woods shook. He shot me a scoutlike glance. The guys in the bunker have spotted us, the radio is dead, no one knows where we are, will we make it back alive? take out the men in the bunker? I looked away, inched back to where I'd been lying and aimed my gun again. I was feeling restless. Restless. Restless. I swear I'm not using this restless, restless, restless thing as a segue to the story of how our daughter brought an itch of restlessness to our lives. Although it may seem like a segue, your honors, it's not. I felt restless on the edge of that meadow, poised for the enemy. I also felt restless when our daughter, whom I often experienced as the enemy, was born. Restlessness has many names but always the same face. It fidgets inside you, wriggles, overwhelms you, freezes your brain, clenches your teeth, hands, gut, propels your heart rhythm into syncopation, raises the hairs on your scalp, sends sweat dripping down the nape of your neck, stretches your lips into a big grin, nudges you to hilarity and tears. My restlessness was sometimes a cry from my daughter during the night, her smile when I had no smile left, and her wide-awake gaze as my eyelids drooped. Yes, my daughter brought restlessness to our lives.

He was often angry, I think, yes, angry. "Why take out a loan to install a phone, who told you to sign the order, who are you anyway?" "Look, we had this chance to get a phone connection though we're only subletters, the landlord arranged it, when we move out he'll take the number for himself, we can pay it off in installments so why not?" "Who needs a phone, who will you call, you have one at school, I have one at work." "Are you crazy?" my hands shook, "our girl will be starting school, she'll be alone at home. When Eka starts first grade …" "When Eka starts first grade! Eka's an infant, what if she never starts first grade?!" We looked at each other. "Whoa, man … you really are a nutcase," this scared me. He was sitting at the table, I, standing by the sink. "Who's a nutcase?" he got up and came over to the sink. He snarled and glanced over at the glass door that divided our kitchen from the landlord's living room. Then he remembered the landlord was away in Slavonia and raised his voice. "Who's a nutcase?" "Why the anger?" the nape of my neck was damp. I was placating a man who had no clue what he'd said, by mistake he'd said Eka wouldn't live to the age of seven, he was sick, crazed, extremely disturbed, who knows what was going on with him, I didn't dare raise the subject, I should've waited until after dinner to mention the phone, he isn't in his right mind when he's peckish, he'd never have said such a thing if something hadn't shaken him up, was he unwell? …"Why are you raising your tone with me?" I tried to speak more softly. I stammered. Wrong, wrong! "The child ..." Wrong again, wrong again! "Don't mention the kid, leave the kid out of this! You wormed your way into my life, you're scheming to get me totally under control, today you'll install a phone in the apartment without asking, tomorrow you'll be fucking somebody while I'm toiling away for you and your lover boy ..." "Wait, what is this movie you're in, what lover boy? Hey, we were just talking about a phone line ..." "We're talking about you barging into my life without my permission!" "A telephone installation is interference in my life, too, if this is about interference," I lowered my tone. "I'll barge into my own life, install the phone in my own name, it'll be my phone, you do your calling at work, I'll make my calls at work and at home, a telephone is ..." Suddenly he slapped me. He struck me across the face with his left hand. I slid to the floor. I banged my head, slumped onto the tiles leaning on the cupboard doors beneath the sink and a weird film began scrolling by in front of me.

We're in a park in Opatija, he runs toward me carrying a big bough of mimosa. We're swimming far out at sea, out in the waves with a violet-colored air mattress floating along beside us, he strips my bathing suit bottoms, we peer into the depths, far below us floats his sperm. I'm handed my teaching degree, I see someone's broad, cheery grin, oh, I fling myself around his neck! We're in the fanciest restaurant in Opatija, his parents have paid for the dinner, he has graduated, the waiters are dressed in these thick uniforms, everyone looks like a South American general, even the waitresses. It's hot, the waiters are sweating profusely. Might there be splashes of sweat in our scampi? The waitress changes three olive-drab shirts an hour. Mama's lying on the tiles, Papa's stomping on her, Nonna's wailing, ayoooooooy, people, help ... We wanted to fuck, he and I, for the first time, and up came a park guard. Right there in front of the strange man under the street lamp I pulled on my panties instead of leaving the park with them stuffed in my purse. I could've pulled them on a few steps away … Lord! What a weird film! Looking back, I realize I was mixing up the years and the men. Why were these images swimming around in front of me with no order or logic to them? The violet air mattress wasn't part of my life with him, I fucked on it with a dentist, a lawyer in training, it was my mother slumped on the tiles, OK there's a logic to that … I was sitting on the tiles, she was lying there, my brain messaged me, old lady, you haven't moved an inch, your life hasn't budged, from lying to sitting is hardly a seven-league stride … But just maybe there's no point in probing too deeply into the images you watch flicker by as you sit on the kitchen floor with your husband's first blow ringing in your ears. It stunned me. Why didn't I sit up straight or jump up? I sat leaning back on the cupboard door beneath the sink, I already said that, I felt the round wooden handle poking my back. "Listen, is it possible to have a normal conversation?" I asked. "I don't want a telephone, I have my reasons. Why don't you ever sleep on these hysterical decisions? Today a phone, tomorrow …" I pulled myself up. The kitchen door, the one facing the garden and the road, was unlatched, I'd scream, run! I'm not locked in, I'm not in jail, I'm free, in a little kitchen, which isn't a real kitchen, I'm fussing over nothing, the door is unlatched, I can go, only a step between me and liberty, this is no prison, I'm not a victim who has no way out, there are people walking around out there, look at those cars zipping by, a neighbor's fixing a kid's bike, there's a dog in the yard pooping on the neighbor's Swiss chard, I'll wrap the poop in newsprint and throw it in a trash container that's not next to our house so the neighbor doesn't see … That's what was flitting through my mind. I'm not certain, the piece about the dog and the poop, I'm not big on animals. "Listen, let's talk, you and I," I sat down on a chair. The gap between us was too small, I felt his smell, sweet and a little rancid, the smell of sweat breaking through his deodorant. I was looking at his chest in a white undershirt. "Trying to prove you can throw me down onto the floor?!" I tried to keep my voice under control, I'd rather he didn't see how scared of him I was. "There's no audience, we aren't in a boxing ring, the audience has gone home, the landlord's away in Slavonia, get treatment if you're disturbed," those were exactly my words. "You listen to me," he was calm, almost courteous, "why ask for trouble? You're asking for it, when you're winning you ask questions." "When I'm winning?" I repeated, "I just won for the first time. Are you planning a repeat performance?" "No, I'm not, if you give yourself a real talking-to. Get yourself under control and we'll live happily for a long time," he laughed. "Duckie," he said, "pull yourself together, Duckie." If you think I'm scared of you, you're wrong," that's what I said. I slowly opened the half-closed door, very slowly, no rush, and stepped out onto the street. Eka began crying, I came back, picked her up. I carried her through the workers' housing project, watched the men and women sitting out in front of their concrete row-nests. Where could I go? The bank had rubber-stamped a mortgage loan for us, soon we'd be moving into a two-bedroom place with a living room, an apartment that would have a phone already installed, why was I in such a rush, I couldn't last six months without a phone?! I circled the house several times and then we went back in. I don't know what Eka did while I was holding her, whether she smiled at the cats and dogs, I don't remember pictures from the life of our daughter. I never looked at them much. Both the kitchen and the room were empty, the car was gone. How awful it would've been if we'd really quarreled, broken it off, if he'd left me?!! She and I would've come back into that miserable kitchen and room. Living without a man?!! If only I weren't crazy, if only I weren't so finnicky about the picky details, if only I were less aggressive, if I knew just how to be with him, everything would be so different. I should've dragged him off to bed, fucked, and after fucking told him, the phone can be paid for in installments, we'll list it in your name, in your name, in your name, in your name! In **your** name!! You're the judge, you'll be president of chambers, a judge must never be without a phone, not even for six months! Had I only said what I should've said my eye wouldn't be swollen shut. When he came home I curled into his arms, nuzzled my head into his armpit and murmured forgive me, forgive me, forgive me. He forgave me several weeks later. They installed the phone, he signed the paperwork in his name. We got the keys to our new place! On my thirty-third birthday, Eka was a few months old. He was seven days older than me. And we already had our own nest?! What a joy that was! To the apartment we moved two kitchen cabinets, the kitchen sink, a bed, three chairs, a little table and a crib for our daughter. Finally living in seventy square meters! We could pack so much into such a commodious space. Our clothes wouldn't be falling out of the wardrobe, we'd bathe in a bathtub, piss in the toilet, goodbye to jumping up onto the kitchen sink! "Oh," I said, when his friends carried in our things and left, his mother was babysitting Eka, "in six months every-thing will be different." "What do you mean?" he said. He was lying on the bed, bare to the waist, in jeans. "We'll buy a sofa and armchairs, a wall unit for the hall, furniture for our little girl …" "Listen," he said, "listen! We don't **have to do** anything, what's the rush, we have no money." "We can take out a loan," I ventured. "I already used a loan to buy a car trailer." "A trailer?" "A trailer, I'll say it again, a car trailer." "What do we need a trailer for?" I was astonished. "A trailer?! For us? What for, for us?" "I need a trailer," he said, "it makes it easier toting the salt to the woods, I need to look after those animals." "You'd look after the animals instead of us, you're crazy ..." He got up, I started moving, backward, toward the door of our bedroom. "Listen," he grabbed me by the shoulder and steered me into the room, "Listen, I'm in a good mood, none of your shit's going to ruin my mood, but I'll set the record straight! If I said I bought a trailer, that means I need the trailer, I don't need a sofa or a wall unit or children's big or little furniture, don't turn me into one of those dimwits who spends his life shopping in furniture salons!" "I'll pick it out myself," I wiggled to shake my shoulder free. "I don't understand you," he said, gripping my shoulder tightly, "how many times do I have to repeat, we don't need furniture, we need a car trailer." He shoved me down onto the bed, pulled my dress up over my head. I tried to wriggle free under his heavy body. He yanked off my panties and shoved it into me. After a few seconds or minutes, he got up. "There," he said, "now you'll be in a better mood. Either you need a fuck or a thrashing, which of the two depends on you, decide, don't play with me, remember, you always have the choice, the prick, or ..." He was nervous, very nervous. All these loans, and now the trailer on top of it, we have to keep ourselves under control, what good will all the wardrobes, beds, sofas, and wall units do us, "Slow down, slow down," I said to myself while I rinsed off my cunt and checked the panties. Torn, useless. I should throw them in the trash. I held them in my hands, anticipating with delight that day when, at the foot of the bathroom sink pedestal, there'd be a trash can with a pedal I could press with my foot, the lid pops up, I'd buy a beige can ... That delighted me. I loved buying little stuff, trash cans, vases, woven-twig waste baskets. Lord, somehow I'm feeling sad. As long as we're alive, we people, we have these plans, plans, plans. When we die, I'm speaking to you from the heart here, I want, this very minute, I want one thing only, get me down off this cloud, your honors.

6

I DON'T KNOW WHETHER you've understood what a crucial role hunting has played in my life. Your honors, do you know the difference between a hunting party and a hunt for two? You don't? People are either hunters or quarry, if you're not hunters, then you don't know much about hunting. A big hunt ... When he and I went hunting as part of a larger hunt, who knows whether I said that correctly, **part** of a larger hunt? It doesn't matter, when we went on a hunt as part of a hunting party. A hunting party? When he and I would go hunting by joining a group of hunters—hallelujah, I found a phrase that's more or less understandable to those of you who aren't hunters—my husband treated me differently. I'm saying husband, I'm tripping the word lightly off the tongue, we were married for eight years, before you're married you dream of little else, of how one day you'll walk through the world and lightly off the tip of your tongue you'll trip the word husband, husband, husband ... While you think about it, while you dream about it, you think you'll always pause a moment before you say "my husband," and then with the knowledge that the words "my husband" mean "my victory," you'll cheerfully enunciate "my husband." After eight years of married life you're forever saying "my husband," you no longer hesitate, you don't think you've come out of the battle as victor, the phrase "my husband" is about as exciting as a kilo of greens, please. Strange how everything changes in the big picture!? Yes, I'm wandering off theme, when only my husband and I were parts of a hunting group pursuing certain animals—most often wild boars—my husband treated me differently. He didn't look at me, command me with his eyelids, shush, say shshshshsh, walk in front of me or by my side. I didn't creep along behind him with my feet in his footprints. I walked alongside a different hunter. This other someone would stop, sip from his canteen, offer me a swig, I'd wipe the mouth of the canteen, take a sip, wipe my mouth with my elbow, and off we'd set again. Then this other someone would fart, softly or loudly. It's *de rigueur* for hunters to fart. The tension is fierce, wild animals are everywhere, you grab any chance to relax. Some don't fart. They spit, hawk, belch, scratch their butt or balls, halt, pull it out and take a piss, shake it off and tuck it back into their green woolen trousers. I seldom take a piss then, when there's a hunting party, I'm the only woman.

The hunting party stops at one point. The hunters take their positions, I mean we take our positions, the wind is always blowing in the opposite direction, we wait, wait. Shots are heard. We know who is where. We know when Mirko took a shot, or Drago, or Mr. Miljenko. Everyone's equal in the hunt except that if a hunter is a doctor or judge, one always adds Mr. to their name, and if the hunter is a village butcher or forest ranger or innkeeper, then the hunter isn't a Mr. When the leader of the hunt signals that the hunt is done, the hunting party stops being a hunting party. The hunters cluster into smaller groups, they fart louder, swagger, and march over to the hunting lodge. There we sit down and eat what's in our knapsacks. When we finish eating, I make the coffee, because I'm the only woman, we drink from

tin cups, and when we finish drinking I wash the cups in water
that one of the hunters has drawn from the well. Why don't I
describe a hunting party for you so you know what I'm talking
about. I'm a hunter, you can't try a hunter if you know nothing
of the hunt. As I said before, pissing was my greatest problem
mid-hunt. That's my way of relieving stress, I guess. I crouch and
I feel better. But you can't crouch among all those men gripping
guns and staring tensely at the other side of the woods whence
the deer will appear. What if the sound of the hissing of my pee
on the dry leaves sends it cantering off? Can you imagine how I'd
feel? If, because of me, the stately, antlered beast were to prance
away instead of dropping with a bullet in its slender neck?! No,
I was careful that such responsibility didn't fall on my deerstalker
shoulders. I'd always pee when the leader signaled that the hunt
was done. I never had problems with stress. Mr. Stjepan, yes,
Mr. Stjepan, he was a misdemeanors judge, had the same issue.
Nearly the same. He'd get the urge to take a shit mid-hunt.
Together we'd sneak off far from the scattered crowd. I'd rustle
in my bush, he'd find relief in his. The sour, heavy stink would
waft my way, but still it was better for us to be near each other
than each in a different part of the woods. As a twosome, we were
stronger, in a way, or at least that's how we felt. We were each
other's alibi. We were letting the others know, it's just that the
two of us have body problems, we have nothing against hunting. This is physiology, I'd pee, and from his canteen he'd rinse
my hands, I his. We'd dry our hands on our pants and meander
slowly back to the hunting lodge.

A little about Mr. Stjepan, though it has no bearing on my
story. I don't want you to think I merely used Mr. Stjepan as
bush-to-bush company, that I knew nothing about him as a
human being, that Mr. Stjepan for me was no more than someone who took a proximate shit. Oh no, that's not true, and I

wouldn't want it to seem so. Mr. Stjepan, although getting on in years, had a mistress, a woman twenty years his junior. She had light brown, thick hair, and a pale, lovely complexion. She and he went hunting together, we all knew it, we hunters, I'm speaking of us. Mr. Stjepan's wife merely sensed this. Poor thing, she had no proof. Hunters are wary people, she searched the pockets of her husband's green jacket in vain. Her voice was that of a shrill, uncontrolled, unreasonably jealous wife. Mr. Stjepan and Mrs. Julka fucked in the hunting lodges. After screwing, they'd replenish with salt all the salt licks—wooden containers for salt nailed to trees. From them the animals lick the salt. This suited everyone. Toting the salt wasn't a job that required much concentration, caution, or imagination. A heavy knapsack on one's back doesn't fill one's veins with a rush of adrenaline. Mr. Stjepan wasn't a robust man. He suffered from stomach pains, and while hunting, during a hunting party, he'd often belch loudly. This was something he couldn't control. Some of the hunters complained. The woods don't tolerate sounds that are alien to the woods, or belching that sounds like roaring and thunderlike farts. That's why hunters farted softly and spread around them an oily, quiet stench. They'd somehow swallow their burps.

That day, there on the meadow, at the end of the hunting party I was telling you about, I should've felt bad because I didn't kill anything. The hunter murderers watched the hunter butchers carve up the animals they'd killed. Yes, hunters fall into categories such as butcher, carver, murderer. The butchers are the ones who put the animal out of its misery while it's dying after being hit in the wrong part of its anatomy. Sometimes they stab the animal more than once. The roles may overlap. All the carvers and butchers may also be murderers, but not all murderers know how to carve up an animal or cut off its head or plunge a knife into the slender neck if the bullet didn't kill it. That day I didn't kill anything, I hadn't done so in the previous days either, and I was expected to ache with disappointment. How did I ache? Misery incarnate. My eyes were open wide, I stared tensely at the green grass. I wasn't hungry or thirsty. A lie! A lie! Ah, what a big fat lie! I didn't feel bad! I wanted to yell, hey, hunters, I'm ravenous and thirsty and give me a slice of pancetta! I want a glass of water and some coffee! Mr. Stjepan looked at me out of the corner of his eye. He hadn't killed anything either but there he was chomping away on cold cuts, no one looked askance at him. Hey, old man, how could you be hungry, why aren't you despondent about not shooting an animal in the neck? Why don't you drop your head between your hands and then your head and hands between your legs?! No! Mr. Stjepan stuffed his face, while I squinted and squinted, then stared, then looked fiercely down between my knees and thought, we'll go home, I'll eat two large bananas, chocolate, a slice of bread, a Griotto chocolate-covered cherry, a slice of pancetta, I'll cook up a sausage, eat a big apple and stewed cherries and chocolate pudding and corn flakes with warm milk! I won't care that it says on the cardboard box that it's for Eastern Europe only. I'll chew softly, as if I'd killed something in the hunt, even though I didn't! We sat under a tree, they chewed and chewed and chewed, there were green hunters' jackets strewn all around, their whiskers were greasy, their lips moist, the dead animals were waiting for the butchers to eat their fill and then pull out their big knives and stab them in the neck. Many a head had to be severed from its body, the warm liver pulled out of the belly and photographed for the *Hunters Herald*. What did my lying on my stomach on the edge of that meadow, that great meadow and the story about the hunting party and my need, my powerful need, to leave school, to stop being a teacher, all have to do with each other? Nothing whatsoever. Yet, nevertheless I need to tell you a few things about myself. Maybe they're important and maybe they're not, but the fact is, do you hear this wording, the fact is … While I was alive, while I was walking around down there on earth, they always used to say: the fact is … This is the favorite interjection the people down there use, they're always saying it, the fact is … And I'm no better, so, your honors, the fact is that I was eager to be done with teaching …

7

TEACHERS, FAT, SKINNY, OLD, young, dense, thoughtless, ambitious, evil, jealous, vile, nervous, pure, filthy, loud, soft, unbearable. And children. Smelly, noisy, violent, numb from glue, groggy with alcohol and cigarettes, half-naked girls, smelly boys, stupid, evil, thick, sad, cynical, depressive, aimless, smart, scornful, sick. Parents, sad, sorry, unhappy, relaxed, wrong, bitter, groggy with alcohol and cigarettes, nasty, distrustful, suspicious, jealous, anxious, ungrateful, raging, evil, helpless, weepy, hopeless. I'd had enough. He went off on a seven-day seminar. The director of the radio station was a friend of his, I heard they needed a journalist proficient in the Čakavian dialect, regional shows were coming into vogue. The radio needed to bring old-style story-telling for the old-men and old-women listeners so they could hear something in their almost forgotten language to foster their slender, neglected but one-and-only genuine Croatian roots. The director was his pal, Čakavian—my native dialect. A failsafe combo!

He came home from the seminar. I took Eka to his mother's. We had dinner. I wrapped my arms around his neck, plunged my tongue into his mouth, then I unwound one of my arms from his neck and undid his fly though I knew he wouldn't fuck till he'd washed. The unfastening of his fly was supposed to show

how much I wanted him, a long week with no sex. He relented against his better judgment or so it seemed. He went into the bathroom, I splashed my cunt, fast, with water in the kitchen, rinsed my feet in the kitchen sink. We staggered over to our bedroom, he naked, I dressed, I stripped off my clothes in the room, my top and jeans. He looked at me, I understood the look, "I washed in the kitchen," I said, "so we wouldn't waste a minute." I tried to wriggle in there around his ass, he resisted, I wanted to give him slow head, he resisted. I posed on all fours on the bed, he stood by the bed. My arms, back, neck hurt, I held the cat pose for an age. For a time I shut my eyes, then I opened them and stared at the scruffy mane of the wild boar, at that point the boar's head was still hanging over our bed. I thought how I'd never been much of a hunter, not a single carver ever thrust his big knife into the neck of an animal I'd killed. Had I killed a wild boar one of the hunters would've pulled out the hot liver from its belly and lay it on my hands, it would've steamed in my hands, puff, puff, someone would've snapped a picture, the hot liver and my happy smile, but I had never yet ... He came, pulled out, I was still leafing my way through the *Hunters Herald*. "Hey," he said, "I'm here, it's over, wake up." "Hmmm. Yes. I'm not sleeping." Take that pig's head, I wanted to add, out of our bedroom. I drew my legs together and lay on my back. He lay down beside me. "You won't wash?" "No," I said coyly, "come be in me a little longer." "Come on, say what it is you're up to, out with it, let's get this over with." I didn't turn over onto my hip, I didn't look him in the eye. Nor did he turn toward me. Should I have attacked? "Why can't you come again, you were away from me for seven whole days yet your prick isn't filled to bursting, whose hole did you discharge it into?!" Pointless. I had no proof but intuition—just another name for a woman's hysteria. "You've read me like a book," I murmured. "While you were on your trip, I switched jobs, now I'm a journalist on City Radio." He froze. We were silent, I waited. For whatever reason I wasn't afraid of him. He felt it. "Fine, your call, your business. Never, never, for a single moment, think I'll lift a finger." "What do you mean?" "Journalists have no real work day," he said, "and you're a mother. Don't count on me. If you work till midnight, I'll come home at 1:00 a.m. If you work until 6:00 p.m., I'll be home at 8:00, I won't say this again." I laughed, "I'm listening closely, no need to repeat." "Bravo," he said, "good girl!"

Work in the media looks phenomenal to those who don't do it. I had awful stage fright on the saint's day for St. Peter, the patron saint of a city neighborhood, formerly a village. For the first time that day I was reporting live for a show. The broadcast was about a donkey race. I asked Natasha, she was the secretary at the radio, to record my report. Tell the technician. I didn't know then that people who work for the radio never listen to the radio. "Hello, hello, can you hear me, hello, hello," I shouted into the microphone. They could hear me, live reporting had been invented fifty years before my debut. The donkeys had odd names, Rozario, Rozamunda, Belami, Meriblu, Anabel. Anabel was the favorite, its rider was Antonio. I went over to Mr. Antonio, this was my first interview. "Signor Antonio, what are you hoping from this race, can you hear me?" I said into the microphone. "Signor Antonio, what are you hoping from this race," I repeated, shouting, the clamor was deafening. "My donkey comes in first," said Mr. Antonio. "Thank you. Dear listeners, the tension is rising, the air is buzzing with excitement, Rozario," I read from the sheet, "Rozamunda, Belami, Meriblu and Anabel are waiting for the pistol signal, there goes the shot, the race has begun! People are yelling. This is terrific," I yelled, too, "Anabel is lagging, can you hear me, Anabel is lagging, Rozario is first, Rozario is veering off the track, Rozario is lost, now Rozamunda is in the lead, can you hear me, Rozamunda is racing, Anabel is catching up closer, closer, can you hear me, closer," I ran out of breath, "can you hear me," I yelled, "can you hear me, can you hear me, closer, Anabel is catching up, can you hear me, Anabel is first, Anabel, Anabel," I yelled! "Dear listeners," somehow I caught my breath, "it's over, the fastest donkey was Mr. Antonio Matić!" This upset me hugely. "Don't you worry," said Natasha, "they don't give a shit, they all like having their name mentioned, old Antonio won't be angry, better he was mentioned as a donkey than not mentioned at all."

Working on the radio is all about routine and boredom. The on-duty service on Saturdays, Sundays, and holidays is a pain in the neck. The technician dozes there behind the glass wall doing crossword puzzles, burning CDs, talking with the crackpots who are forever calling in. "Sorry you can't reach her, she's in the studio now, editing a piece, sorry she's on the phone with a transport official, sorry, the mayor's with her now." Meanwhile the woman the crackpots can't reach, meaning me, the journalist, is evading her fans. Ah! You may get sick of the crackpots but the fame does feel good. It's an odd sensation, a stranger comes straight up to you on the street and wants to shake your hand and you long to get away. Who is this man? Yet when no one comes up while you're at a store, when the saleslady, while you're fingering the clothes hangers, doesn't realize you're a radio journalist and local star, you start fidgeting, is it possible, is it possible? I despised them all who saw in me what I wasn't: a smart, young, witty woman who adores people, village fêtes, donkey races and the Little Miss beauty pageant in the Crystal Hall of Hotel Kvarner in Opatija. I knew that I was someone who flogged hot air, equally ignorant on all topics. When a show began with absolutely nothing new to say, when yet another routine brainwashing session for the mindless was broadcast, it was difficult not to send to hell the listeners who were thrilled to hear the sound of their own voice, for a few seconds, in all the city shops. I had no mercy. I cut off their joy, with my help they almost never managed to send out greetings to relatives and friends, they didn't get to wish their folks a happy anniversary. I quickly learned that I hated these people with the same fervor I'd felt for the kids at school and my colleagues, the teachers. There they were smelly, here they were chatty. Is it normal to loathe human smell and speech? Smell is what defines us as animals, while only humans can speak, so in a way I hate both animals and humans. A person who hates both humans and animals?! Is it possible to live far from humans, far from animals? Yes, I still can't handle myself, or that's what I'm telling you, your honors, I can't speak sincerely even when I'm alone. While I'm bucking on this madcap, billowy horse, I want to portray myself as a creature who's spent her life asking the big questions and seeking the big answers. Is a person an animal? Or is a person a being with a soul? Or an animal with a soul? I didn't do myself justice in seeking answers to these questions. If I hated—and I hated all my dimwitted fans, smelly seventh and eighth graders, the miserable teachers and journalists who knew nothing about anything yet spoke with the tone of a top expert—that doesn't mean I was obsessed with feuding. I wasn't, it's just that I'd had it up to here with life.

My depression had nothing particularly special about it. In that little country, your honors, some thirty people killed themselves every day! Depression was all the craze. It was a Croatian fad. If you weren't depressed there was something wrong with you. Every normal woman simply had to go out and buy a bouquet of little pink plastic roses, lock herself in her bedroom, stare at the roses, and sob. I stared. I don't like roses so I bought myself a big, white, plastic lily. They can be found at all the open markets and on the graves of those whose relatives don't have the money for the genuine article. I'd shut myself in the child's room, clutch the lily, sob. I like it, I really enjoy, now, from this celestial perspective, thinking of myself, of myself as a being of spirit, depression, lilies. But still, damn it, I have to admit, both to myself and to you, that while I was still alive and a journalist on the radio, there was a lot more meat and fewer lilies to it than I dare admit. Dare admit?! Sin, sin, sin! Guilty! Guilty! Guilty! I didn't go to church nor did I believe in any sort of supernatural, skinny, bearded being. Do not kill, do not lie, do not desire someone else's spouse, do not steal ... Those were my rules, too. If you do those things, ache, feel bad! Fuck yourself in the head, bitch, even if you don't believe in me! Sinner! Liar! What lunacy! God fucks you even when you don't believe in him! The Catholic Church is the biggest multinational company, its managers could teach the managers of Coca-Cola a thing or two. Indeed they've been selling their product longer. Coca-Cola has us feeling thirst while the Catholic Church has us feeling guilt. My whole life was about drinking Coca-Cola and fucking myself in the head!

Fame! Fame! Fame! My fame was small, local, urban. Madonna would smile if I were to tell her, Ma'am, I was famous. Is there a difference? No, but ... Ah, you recognized me? Gee, wonderful, thank you so much! JOY IN YOUR BELLY FEEDS YOUR SOUL ALL THE LIVELONG DAY. Fame! If there hadn't been this fame, which Madonna would have sneered at—and she would have been wrong—I would never have met my lover. I know that worldwide there are wives of all pigments fucking with lovers and they're not all of them broadcast journalists. Perhaps I exaggerate. But people—all people—are fascinated with those who work for the media. When faced with women from the media men pull their hands from their pockets, stop scratching their balls, the wives smile a tight smile, like, we all could have been sluts but some of us have taste. Their rancor is wasted. Even the ugliest woman is a babe if her voice resounds through cafés or her mug glows on the TV screen. This can make you worry. Is he fucking me because I'm a Voice? He might be spreading the word, I'm fucking the Voice, I'm fucking the Voice! Did I think of myself as a Voice? When I think of them calling Lauren Bacall the Voice?! The Voice?! I never called myself the Voice, the Voice, the Voice, out loud. I whispered it voicelessly to myself. I hid, as much as I was able to, once and for all, my new-born self-love. Here my husband was a huge help. On Sundays while we sat around the table he'd get up after dinner, take a wooden spoon from a drawer, hold it theatrically to someone's lips, and say, "Well, then, sir, would you like to fart for our dear listeners?" With his lips he'd make the sound of a long fart. Eka would scream with laughter. "See what your mama does?" Every journalist had his sector. I edited a monthly show called *From Our Corner of Croatia*. They needed to give me another segment. My husband was a judge so they thought the courts would fit me best. "Don't do it," I told my boss. I said the same thing when they assigned me a judge. The listeners were overjoyed when they heard the show would be broadcast, the judge would give out free legal advice. Lawyers were expensive. "Sir, my mother died in 1961, we never had a probate hearing, then my father married again ..." "Now that problem is a tricky one," said the judge. "My wife, my former wife, we no longer live together, she ran off with her lover, left the children with me, and now she's demanding half the house ..." "Now that problem is a tricky one," said the judge. "I worked in this big supermarket, no days off, fifteen hours a day, I was fired, they paid me no benefits ..." "Now that problem is a tricky one," said the judge. They railed and railed. "Hey, listen, what's this moron doing in the studio, is there any question he knows an answer to ...?" We played music, handed the microphone to callers only if the technician swore on the health of his two children that the caller was benign, but in vain. "Hey, what the fuck is that ape doing up your tree, he has no clue ..." They're agitated, I told the judge while ads blared, must be a full moon, dips in air pressure, high humidity, what music do you prefer? Bagpipes, he said. The music editor rolled his eyes but played the song, "The Black Bear Bagpipes." This was a bad move. The listeners went berserk! "Fuck the black bears, you ape! This isn't the backwoods, we're on the coast ..." We barely made it out alive. At a meeting of my colleagues they pilloried me. "Why did you invite that clueless dolt to the program? You enraged the listeners!" "Whose idea was that?" "Mine," said I. "Where did you find the cretin ..." My colleagues simpered, my boss and director raked me over the coals. And then barely a month later Bagpipes became president of the County Court. "Cat got your tongue, douchebags?" I strutted around the studio as if I had a broomstick up my ass. "Why don't we give the cretin a buzz so I can let him know what you think of him?" Later he was a frequent guest in the studio but the microphones were never on. Listeners are generally of weaker fiber than journalists. "I don't want to follow the courts," I told my boss. "Ignore that I sleep with a judge. Would I be assigned to follow cows if I were fucking a butcher?" "Watch your language," said my boss. "How about ecology?" I said, "now that's a blessed sector."

Natural-gas pipelines were frequently in flames, on better days whole neighborhoods blew up. The refinery in the center of town was always belching dense, black or gray smoke. People were choking. The journalist who follows ecology is always a champion for human rights. A fabulous position, you thunder on about injustice as if you're the lord god but you're no threat to anybody. The politicians don't give a fuck about the sky overhead. Gypsies at the city dump serenaded me with songs while the seagulls ferreted out trash, winged off with it in their yellow beaks, squawked. On the radio, sound effects matter more than speech. The Minister for Ecology often came through our town, he must've been screwing someone in Opatija. For the newspapers and television he'd always have his picture taken in front of some big Russian oil tanker that'd never pumped off so much as the piss of its drunken crew, let alone any oil. Some ecological topics were out of bounds. Near our city there was a small town. A huge smokestack from the factory on the shore had been belching poisonous gas and fine, black particulate matter for decades. It settled on the wells and gardens. The little town on the hill was somehow the most exposed. Its inhabitants were dying daily. People and pets. Dogs died of liver cancer and leukemia, women of breast cancer, men of all kinds of cancer, the leaves came out red instead of green. We didn't mention that. The journalists and the doctors and the opposition politicians all kept their mouths shut. Even during political campaigns politicians never went to the town on the hill. They were afraid of being poisoned by a glass of clear, well water. The listeners liked me, I was on the side of the so-called underdogs, whom we called the so-called underdogs but they were, in fact, genuine underdogs. They suffered from the smoke, fire, gas, stench, I didn't give a shit. Like all journalists I knew squat about the subject matter I reported on. I let my guests chatter on about protecting the drinking water, water sources, trash dumps, passing lanes, they thought I found all this riveting, I looked them in the eyes and nodded. While they were speaking, the technician would give me the "scissors" gesture, snipping his index finger and middle finger like scissors. Time for them to shut up and run an ad, or the news, or sign-off. I'd interrupt them as soon as I saw the scissors, regardless of the stage of the guest's logorrhoea. I couldn't say, now, from this perspective, that my life as a broadcast journalist was wildly entertaining. Mainly I found it deadly boring, and then …

It was a Tuesday. An hour-long show about the Krško nuclear power plant. This theme had its up side and its down side. The down side, everyone living and dead had already jerked off on the topic of the power plant so there was nothing new to say. The up side, although everyone had already said everything there was to say about the power plant, there was always room to sow a little anxiety. Is there or is there not radiation? Are there explosions? Uranium leaks? Cracks in the dam? Disposal of nuclear waste, are we too near or far enough away? "Yes" for the power plant? "No" for the power plant? Croatia doesn't have enough electric power! God bless the power plant! I had an hour to fill between the music and ads. In the corridor by the studio waited the guest. My boss said he was a "promo" guy. That's what we called the pretentious jerk-offs who liked coming to talk on radio shows, but who did nothing concrete, had a Ph.D. in some branch of science or were high-school teachers who wrote diddly-squat in the local papers and appeared on community TV. My task was simple. The guest would speak, the technician would give me the "scissors" gesture, cut to music. Then blah blah blah, then the scissors, then cut to an ad, then blah blah blah, then the scissors, then music, then an ad, then, then blah blah. If we had some-one on the line, you're on the air, hello, yes, we can hear you, go ahead, hello, then the scissors, then an ad, then music, blah blah, scissors, ad, music, the last blah blah, and then goodbye till next Tuesday. To come out of the studio into the hallway where the promo guys were waiting had its good and bad sides. If the guest was informed about the topic to be discussed, this helped the journalist make a reasonably palatable show. But if the guest was overawed by the media, the microphones, the bustle and the journalists, then a ten-minute session would turn into agony.

When I went down to the editing room I never knew what sort of promo guy I'd stumble on. I couldn't rely on my colleagues for their opinions, journalists never think highly of anyone. As far as we were concerned, all the guests were cretins, morons, talkaholics, crackpots, trash, dumbasses, jerk-offs. My boss had said only that the man was "good-looking"—an eloquent description. A younger man was waiting downstairs and he was indeed looking good. Anyone can talk about nuclear power plants for an hour. The young man and I could get away with anything while they played Slovenian music—the power plant was half in Slovenia, half in Croatia. I told the music editor polkas would do, and waltzes. He was sitting alone at the table and stood up when he saw me. The boss was right. He gave me his name, I gave him mine, we sat. Short, slender, small eyes, thick brown hair, corduroy pants, nice shoes, nice eau de cologne. "How should we start?" I asked. "Listen," he said, "I'm a judge, I work with your husband, I know nothing about nuclear power plants, I've only been working on ecology for six months, I'm a member of the Municipal Council, I was hoping this'd be a way to meet you." Holy shit, holy shit, holy shit! Every crackpot has his method. "You're crazy," I said, "how do you mean that?" My vanity was tickled, the promo guy was different than most of the crackpots we saw. The power plant had already been announced, but it occurred to me he might not have much to say, I would have to fill in the gaps, about what? how? I couldn't just play Slovenian polkas, or maybe I could, damn the promo guy! "You've already been announced," I said, "this isn't fair, you're making me look like a fool, I'll make fools of the listeners ..." The technician called us in. The gentlemen spoke with ease. Judges are people who are always talking on their jobs, dictating, asking, wrangling with attorneys, defendants, witnesses, spouses. How could I forget that? Judges are professional gabbers. Listeners called in. He had answers for everything they asked. How long would the power plant run? Did it radiate? What if there were a meltdown? Why was the waste being sent to us? Were the Slovenes exploiting us? When would the Hrbat family be allowed to retrieve their foreign currency from their Ljubljanska Banka account? He even had an answer for that. He told the mother of a girl who was stricken with cancer that the cancer was not due to Chernobyl ... Even the technician listened. He forgot all about the scissors. We went for coffee. Behind me was yet another totally failed broadcast with which everyone would be deliriously happy. The listeners got all the answers to all their questions, nothing was said that might excite anyone except the Slovenian government, which local Croatian radio could badmouth to their heart's delight because no one from the Slovenian government ever listened to regional Croatian radio. I rarely had run-ins with my boss. We were on the same side, against pollution, smoke, exhaust fumes, rusty tankers, oil that was floating on the surface of the sea or smeared all over a penguin, or matting a seagull's wings. When something happened and there were foul smells in the air, or a black seagull's beak, the phones would ring. Those were my favorites. The listeners shat bullets live, they raged and fumed, and I did my nails in the studio. Win-win. I loved ecology.

Help me, your honors, I'd like to leap from ecology to my lover, tell you our love story and I'd definitely like to tell you the story of the hunting party, I have so many stories to tell, but so they flow from one to the next with no cuts so you can listen to me, relaxed, so my story entrances you, so I can be a Scheherazade who softens your heart, my light prattle will dull your attention and your need to condemn me for committting a serious crime. I'm transparent, I see that, and you see that, yet still I can't resist. I'll take you and myself back to the hunt, now I'm there by the hunting lodge, remember, there were green, thick hunting jackets flung around on the meadow. And the dead carcasses of the animals killed. The hunters had eaten their fill, all of them but me, they stood up, brushed off their pants, the butchers took out their knives, each butcher went to his animal, the rest of us choosing where we'd stand to watch. By Mato, the strapping, swarthy hunter who'd cut off the little boar's head, or by Matko, a butcher's helper and son of the owner of a village inn, who'd sever the head of a deer. I turned toward the group gathered around Mato. I didn't like the smell of fresh blood nor the little, glassy eyes of the dead wild boar, but I had to opt for a group. It was unimaginable that a hunter would stay sitting while others watched the dead animals being carved up. So I watched. Mato had a big knife. He stabbed the little boar in the neck with it and cut off its head. When he severed the head from the body he grabbed it by the snout and showed it to us. We clapped, I don't know why. Then Mato stood up, brandishing the bloody head, and Mr. Stjepan photographed him. Be careful, said Mato to Mr. Stjepan, last time my eyes came out red. Victor, Mr. Victor—a cardiac surgeon, a tall, fat man—had killed a boar but hadn't had his picture taken holding its head, he had a picture taken while he stood by the dead boar while it still had its head. Mr. Victor had planted his foot on the head and gripped his gun. Mato set the bloody head on the grass and went back to the body. He gutted it and drew out the liver. He cupped the liver in his hands, picked up the head and looked at all of us standing around him. I smiled at him. I thought I should. He smiled back, stood up, placed the red, hot liver in my hands, the men clapped, Mr. Stjepan said, "Look at me," I looked at him, the hot liver wobbled in my hands, poopoopoo or something like that, his camera clicked, my smile and the liver and my hands were caught on paper. I have the picture somewhere.

So now you tell me, explain to me, Does a hot liver have anything to do with my lover? Is a story about pig liver the proper segue into my love story, which did happen, yet shouldn't have? It's a ridiculous segue. The link is pointless. But, your honors, if we say one link or another is pointless, this would suggest that we believe life has a point, that life isn't merely an assemblage, a sequence of pointless snapshots, moments that hurtle one after another without order or logic. Without logic is something we mortals understand. We mortals?! I'm dead and understand nothing! Even when dead, man is stupid. This isn't a gratifying insight. There in my mind's eye the hot liver is wobbling in my cupped hands, I'm looking at the lens of the camera in Mr. Stjepan's hands but I want to be telling you about my lover. I'll make a huge effort, I'll throw the liver away, I'm chucking it, my hands are clean, if I were alive I'd wipe them off on my jeans, if I were wearing jeans, and not lurching on this undersized rubbish that seems to be egging me on to storytelling. If I felt well, if I weren't rocking so awfully, if my soft horse were a firmer something, I wouldn't be telling stories, I wouldn't be talking with you at all. I'd sit back in a solid wooden armchair, light a cigarette—something I never did while alive because I feared death—I'd smoke, watch you out of the corner of my eye, and brace for the questions. As it is … I'm telling stories because I'm lurching. Lurching something awful.

8

He called me every day. I was hooked. When he didn't call, the day had no sense to it at all. He was short, a little taller than I, his muscles were soft, his thighs not much firmer, he had a small, hard tongue, still does, I know it's small and hard, I held it in my mouth. While I was with him I'd sometimes say to myself, hey, old lady, what a master you are, what a hunk fell into your net! Still, don't anyone talk to me about how nice it is when you're being fucked by both your husband and your lover. It often happened when, after screwing with my lover, when I walked along the street, a wall would materialize right there. A wall! I'd stare at the gray concrete surface, shake my head left, right and look for an opening through which I could catch sight of a store window or a neon light. The wall wouldn't move right away. A ghastly feeling. In my marriage I'd often dreamed, in bed, of a great love, a true love, a hero who wouldn't beat me but would listen, talk, bring me a banana mash in bed. I love banana mash but dislike mashing bananas. When I found a lover I didn't magically transform into a joyous filly who flicked her tail and welcomed a big boy between her hot haunches. Instead of joy I was swamped by depression, I asked myself a million questions. Yes, fear welled inside me. Fear of seeing myself as just one more slut who walks the world and explains her side-fucking as a need for love and fear of my husband who, when he figured it out, would beat me silly. But there I go again looking for an alibi, when my husband whacked me over my kidneys with a plastic cutting board, I'd stuffed a dish towel in my mouth, and often, while howling voicelessly, I'd long for it to stop, and then after a day or two I'd scratch my lover's back with my nails so his wife would see it.

If my husband hadn't come home, I never would have found a lover. By day, while he was off at seminars or judges' competitions, I lived alone in our concrete bedroom, kitchen, and living room, Eka was there nights. She only came to the apartment to sleep. Otherwise she was either at school or at his parents'. I cheerfully made my peace with married-saint status. When he was away traveling we couldn't fuck, when he was home for a day or two we didn't fuck because he was getting ready for his next trip. Those were the happiest days of my life. I forgot about his little prick, the ass-fucking, the panting, I had my job, Eka would zip through my life now and then, not often and not overmuch. The girl grew up right next to me, but without me, his mother was always with her. I was amazed by how lanky and lovely a creature she was.

Some mornings with her were wonderful. You wake up, alone, your daughter's still sleeping, she has school in the afternoon, all morning she's yours. You can see the neighbors through the window as they stare out at the neighborhood, elbows on the window ledge. My daughter would get up, come over, kiss me on the neck, she loved snuggling, the gangly girl, then she'd dress and off she'd go to her nonna's. I'd boil myself an egg, eat, and leave for the radio to repeat, "Hello, hello, can you hear me." What a marvelous life! No one hanging over you, no norm, your salary guaranteed, local fame, no stress, no boss, sponsors bring you T-shirts, lingerie, socks, cured meat, movie and theater tickets, coupons for laundry detergent … Then suddenly! It was all over! A year or two ago …

He appeared at the door, lingered, began fucking me three or four times a week! Jesus! Water splashed in the bathtub, he sucked it in through his nose, then snorted it loudly out through his nose, shshshshlyup, shshshshlyup, something like that. I lay there tense, in pajamas, flannel, unappealing, I thought the washed-out bathrobe would dissuade him. A headache, trichomonas vaginalis, cramps, bleeding, bleeding … In vain. He stepped out of the bathtub, toweled off, wielded the hair dryer, came into the room, grinned, flashed his big, white teeth. Horrible! Horrible! I ought to write a book, *What Happens to Me When My Husband Gets into My Bed?* A bestseller! Millions of women's cunts shrivel up at the very thought of screwing with their husband! I'm assuming. Almost certain. I could swear! I spread my legs. A woman plays thousands of games while her husband screws her. Which should she buy, a king-sized mattress cover for the double bed or something queen-sized? What about some new bedding—a down-filled duvet—on a payment plan, something light but bigger and warmer. A complete set of a duvet plus a fitted bottom sheet, a bedspread, and two pillowcases, 500 kunas a month on our Diners card in five installments? That wall needs painting, I should buy a sprayer, painting with a roller is such tedium. No, I'll pay someone. Painting isn't as simple as the people selling paintbrushes would have us think, "Call us, this magic brush does all the work for you!" Not so, it's better to call a guy, never pay in advance, nothing up front, if you pay him up front he won't show for weeks, they always schedule dozens of jobs at once. High time to move that guest bed out of Eka's room. One of those inflatable mattresses would do the trick. You pull the plug and stow it back in the box. My jeans are cutting into my cunt, there's a tailor in town who'll sew a gusset in, a

patch of cloth, you can sit with no discomfort, stretch jeans are
the best, the weather is too hot for jeans, I should buy a pair of
khaki, lightweight pants … His moaning sometimes interrupted
my train of thought or my conversation at the Indian shop with
the young saleswoman. While he was panting, I, with my eyes
shut, was unclasping a turquoise necklace and putting it back.
And a light khaki-colored blouse to go with the pants, a jean
jacket, flat-heeled shoes, the kind that breathe, a store opened
for shoes that breathe … He was poised to come. He rolled off
me. "Did you come?" I nuzzled into the dip by his collarbone,
"Oh, honey," I said. I've discovered that a person can fuck with
her husband meanwhile making the rounds of charming shops,
doing up her apartment, settling on a new hair color and hair-
do. Fucking with one's husband can definitely be worthwhile. In
those moments I could've passed the entrance exam for nuns, his
prick was the last thing on my mind when it was up my cunt. I
knew, I'd learned from Mama that one must never speak candidly
with men. Don't look them too often in the eye, never tell them
the truth, never expect fair play. Life with them is the only possible life but there are rules. Short sentences. Have you eaten?
When are you home? Your shirts are there, I rinsed my cunt, I
had a gorgeous orgasm, you're terrific, no one understands you,
beer or wine? cold, warm, ice, I'm off to the hairdressers, haven't
been for a month, Mary gave me this blouse, I got these pants
from Ana, Mama gave me the shoes for my birthday, what perfume? I was given it by a sponsor, Koka's divorcing, leaving her
husband, sure she's a slut, the whole town knows that, no, she's
not my best friend!

Your honors, enough of this fluffy horse, I know, I'm repeating myself, I'm a pain. I won't even mention the queasiness,
though I should. My job has taught me that human speech must
be coherent if you want the person listening to you to follow.

Skipping from topic to topic puts the person across the table on edge, prompts them to tune out or walk away. Don't do that, stay, hear me out, I'll be brief, I'm queasy, but this queasiness isn't my worst queasiness. I keep saying queasy, queasy, queasy, sorry, but somehow I must push on to the story of our first outing. I'll tell you how my lover and I went off by boat on our first and only adventure.

We went to the Brijuni islands. The idea was his. I couldn't make sense of how to walk through life, arm-in-arm with my husband, meanwhile with a hand on the pricks of multiple young men. I'd thought I'd find happiness with a single prick so I was nonplussed. Gentlemen, I lie! I was only a saint because I'd never been tested. The men strutting around me didn't interest me. I can also say something else about myself. Thinking his was the real thing and would be my last, I'd stayed with my seventh prick, if I've counted correctly. Now this really is the truth! I should describe, I believe, the path from the first coffee with the unknown gentleman to the first screwing with the unknown gentleman. Phone calls, trysts, mainly downtown, only people with something to hide meet up in motel rooms, Ena told me that. After a year—see, I'm no slut—I mustered the courage. A second prick entered my terrified body! My audacity astonished me. Or was it madness?

Poisoned by Catholicism yet with no formal sacraments, my mind was dead set against me. You have a husband, it said, he hits me, I answered. You have a daughter, how would your child feel to know her mother's sleeping around with unknown men? Just one, I said. And what about if that one you've allowed between your legs has AIDS? Hepatitis C? He's not fucking just you! Who knows who else he's fucking? You're just one in a series! Who knows how many terrible men are fucking you through their front man? All his lovers fucked someone and who knows all who've fucked his wife?! Woman! This isn't just one person fucking you, hundreds of unknown, diseased pricks are fucking you! How will you keep under control the frightful afflictions that all manner of sluts are delivering to you through him? Syphilis, gonorrhea, trichomoniasis, candida! You'll be scratching your crotch till you die! You'll collapse! Your body will turn into a massive ball of pus! Don't give in! Don't give in! Major struggle! Lost struggle! I gave in! I forgot all about the AIDS that would turn me into a heap of featherweight bones, I didn't worry about our hospitals that have no treatment available, nor about the money I owed and that had left not a kuna in my pocket to pay for a decent hospital bed! I lay right down! Stretched out! Gave in! Closed my eyes! Forgot! Snapped! Spread my legs! Gripped the table edge! Hugged a big rock on the city beach! Rode him! Writhed under him! Moaned by an open window in the building where the couple lived who were witnesses at my wedding! Scratched the bark off a camellia in an Opatija park! Clutched the railing on the terrace at the top of the tallest city building! Bit a towel in my mother-in-law's bathroom while she was away at a hot springs! Stared at his picture from his wedding while his wife and children were off visiting her mother—the lady was on her deathbed! Moaned in the bathroom of the Union Hall while people were hotly discussing "Whither Croatian democracy?!" Your honors, I was a slut! No dispute!

Only in nice stories do fuckers who screw someone else's wife have no wife of their own. The heroes in the nice stories also have no little children. In our real-life adulterous lives it's all different. We talked about my husband, and his wife. I didn't go into detail. He was brief, his wife had begun to bore him. He showed me pictures of his little girls, big teeth, big eyeglasses, elementary school. Sometimes my imagination would get the better of me and I'd picture him licking me with our three little girls, his wife and my husband waiting for us to orgasm, it coming, them wailing. Your honors, we weren't even screwing yet at that point. If we were to begin fucking, I thought, who'd be orgasming in that particular audience? I imagined us marrying, OK, I knew it was silly, but a person can't live from life alone, we need dreams about forgiveness of sin. I dreamed our wedding but even in my dreams it didn't work out. We were in a black old-timer car, we stepped into it—brushing off the rice, how silly is that, we with our three daughters?! Anyway we stepped into the old-timer, I already mentioned the rice, it was even up our noses, I shut the door of the car on my side and then opened it again to pull free the twelve-meter-long white train that had gotten caught in the door, I shut the door. We pulled away from the curb. The wedding party stayed behind, they waved and laughed, many teeth flashed, my bridesmaids, my mother, his mother and sister, they were in pale-lavender dresses, the bouquet, a bough of white orchids, was caught by my sister and I don't even have a sister. He was driving but looked back once more to see the radiant, splendid wedding party, to flash his little white teeth again. He turned, flashed his teeth, I, too, turned, flashed them my teeth, then we both turned back to look at the narrow, village road, you could see the tower of a charming, oh so charming little church, we looked from the church tower to the road. Too late! Under the wheels of our old-timer lay our three daughters, dead! Cut!

What I want to say is that before I fucked I was wracked by doubts, remorse, pangs of guilt and fear. And still I did it anyway! At the court, in his office. The building of the court is in the center of town. The court doesn't work evenings or nights. I was a journalist, the whole town knew me and half the town knew him. I was scared. He and I had to go, together, into the building of the court at nine at night?! Off we went. My colleagues shielded me. The radio was a fortress. The door was

always locked, the doorman never let anyone in without the permission of a journalist. Our spouses had no idea that—during a
broadcast—some of us, in fact nearly all of us, leave the building. The routine was simple, we'd make pre-recorded messages
to intersperse with the pre-recorded material, our voice could
be heard on the radio but we were off romping with someone.
If a husband or wife felt the need to call at the wrong time, the
technicians had millions of excuses up their sleeves. In a sharp,
nervous voice—the voice of a hard-pressed media staffer—they'd
say, "Sanjin's busy, ma'am, prepping for his show, call back later
please!" She wouldn't. While we were screwing, the musical editor played our favorite songs. We coupled in cars, the apartments
of friends, the capacious bathroom at the City Café, there were
speakers there. The two of us fucked to a silly song by Franci
Blašković and Drago Orlić Nikoleto with the nonsense lyrics,
"*Ana-ita-ke, žinga-lo, oto-blo, tuba-ele tuba-ul, pi-ždrul.*" They
had gorgeous bathrooms at the Court. I'd sink into the president-
of-chamber's armchair, while he'd …

I didn't talk about how he fucked. My colleagues and
acquaintances loved discussing their husbands' pricks and how
they fucked. Mainly there wasn't much to tell. The husbands
were often tired, nervous, and had little imagination. They'd
fling themselves, naked, onto their double bed. They had to be
asked to wash their prick, or maybe their prick and legs, at least.
They said, "I washed yesterday or the day before, I'm not dirty,
you always harp on 'clean this and clean that,' you're nuts." So
they'd lie there on the bed, on their back, naked, legs spread, and
entrust their prick to the mouth of their poor wife. The wives
suck, suck, suck until they sprain their jaw. Then they get up,
all panting, they mumble something, mmmmm or grrrr, they
lick the ears of women who don't want their ears licked, nibble
the bottoms of women who don't want their bottoms nibbled,

tongue the women who don't want to be tongued and shove their prick into the women who prefer the tongue. The poor wives liked talking about that. Their husbands' pricks were average but this was something the men couldn't be told. The poor things had to refer to these little pricks as "beasts," "animals," "cudgels," "hoes," "sticks," "poles," "mallets" … There were times when we howled with laughter in a café that was later made over into an Austrian bank. In the city, when they opened the bank, they put on a lavish fireworks display instead of reducing the interest rates. Morons! Listen, Anita would tell Meri—Anita and Meri worked at the radio in bookkeeping and marketing—"So say to him tomorrow that his prick's as hard as Ivan Zajc's baton." Ivan Zajc was the bronze statue of a musician we could see out the window of the café. "Not tomorrow," said Meri, "he only fucks Wednesdays, I'll tell him if I don't forget. What if he asks me who Zajc is?" "Tell him the point is the baton, not Zajc, could he be that dumb?" Meri said not a word. On Wednesday Ana, Anita and I asked, one after another, "How's the baton, what about Zajc …" While I was still crazy about my husband I didn't go around telling my real-life stories, but once I'd cooled off on him even his little prick made its appearance at the round, tin café table. I'm not much of a raconteur, I'd only say his was really small, that I had to tell him it was big and he believed it was big, as if he'd never laid eyes on a bigger one, yet he played basketball, they took showers there, how could he not know it was small … My friends didn't laugh, they said maybe he knew his wasn't the longest in the world, but he figured I didn't. "He's mocking me," I said "he knows his is small, he thinks I don't, he's laughing at me when I say things like, 'where's my big baton?'" "No way," said Ana, "they always think theirs is biggest, no way, men never, when they pull it out, believe what they see."

We ventured into the building of the court that night around
9:00 … When I was very young I read romance novels. In these
novels the women heard music while they fucked. I paid no
attention to whether it was jazz or pop, rock, opera, they heard
beautiful music. I could hardly wait for someone to fuck me so
I could shriek to Elton John. Many fucked me, if seven, maybe
eight, men is many, but never did I hear music. Not even when
I first fucked with him, meaning my husband. We were in a car,
he didn't know how to lower the seats, it was this ancient Opel.
He wielded a wrench but the seats stayed stuck. I sat on the back
seat and waited, bare under my skirt, my panties on the back
shelf, it was hot, high noon, next to the highway in a wooded
area where there were hundreds of scraps of toilet paper people
had used to wipe their asses, they left condoms dangling there,
snared on weird brambles. He gave up on the seats, pressed me
down on the back seat, the heat was sweltering, we were soaked
in sweat, yes, he pulled on a condom, it seemed a bit large, too
roomy, the wrong size, I could hardly wait for him to come.
While he moaned and thrust into me, the right seat suddenly
released and cracked me on the temple. When he came he saw
the seat had dropped over my head, "Did that hurt?" "Not at all,"
"Did you come?" "Of course I did." I wanted to say also: "I didn't
hear any music." Where was the Elton John? I didn't know then
that life is long and unpredictable. So there we were, venturing
into the court building for the first time, with a very obvious,
oh so obvious intent to fuck. I'll skip the details. Climbing the
stone stairs in the dark, pushing open the door to the Court in
the dark, shutting the door, switching on the light, entering the
palatial bathroom, he, then I … He put it in me, it was in me,
then he pulled it out, pushed it in, then … Classic.

I'd be lying if I said I'd met a master that evening. But your
honors! I heard the music! I heard the music! Loud! Deafening in

fact! Oh, I thought, oh, so this is it, this is what the books were talking about! I was bewildered! I hadn't come yet I heard music?! Fuck it, all those writers had written about the music, none of them said anything about orgasms, so did that mean women never came when they fucked, they just heard music?! Was this being offered to us women as a choice? It's either an orgasm or the music?! While I listened to the music I had to listen to it, the whole building shook, I couldn't answer the question of which I'd choose if I had a choice. An orgasm? The music? Well, the orgasm. The music was insufferable. But who was in charge? Whom to tell? Can one choose? Are we women divided beings? When our husband fucks us we come, when our lover fucks us we hear an orchestra? The chorus chimes in?! Some particularly earnest singers begin singing very loud?! Oof! I couldn't concentrate on the screwing, I moaned for the record. He pulled it out, straightened up, panting. Oof, damn, will I go through life to the accompaniment of a chorus and an orchestra? Is this awful racket punishment for my sin? I was silent amid the hellish thunder. Why had my feeling of guilt turned into Republic Day festivities? And then the music stopped! All at once! "Did it bother you?" he asked. "What?" I asked. "The music." He'd heard it too?! We were listening together yet he came and I didn't?! I looked over at him, drew my legs together so his sperm wouldn't dribble off onto the parquet flooring, rose from the armchair, leaned on the table and crossed my legs like a model in a car ad. "They always practice Thursdays." "Who?" I asked. "The pit orchestra from the theater, the theater's being remodeled, they have nowhere else to go." "They sure are loud, what were they playing?" I was squeezing my legs together tightly, I really didn't want the slurp to ooze down my legs, I was probably shy, I no longer remember exactly. "It's the Šubić Zrinski opera, that was the famous 'To battle, to battle' chorus." "Oh," I said, "how nice." "I wish they'd stayed at home, it slipped my mind, I forgot, forgive me." "You're forgiven, I'd thought they were only playing in my head, because we were fucking, as an accompaniment to my orgasm." I was bullshitting, of course I knew perfectly well that some cretins were rehearsing a floor or two below. But when you're fucking with someone for the first time you have to be just a little help- less, coy, anxious, a little ignorant. I recognized the choral num- ber "To battle, to battle," everyone's heard it a hundred times, but, there, I thought, if I was …

If I was thinking at all?! Simply put, I felt that the unknown man was fucking badly, that I hadn't come, I was scared he'd given his all and his all was not enough for me. I was being screwed by guilt pangs, too. Hey, old lady, you cheated on your husband, you're fucking to the thump of drums and the rattle of dishes and you didn't come?! You're better off at home, what the hell do you need this for?! Those are the thoughts that tor- mented me, but we're going for the truth and nothing but the truth. There's the truth, your honors. "Your orgasm," he said, "you didn't come, next time I'll do better …" No, he didn't say that to me, it'd be awful if men knew when we came and when we were pretending. Luckily, they can't know this because we, when we don't come, howl like stricken beasts, we imitate actresses in the movies, we bite his hand, rock our head from side to side, chew our lower lip, squint, buck, and meanwhile we're thinking, while he comes, I'll get my hair done, time to have the highlights refreshed. "Let's go somewhere quiet," he said, "without the musicians and the trumpets, let's go to Brijuni, next weekend." So we did.

Three weeks before the Brijuni trip, he whacked me with the curtain rod on which I was going to hang the just-washed cur- tains and basically broke my leg. I was in a cast for seven days. No, no, not at all, this isn't an excuse, it's not why I cheated on him, I cheated on him … I'd rather not analyze why! When he smashed my leg I went to Mama's. Mama's? Yes, Mama's! Mama's! It was like this. I showed up on the doorstep. "What's wrong?" she said. "He broke my leg." "You can't stay here," she trembled and kneaded a dish towel, "your father doesn't tolerate such things, it'll upset him," "We have to tell him something," "What do we have to tell him? He'll be home any minute, it's three minutes to one." The soup was steaming on the table, Papa was in the air, he'd soon be in the kitchen. "You didn't say you'd be coming, why did you come, you'll aggravate him, keep calm…" She looked at me with her faded, light-blue eyes and glanced at the door. Somehow I settled in where the wood stove used to stand. He came in. "What are you doing here?! Where's your husband?" I didn't answer. "What's she doing here," he glared at Mama. "She broke her leg, her husband's away on business, she'll stay a few days." "She can stay until tomorrow," he said to the dish towel Mama was holding with one hand, her other hand hanging alongside the sleeveless housedress she wore on her slender frame. "I have no need for battered sluts here," he said! Mama put the dish towel down by the kitchen sink and stayed standing with her back to him, her side to me. He looked at her back. "This is no hospital for limping sluts!" "This house doesn't belong to you," I said, "I came here to be with my mama," I said, "I came to Mama in her house, this house belonged to my nonna, leave, why don't you, if the guests don't suit you." He turned toward me, I grasped my crutches firmly. He strode out of the house. "I'm asking you," Mama said, "don't turn up out of the blue with problems that are yours and only yours, why are you poisoning my life?" "Who's poisoning your life?" my eyes were full of tears, I can't bear attacks of self-pity, I reined myself in fiercely, I'm good at this, but my leg really hurt, there are many steps from the street to the house and my back and wrist and elbows ached, that's why my eyes were full of tears. "You poisoned your life all on your own," I said, "leave him, send him packing, you own the place, sell it, buy an apartment, live!" She looked at me, snatched the dish towel and crumpled it in her hands, "Why aren't you tending to your child, where is Eka, who's looking after her?" "Her father," I said.

I spent the night there. I lay on my bed up in my room. There was no noise to be heard downstairs, just his snores, I locked the door and propped a chair up against it. In the morning I inched down the wooden stairs on my ass, opened the fridge and found in it a few slices of *Gavrilović* salami, I really love *Gavrilović* salami, I popped them into my mouth, I knew they were his. I made myself coffee and took it up to my room, up the stairs I inched on my butt. Mama came into the house, in came Papa after her. It was time for his mid-morning snack. He opened the fridge, shut it, I heard it, how odd, he was on the ground floor, I upstairs. "Where's the slut? I won't feed the slut! She ate my salami!" "Calm down," said Mama, "calm down, please, the neighbors will hear you, I'll go right out and buy some more …" He hit her, I heard, or thought I heard, how she choked "ghhhh" and slumped onto the tiles. I wanted to leave the room but then I'd have had to inch down the stairs again on my butt … I stayed upstairs. He opened a cabinet, took out a bottle and a glass, poured himself some wine. The smell of frying fish wafted up. Probably two or three little squids that hadn't even been cleaned, he tossed them straight onto the hot burner and the black ink and mud sprayed onto the tiles as it had a thousand times before. I felt pangs of hunger. There was no sound from my mother. I got up on one leg, held onto the bedside table and hopped over to the window looking out onto the street. It was early spring, there were crowds. Parents with their little children in tow, I stuck my tongue out at the kids. They stuck their tongues back out at me. The parents followed the gaze of their children. They saw me at the window looking out, my expression consumately serious, tongue tucked safely behind teeth. A fat mama in yellow pants smacked her plump little boy on the nose. He cried and looked at me. Quickly I flashed my tongue at him. The charm of this is lost in the retelling, but it so relaxed me. I stared and stared at the narrow street, the weather was strangely hot, April yet hot, or was it early May, I hobbled over to the bed, lay down, stared at the ceiling, and self-pity filled my breast. I felt like a wolf stuffed with stones. I fell asleep and dreamed of Anita and me … in the dream Anita was my best friend …

Anita lived in the house next door to my folks, we were never close, we'd have coffee together at The Bar from time to time. Still, in my dream Anita was my best friend. I cried and cried, sniffled, and said to Anita, in the dream, "Anita, Anita, my childhood was so sad." We sat at The Bar, out on the terrace, little gypsy kids were hopping around on the square and licking their noses that they'd dipped into their ice cream. They were chattering away in the local Čakavian dialect. "Sure," Anita said, "your childhood was sad, still I'd thought a sad childhood would mean having a mother who's a slut and a father who's a drunkard, yet your mother wasn't a slut, nor was your father such a drunkard." "My father was no drunkard," I said, "nor was my mother a slut, she didn't put out for anyone." "Yes," said Anita, looking at me with her small, brown eyes. Anita has a long nose. "And what's the opposite of slut, what's your mother when she isn't a slut? How do you define a woman who's not a slut? You can't speak of your mama and say, 'my mother wasn't a slut' and then think you've said it all, somehow you want to say she wasn't a slut, yet still you're saying she was a dirty rotten slut? When your mother isn't a slut, what is she? You have to define a woman as either a slut or something else, I'm missing the apt word, is there one?

To say for mama she was a shithead, that's not it," that was Anita
talking. "My mother was a decent woman, a saint," I said. "Yes,"
said Anita, "some think that to be a saint and a decent woman
is something good, your mother wasn't good." "My mother was
a coward," I said, "a slug, slimy, soft, someone soft, no balls."
"Don't," said Anita, and ordered ice cream, "don't define your
sad mother as having no balls, it ends up sounding as if having a
prick is a quality in and of itself. Your old man had a prick and
yet he was hardly a person to whom one would write a bucolic
letter from a windmill." One little gypsy kid said to another
little gypsy kid, "Hey, let's go buy us another ice cream cone."
Another little gypsy kid said to the first, "Get one for me, too."
"No way," said the first little gypsy kid to the other one, "I ain't
got the money, give me some, I get you a cone." "I don't know," I
said, "I'd like for my parents to vanish, for them to rest in peace."
"That's phobia speaking," said Anita, "Phobias should be faced.
I fear the deep sea so I lie there on the beach, stare and stare at
the waves, and feel relief," said Anita. "I still haven't read Orwell's
1984," I said, "because I'm scared of rats, I have this thing about
rats, I haven't read to the end of *1984*." "Let's go visit your folks,
check them out, examine them closely, that'll cure you," Anita
paid for our two coffees and said to the gypsy kids, "How come
you speak in the local dialect?" "We was born right here," said
one of them, Anita gave him ten kunas, "Will you look," she said,
"at who's cultivating our otherwise neglected linguistic heritage."
"Come on," I said. We didn't go to our house that was just a
few steps away from The Bar. We flew all the way to the two-
bedroom apartment with the living room where my husband and
I lived. Our apartment?! My parents were living there? A cheap,
transparent message, but dreams are what they are. We stood at
the front door. I was trembling. "I don't really feel like checking
them out," I said, "I get my dad, but I can't even think about

her!" "Oh, cut the bullshit," said Anita, "don't you give me that shit! Your father was a shithead, a real live shithead, he beat a little girl and told her she was a slut on her tenth birthday! Look, old lady, you're certifiable, you should've cut off his prick, stuffed it in his mouth, hanged him from the mulberry tree, let his filthy body swing, swing, swing, swing. What's there to understand? He did a number on you with the guilty-conscience thing and you're trying to understand him. After a hundred years you still feel **guilty**?! Oh, you silly cow," said Anita and kissed me on the hair there in the little hallway in front of the two-bedroom apartment with living room. "I have to tell you something about my papa," I said. "Just don't give me any of that 'my-poor-papa, my-poor-papa' bullshit, don't give me that shit!" "My papa had a sister," I said, "she was this amazing seamstress, she sewed for the whole town and all the villages near-by, she was an artist with needle and thread, and then she snapped, she took off for Trieste, she was a slut there at a bordello, contracted syphilis, died of it, my father loved his sister, he loved her so much, he was crazy about her. So that's why he beat me," I said, my hands were trembling something terrible, I steadied one hand with the other, "He was scared I might take off for Trieste." "Old lady," said Anita, we were still standing there outside the front door, "that's not what was bugging him. He saw, he knew for sure you were no seamstress. It took you like ten years to embroider a single tablecloth, your aunt was a seamstress and a skank. For you from day one of your little life everybody knew you'd never be a seamstress, a knitter, a needleworker. Forget that story! Your old man beat you because when something helpless and little squirmed at the blows of his belt he got a hard-on. That's the whole story. You've got a story and a guiding idea, don't be handing him an alibi! Come on, let's go into the apartment, maybe it's not too late, we'll heave him out the window!"

We buzzed at the door, someone clumsily undid lock after lock. The door opened. My mother was at the door. "Hello, ma'am," said Anita, "I'm Anita, a friend." "Yes, I certainly remember you," said my mother, "we were neighbors. Do come in." She was so formal with anyone over fifteen. We stepped into the living room that was my living room. "Where is he," I asked. "Who—**he**?" she asked. "He," I said. "Your father's sleeping," she looked at Anita, "my daughter's very rude," she said. "No she's not," said Anita, "why don't you make us some coffee, I take mine with hot milk." While she was making the coffee we inspected everything. The sofa, two armchairs, a low bamboo table with a glass top, a photograph on the wall of me when I was little. I have a big bow in my hair, he and she are holding me by the hands. The curtainless windows. Through the glass balcony door you can see several men's pajamas on a drying rack, the balcony is crammed with flowers, my mother doesn't like flowers, I'm the one who likes them. She brought in the coffee, hot milk, a white pastry. Anita sipped the coffee, nibbled at the pastry and said, "Yum, I didn't know you baked, I thought you just smoked up in the toilet on the second floor and went 'smack, smack.'" "Not anymore," she said, "So what else has my daughter told you?" "She told me you're soft like a slug. While her father beat her you didn't give a shit, you had no balls, you never stood up for her, you were a ball-less coward." "Not so," she said, "I always had the balls for things I cared about. My daughter didn't interest me, she doesn't interest me now, you children think you're the center of your parents' world, well you're not." "Oh," said Anita, "do tell, dear lady." "Dear Anita, you children are selfish, first you're a little creep, then a bigger creep, then, ultimately, the biggest creep. As the years go by you look back on your childhood more, on your parents, you ferret out the mistakes but you don't have the balls to walk away, so instead you keep coming back to whimper in our laps! And when our laps dry up, when we have nothing left to offer, you no longer come to the door, call us, bring your grandchildren around. Your analysis of your tough childhood is just another excuse to dismiss us." "Ma'am," said Anita, "these are weighty words, you've changed." "And what's this story about a tough childhood," said Mama, "there's no such thing as a tough childhood! If your father beat you and your mother was a slut, if papa drank, if papa didn't drink, if mama drank, if they both drank, if they both beat you, why would that be a tough childhood? That's merely the best possible preparation for a life in which people drink, beat, sleep around and drink, or only sleep around, they don't worry about you, worry much about you, and on spins the world. The assumption is that a papa who holds you on his lap until your fifteenth birthday and your mama who makes you breakfast until you're thirty are a winning combination," said my mother. "If I'd made cocoa for my daughter every morning, she wouldn't be happy. Are you happy?" she asked me. "Oh yes," I said, "I'm grand." "There, you see, Anita," said my mother. "Fine," said Anita, and wiped her mouth with a thick, green paper napkin, "you could've stood up for her at least once. Why did you just hold your tongue and do that smack-smack thing in the toilet up on the second floor?" "I didn't want to pay with my cunt for what my daughter imagined happiness to be, that's why. I had my principles, I didn't feel like screwing with my daughter's father. He begged, crawled, stroked my hair. I wouldn't even open my eyes, he knelt by our bed, I liked sleeping till noon." "I'm thinking," said Anita, and looked out the window, it was snowing, "I'll tell you something, we're only here because this is a dream, if this were real we wouldn't be caught dead here, correct me if I'm wrong," Anita said to me. "That's right," I said. "Why are you, Anita, doing all the talking, why don't you say something? You're always waiting for others to do things for you, speak up, say something," that was my mother to me. I said nothing and stared into her small, blue eyes, I'd thought her eyes were large and brown, dear god. "My dears," she said, "we think far too much about ourselves, we people, I heard on television that between us and rats the difference is negligible. Why do rats not analyze their childhood? Research has also shown that between man and yeast the similarity is astonishing. Perhaps my daughter is some variety of yeast that screws around and thinks that she thinks that she thinks she has memories. Did your papa, my dear Anita, say to you, 'You're my princess, my little princess?'" "No," said Anita, "he said, 'My little mouse.'" "There, you see, you were a little mouse, my daughter was a slut, would you say you were happier?" "I don't know," said Anita, "but when I look back ..." "Why would grown people, responsible for their life today and tomorrow, look back anyway? This is the path of least resistance, you, the young, today, don't seem able to take your life into your own hands so you endlessly repeat how your papa said 'slut' or 'little mouse' and you think this has defined your life. My dears, your papa is no papa anymore, as little girls you're history, make your peace with that. Papa's an old geezer in a wheelchair, you're mamas in someone else's childhood, you're a tale from the past, teach your children not to look back ..." "Great," said Anita, "you, bubbling with optimism, you're an old woman, soon you'll die." "I won't," she said, "there are no rules for death, look at the news, the dead are getting younger and younger, and we old folks die last because we don't look back. Forward, tomorrow, that's all there is." "Ah," said Anita, "you're a mama like any other daughter's mama, shit, always prepared to dump guilt on your daughter. Mamas! Who gives a fuck about you anyway, why didn't you teach us not to look back," said Anita. "I love my mother," said Anita, "she suffocates me, forever calling on the phone and whimpering full of self-pity, 'Come, come visit, I'm alone, I don't feel well.' I want a different mother." "That's not true," said my mama, "you're just bullshitting, you daughters, all of you want mothers you don't have, and you want the mothers you think you want ... My dears," she said. "If we were the mothers we aren't, we'd tell you, 'hey, you little bitch, who are you to spit on us when you're worse than we ever were?!' You fuck with husbands you don't love, you write homework for children you can't stand, you give your boss blow jobs yet you despise him, you answer phone calls from your mothers who suffocate you. Hypocritical cowards, servants, slaves, blind women, cheap sluts, you're afraid of us parents and your children and your husbands and lovers and bosses and the state, you're scaredy-sluts, you only have the balls to slam down the phone in your mother's face. Why have you, blind women, such a lofty opinion, why waste your time analyzing your mothers' mistakes, grow up, little bitches, grab hold of your lives in your manicured little hands, tell the fuckers you don't desire to fuck off, don't go to school to hear what the miserable teachers think of your stupid offspring, do something for yourself," that's what my mother said. The hairs over her upper lip beaded with sweat. Pale hairs. "I was smoking in the toilet precisely so the smoke could be smelled on the first floor! Which of you has ever smoked to her heart's content?! Your slut mouths are full of what you don't want! Oof," said my mama. Anita and I exchanged glances, she was red in the face, her small, blue eyes shone. "Oh," said Anita, "dear lady, you're right, no one would ever want such a mama." She looked at me. "Am I right? No one would ever want such a mama?" "No one," I said. She got up and took the cups into the kitchen. "Ma'am," said Anita, "I'll wash the cups." "No need," she said, "I have a dishwasher. I need to give your father his medicine," she looked at me, "do you want to see your papa?

We'll wake him, he'll be glad you came." "No way," I said, "I don't want to see him." I was becoming agitated. "Aw, come on," said Anita, "the two of us are here together, come on, let's go see your papa." We went into the child's room. "We sleep separately," she said, "it's more practical that way." Papa was lying on his back, his empty mouth gaping, a thin stream of spittle drooling onto the pillow. "See, girls, how sweetly papa's sleeping." "Yes," we said, "so sweetly." There was no trace in the air of the smells of an aging body, urine, medicine. "The air is clear," said Anita, "how could that be?" "I do my best, I work like a dog, a woman comes in to help. See," she said, "I keep your picture on the bedside table, that's you when you were eight." "Oh, you were so adorable," said Anita, "long and lanky." He'd lost almost all his hair. A light, wispy fringe covered his bare, gray skull. She shook him, held his shoulder, "Wake up, wake up." He opened his eyes, big, brown, wait, weren't his eyes small and gray? "Sir, sir," said Anita. She and my mother grabbed him under the arms, "Give me a hand, Anita." I stood in the doorway and watched. They sat him up, his spittle, in a thin stream, dribbled to the edge of his jaw, down his neck, into his pajamas. "He isn't heavy," said Anita, "and there I was a minute ago telling your daughter, 'let's heave the creep out the window!' Now that seems silly." "Don't," she said, "he's my little baby." He opened his eyes wide. "Look, look who's here," she said and dabbed at his spittle with a patch of gauze, "Look, look." "Ba," he said, "babababa." "Marvelous, see how well he talks, wonderful, my little snookums." "Bababababa," he worked his toothless mouth, he looked at me and smiled. "He's able to speak," she said, "he just needs a little time." "Who's going to have a little juicy juice, who?" she said. She leaned a pink plastic dish to his lips, I saw his slender Adam's apple go up, down, up down, stop in the middle. "Thaaaaataboy," she said, "wipe up, baby." He laughed aloud. "He's in good spirits," she said. "Do you recognize your daughter?" asked Anita, "this here's your slut, slut, slut, slut, slut. If we keep saying 'slut' maybe that'll jog his memory. Let's try it together," so the two of us chanted "Slut, slut, slut …" "I'm you're little slut, slut," I said. "Babababba, ba …" He was looking at me. "Bababab, ba, ba …" "Change him, change his diaper." "OK," I said. "Great," said Anita, "let's change his diaper, let's see what he looks like naked, the man who used to be so scary. Papa," said Anita, "we're going to see you naked and then the slut won't be scared of you anymore." She pulled back the covers, the heater hissed, she pulled down his pajama pants, he laughed aloud. "Eeheeheeheeheehee." "He knows," said Mama, "that I'll wash him with warm water and shake powder over him, he likes it when I use talc, it tickles." She rolled back his big, plastic pants, he lay there quietly, two scrawny, yellow legs, sheep's legs, his little prick barely visible, scant, gray hairs. "Oh," said Anita, "how touchingly sweet, these fathers, these evil fathers, if a person knew the truth everything'd be easier. If you'd known your papa would, one day, be two skinny yellow legs and a teensy prick, would you have screamed 'ayoooooooy?'" Anita asked me. "No," I said. "There, you see," said Mama, "no point in looking back, look forward, only forward. All the men in our lives end up with skinny legs and a teensy prick wreathed in gray pubic hairs, and that's how we should see them. I adore my cute little baby. Come on," she told me, "put on his diapers." I guided his legs into the diapers, he smacked his lips. "How great is that," said Anita, "once it was you smacking your lips, now he does it, someone's always doing it, why doesn't anything new ever happen?" "That's right," she said, "everybody's life is nothing but a re-run, relax, enjoy life, find a hobby." "Such a shame," said Anita, "that the two of us can't find a pair of yellow legs and a dried-up little prick so we can dress them in crinkly plastic, it'd be so relaxing. Our household pricks are big and they think they're big, they don't want to put on plastic pants and be our toy, they want to be our masters. We need to bide our time, bide our time." "OK," I said, "I'll cover him," and I covered him with a brown blanket speckled with pale stains, Mama had given it to me as a wedding present. Bang, bang, bang, bang, someone was pounding on the door, bang, bang, bang! I woke up. The door to my room was shaking. "Get out of here, slut!" Father was howling! "I've called your husband, go home, slut!" I looked coldly at the door, somehow for the first time in my life I wasn't scared of him. "Fuck off," I said to him in myself, "Fuck off, Sheep's Legs!" If the door doesn't hold, I'll conk him on the head with a crutch, if it does hold, I'll go out later and call a cab. It held.

So you see, your honors, do you see what I see? I'm lying, I'm fabricating dreams and friends. I never had a friend, either in my dreams or when I was awake. My little friends were chased away by my father, my big ones by my husband. I made up the dream so I could put my ideas in my mother's mouth. My mother would rather die than say what she said in the dream. Never would she say such a thing. There's no dream in which she'd dare lecture me on any topic. Not she! Not me! She and I are, for each other, books we read cover-to-cover a very long time ago. Evildoers, murderers, they can be cunning, fabricate dreams, insert stories about hunting parties, sell judges the idea that they're fragile, bewildered, scared, they can't understand their guiding thread, as if there's anything essential except the bare facts, in my case there's only one truth, I murdered my husband! How much will my crime be mitigated by stories about dreams and a mother who was a champion for women's rights? My mother, a feminist?! That timid, trembling, broken creep?! Who in summer wore a thin housedress made of calico, as we used to call the cheap material, calico, calico it was called! In winter she wore a housedress made of flannel, if it can even be called a dress. Her so-called dress buttoned up the front and had to have two pockets. Winter and summer. In the pockets she kept matches, a pack of Fifty-Sevens, several of them broken in half—she always only smoked half—and a linen handkerchief. She used it to wipe her dry nose. She was always wiping her nose, blowing her nose, but nothing ever came out of it. What do I mean to say? I made that dream up, never in a dream, even in the weirdest dream, would this skinny, oh so skinny woman from my childhood be able to speak to me like that. Seldom did she speak at all, through my whole childhood I never heard her say more than ten sentences, I told you, all she did was wipe her dry nose. So much on my mama and her nose, now I'll tell you how my lover and I ventured off on our first and last outing.

9

I'D NEVER CARED MUCH for the collective outings organized by journalists, I have no tolerance for alcohol, bus travel, fish stew. They traveled to places far from the sea, but even there they couldn't be fishless so they ate what had simmered for hours in some sort of cast-iron pot. Greasy chunks of animal, peppery, salty, spicy. Travel for a great distance in some direction just so we could belch fire?! I stayed home. When I went with him to Brijuni, I told my mother-in-law, she was looking after Eka, that I was going with my colleagues to observe fallow deer. He was at a seminar. To set off with one's lover on a trip is more exciting once it's over than while it's on. I stuffed a new teddie into my bag, a pair of panties, jeans and instead of a wild thrill I felt pure terror. I was sure he'd come to Brijuni and murder me. My lover was bemused. Murder? Think about nicer things. We'll screw ourselves silly until we're stiff as boards and then we'll have an alibi, I'll not have to fuck my wife, you'll not have to fuck your husband! Life is good, if you see it from the proper perspective. He chuckled and studied his strong coffee with no sugar and I studied his little teeth. We were sitting on the terrace of a hotel in the center of town. "You men ..." "Don't," he looked up, I saw his little eyes, "Don't start with the 'you men' thing, don't be petty. We men—pigs, you women—seduced saints. Let's be frank, I want to fuck you, you want to fuck me, everything else may be a head fuck but it needn't be. Let's not drag the whole of society into this. I won't be guiltstricken while we fuck. Hey, lady, so few people love each other, so few people have someone they'd like to come to Brijuni with, nobody's knees should be knocking today, let's enjoy our good fortune, let's think of this as a miracle! Imagine, what if we'd never met? We're not at a movie theater or the marketplace where we'd have to hide from our partners. I'm not running from anyone, I'm **coming** to you because I love you, I need you. All I need are you and your cunt." "Oh," I said, "I'm wild about this romantic stuff." He took me by the hand, next to us were sitting several journalists, they nodded in my direction, I nodded in theirs and patted his hand, giving him a compassionate look, let them think he was my brother, or a relative whose mother had just died. I knew they wouldn't be thinking anything at all, journalists aren't interested in people, they're sick of them.

I arrived at the building that housed the radio. The day was gorgeous, early spring, a slight breeze. An official car was waiting. All my colleagues knew where I was going, I felt safe as I rolled my bag toward the Municipal-Court limo. He stepped out. The president of chambers—a lady judge—and a driver were leaving for the weekend, they'd drive us to the coast, we'd come back by bus. Off we went. After two hours of driving we took a break. In the ladies room the judge told me, "Terrific, you, too, are on the road to freedom, I dumped my asshole six years ago, I left him everything, be smarter …" "I'm not at that stage, ma'am," I pulled the bathroom tissue from the dispenser, the water flushed from the toilet bowl. "Still," said the red-haired judge, "what did my asshole get? He died of colon cancer and I'm being fucked by a guy fifteen years younger. I did my best to be sure he heard of it, stress has a way of accelerating disease, maybe he'd kick the bucket faster." "Oh," I said, "ma'am, hatred takes its toll, I read about that in the newspaper, obsessing about one's enemies cranks up the blood pressure and may spur arrhythmia, relax, ma'am, what if you get sick? I don't want my husband to die of cancer," well in fact I did, but I wasn't about to share my dreams with a stranger, "Hatred kills, ma'am, be careful." "Hatred cures," said the lady judge, "a person must release all the hatred, let it prance about, let it reach who it's meant to reach, let it grab, squeeze, choke him, let him croak!" She was shaking, she was holding her lipstick in the fingers of her left hand and touching up her lips. "Hatred's a cure, hate him! Take everything from him you can, they value a woman who hates them, they respect that because that's what they themselves know best! They deserve it, the bastards! Curse, howl, hit him." "I'm scared he might kill me," I said. The flushing mechanism was broken, the water kept sluicing down, you could hear it gushing. "Yes," said the lady judge, "that's possible, every day people are tried for that in court, this is a risk that goes with what we sign off on in the little hilltop chapel." We left the toilet and got into the car, they were already waiting.

After an hour we stopped on the waterfront and took our bags. We clambered into a little boat. The waves were huge, white foam on the crests, then a dark blue pit, and then the white foam again, I hate waves, I'm afraid of both heaving waves and a peaceful sea. The captain was twenty, possibly younger. I vomited over the rail in the wrong direction, and the banana pulp, Coca-Cola and bile all flew back into my face. He held my head, I was glad we'd drown together. On the walls of our house there'd hung pictures of old boats. Little steamboats rearing up on waves the size of mountains or plunging into the depths. Disgusting! I was never afraid of the sea until I climbed up onto the Kuk.

The Kuk was a big rock on the nicest beach, not too far from my house. It towered up skyward, twelve—maybe fifteen—meters tall. Everybody climbed it. You had to step onto the first out-cropping, then reach for the one above your head, and up you'd go to the top. There was a flat surface up there where one person could stand. No one could climb down from the Kuk. The rock veered at a ninety-degree angle. You had to leap into the sea. It was pooled below, a dark, dark-blue surface. Children climbed up and jumped off, feet-first. Only Rudi did a swallow-dive. To dive like a swallow means to leap off the rock and soar birdlike through the air, drop to the water's surface, move your head, plunge torpedolike into the water, shallowly, the feet mustn't be spread apart, the back mustn't bend or touch, no belly-flopping. A swallow is … a swallow. When I climbed up onto the Kuk, the first and last time, I knew I'd never do a swallow-dive. I'd pinch my nose and jump. It was hard work scaling the Kuk, you had to look straight ahead. If you looked over your shoulder you might get dizzy, feel terror, fall off and plummet. I made it to the top. I crouched on the warm rock and then straightened up. Instead of closing my eyes, pinching my nose, jumping, I looked down at the water. It was waiting for me, way down there, dark-blue, still. A fat, blue surface! I died of fear! Shit my pants! I won't jump! I crouched down, that way the sea seemed closer. You can't jump from a crouch. I straightened up. The surface was waiting. I crouched, back to the sea and eyes to the gray rock forming a craggy pinnacle. It rose skyward. "Jump, jump, jump," shouted the kids. "Jump, jump, jump, jump, jump," shouted the kids. I knew they'd send Rudi up if I didn't jump soon. I didn't jump. Rudi was a short blond boy who found jumping off the Kuk or pulling an apple out of someone's mouth equally challenging. His pale-green, almost transparent eyes were like ice. They didn't instill fear. When Rudi climbed up to the kids atop the Kuk who were stuck, he wouldn't threaten, he'd just tell them with those green ice cubes, "Jump by yourself or I'll push you." The kids jumped. I crouched. I'd spread out like a big frog. There was no more room on the flat surface for even one foot, let alone two. Rudi started up. He climbed quickly, he knew each bulge in the rock face by heart, his white hair inched up closer and closer. I waited. I knew there was no force on earth that could push me into the depths. The sun was burning the nape of my neck, my eyes were tearing, my back hurt, my calves were cramping up. I waited. Two white-green ice cubes suddenly found themselves by my salty eyes. "Jump," said Rudi, "jump." "I won't," I said, "go back down, I won't!" "How can I go back down, you know I can't, it'd kill me, jump." "I'm scared, I can't, I can't," I panted! "My arms hurt, there's no room for me to stand on top, you're on top, so jump." "Why did you come?" I said, "I didn't call you up here." "You can't crouch up here for hours," said Rudi, "jump, stand up and jump, close your eyes and jump!" I looked at his white wrists. He was clutching the rim of the rock I was crouching on. "Go down," I said, "I'm scared, you're scaring me, go back, when you go down, I'll jump!" I screamed. I looked at Rudi's wrists. "I won't, I won't, I won't, why did you come, I didn't ask you, I'm scared, I won't, I won't, I won't jump while you're here, I won't jump while you're watching, I won't, I won't, I won't!" It was hot, the sun was burning the nape of my neck, sweat was dripping into my salty eyes, Rudi studied me with his ice cubes. "You're mean, give me some room!" The joints on Rudi's fingers were more and more white. "You can't stay up on the Kuk all day." "Why?" I shrieked, "why can't I stay up on the Kuk all day, go back, go back!" "You can't stay up on the Kuk all day because I have to jump," said Rudi. "You didn't want to jump, you were swimming, you wanted to jump when you saw me here on top, if it weren't for me here on top you'd be in the water, I won't jump, go back!" "Jump," groaned Rudi, "jump, save me, jump!" My head pounded! Suddenly I no longer saw Rudi's white wrists, just his light, almost white eyes and body hurtling down the rock face like a big rubber doll. I screamed and screamed, "Rudi, Rudi, Rudi, I'll jump, Rudi, I'm jumping, Rudi, I'm jumpiiiiiing ..." I dropped into the depths, felt the blow of the chilly water on my feet. I sank away, and then flailing about with my arms and legs and fighting for breath, I swam out. "Aaaaaaaaaah!" "Wake up," Nonna told me, "wake up!" There was a cold compress on my forehead. "Where's Rudi?" I asked. "Rudi who?" asked Nonna. "Rudi," I said, "Rudi Boy." Rudi's nonna called him Rudi Boy. "I don't know where Rudi Boy is," said Nonna. "You're feverish, go back to sleep." "Where's Rudi Boy, where is he?" I yelled. I cried and hollered so Nonna went down the beach and dragged Rudi back to my room. He was furious. Under his wet, yellow hair his green ice-cubes flashed at me. "What do you want?" "Nothing," I said.

What does the story about Rudi have to do with the tale of my crime? Erase it from the tape, forget it, skip it, never mention it. Who gives a fuck about little Rudi! Sometimes our memories mean nothing.

The boat finally motored into a little harbor. I wobbled behind him over the little bridge that linked the boat and the waterfront. He had his bag over his shoulder and was holding mine in his right hand, pulling me along with his left. Oof. The hotel was vast, a lady at the reception desk, not another soul in sight. We stepped into the elevator and then into the room. In the bathroom I carefully brushed my teeth and rinsed my mouth, changed, showered, washed my hair. My neighbor on the third floor, Ms. Horvat, told me a hundred times that I antagonize men, I don't like taking my clothes off in front of them, I have saggy breasts, my belly is crisscrossed with stretch marks, the cellulite in my ass is like a sponge, some of us can't be sluts because our bodies look so appalling. She grinned at me, she had a pretty smile, her teeth were broad, white slabs, the two in front a little larger. She lured me into her club of the saints of the sagging breasts. In that hotel room I flung away her fears and mine. I dried my naked, skinny body with a thick towel, the two little flaps of flesh stuck hopelessly to my ribs. Marlene Deitrich never screwed naked. For the purpose of fucking she had a handmade teddie with an underwire bra. The bra had steel underwires that boosted what couldn't stand on its own. When she was alone in bed, she'd wear a man's wide-striped pajama. I came out of the bathroom. I liked him. Hairy calves, a hairy chest, curly, brown hairs between his legs, hairy upper arms, hair thick but not too thick, nice teeth, lovely, small brown eyes and a big prick. He was lying on the bed, reading. He looked at me, this was the first time he'd seen me all naked. The two little deflated pup tents didn't perk up at his glance. His implacable supine posture delighted me. "Why are you laughing?" "I have terrible tits." I pressed my nipples between my index finger and thumb, pulled my tits up and pranced naked around the room. "Bring your little tits here so I can suck them with my big mouth," he said, so I lay down next to him. I felt good with a man who chewed my little skin flaps. I didn't want to be the heroine of a fantasy he'd jerk off to when he was depressed, nor the woman who'd be with him until death did us part, I wanted him to be my man for the weekend. I admired women who didn't take men too seriously, they floated in the seas while not thinking about their husband's broken heart and their mother-in-law who was looking after their underage children. Then they'd rush home, their husbands would meet them at the airport or on the threshold to their home. These weren't unknown women, they lived right next door. "Sluts," said my husband. "You're all sluts, though some of you have a brief interlude of self-control." How long would I be under control? He looked at me with his light-gray eyes. "I couldn't bear for someone else's prick to be in your body, that your mucus membranes encase someone else's filthy prick." "Why do you think only you wash?" We talked when we were at the construction site of our future home. In my hand I crumpled a fig leaf and the sap dripped onto a tiny wart on my thumb. Fat hornets zipped through the air, the workers had stayed home, it was a holiday, he was holding a big board, looking for where to toss it. Hot. He looked at me, I felt it, I didn't look back, I squeezed the fig sap onto the wart. "I know other men wash," he said, "but, knowing you, you'll definitely run into someone who doesn't." I flinched, then moved the fig stem back to the wart. This was meant as an insult, I tossed the fig leaf onto a heap of tiles and pulled another leaf off the tree. "Hey," he said, "a joke, you're way too sensitive." The day was beautiful, I didn't want self-pity to eat at me, we'll move into a beautiful house and I'll plant two cedars in the garden.

My lover's prick enters my body, there in that hotel room. He didn't shower, my husband was right. A dirty prick entered my body, he wanted to wash, I wouldn't wait. Before I came, it hit me, my husband knows me better than I know myself. He knows that a stranger's prick would, sooner or later, slip into his hole. While I was coming, I thought, if he really loves me, then he's glad we're fucking so nice, so nice, so niiiiiiiice! I laughed. "What's so funny," asked my lover. "Nothing," I said, "I get ticklish when I come, it's your lips on my neck." That evening we sat by the sea. A herd of fallow deer passed us by, no matter how unlikely that might sound. I knew, I'll never forget the feelings that raged through my veins. Today I still remember that even then I knew I'd never forget the feelings that raged through my veins. The feelings, I mean their ferocity, I've forgotten. What do I remember? Taking a shit was a huge problem for me in our shared toilet in such a way that he wouldn't hear or smell it, the toilet had no window. Agony, such agony! I didn't move my bowels till I got home. I've often sought advice for how to live my life in books, but the heroes in books never seem to shit, except for Ingmar Bergman in his autobiography. He, with one of his women, ate kidneys flambé in Paris, and they were suddenly overcome while at the top of the Eiffel Tower by a powerful need to shit. There were no bathrooms up there, the elevators weren't working, and while they were hurrying down the stairs they shat in their pants, got into a cab, the driver laid newspaper on the back seat, they shat together in the hotel room, he on the toilet, she on the bidet. It brought them closer. Bergman! Bergman's shit fest could be a story, I was no Bergman, when I take a shit I empty my bowels and I smell bad. And I'll never write an autobiography. My lover didn't have these problems. He went into the bathroom. I perked up my ears to hear how soundless he might try to be. It took no effort. He farted as though there were no flimsy door between, he shat as if he were on a deserted island, he didn't flush the toilet while he was relieving himself, he didn't spray the room with my hair spray when he finished, he didn't lower the toilet seat, men are so much more relaxed. While I was sitting on the bed and listening to him shit, I leafed through a biography of Marlene Dietrich. I love movies and actresses. She said, if you can stand your husband while he's taking a shit, he's Mr. Right. My boyfriend with thunder and a totally new smell for me, passed the test. There, I remember that and our plans about how we'd walk around Brijuni on Sunday morning, inhale the sea air, soak up impressions we'd cherish in our hearts forever. This would be nourishment for the soul until the next weekend, the next tryst, or death. It was a gorgeous plan. On Sunday morning I was woken by the hellish clamor of children.

While I was only half-awake it felt as I were the teacher and the children were yelling at the Plitvice Lakes state park, borne away along a cold river, drowning in the most beautiful waterfall in Europe, and I was sleeping instead of saving the little vermin. I woke up horrified, he was breathing lightly, my shudder stirred him, we sat in bed and looked at one another. "What is this?" I asked, hoarsely. "Where am I?" he asked. "You're with me," I said, with inspiration, "what is this?" He got up and peered out the window. "I don't know, thousands of kids wearing helmets are riding bikes. I'll check it out." He got dressed, left the room, came back. That Sunday on Brijuni there was a county bicycle race for children under fifteen years of age. All those who had studied or worked with me, thousands of teachers, were only two floors down or just several meters away as the crow flies. I don't know why I turned floors into flying crows, but, I clearly remember, that's what I did. Damned children! They shrieked and shouted. We had our breakfast in the room, fucked and fucked, what else can you do when the county bicycle race for under fifteen-year-olds was going on just outside your window? I called my mother-in-law from a phone booth, I'd deliberately left my cell phone at home. "Eka's fine, have you seen the deer?" "Yes, we have," I said and was tickled that I could tell the truth.

Your honors, you might have the impression that I'm a soul-less slut. Wait a minute! One lover? Just one lover?! We were married for eight years, and only one lover? For fifteen we were together, just one lover? Isn't that practically nothing? Wasn't it my great sin, my only true sin, that I didn't love my daughter, my daughter Eka, enough?! I didn't like children very much. When you spend years in the classroom, you sour on little kids forever. I didn't anticipate Eka's birth full of sweet hope. I thought that once you give birth your troubles end. Your belly is flat again, you don't have to screw lying on your hip, he'll stop shoving it into you from behind, you'll be a girl again. But he thought her birth was the end, and not a beginning with no end. When he saw he'd been duped, he left me, threw up his hands and his prick. He came back when Eka started school. I was with our daughter day and night. I wondered how many women know what it means to have a child. Why didn't somebody tell us?

Now that I'm dead, your honors, I have something to say to you, I often wanted to heave my daughter over the balcony railing or smash her head into the wall, let her brain dribble down. I saw her eternally gaping mouth like a hole to be stuffed with a greasy rag. I got nothing with her birth. No male specimen, no sense of security. Quite the contrary, for years my pale face and greasy hair stared at me from the mirror in the bathroom where I spent most of my time. I ran a bath to treat her bronchitis. When the bronchitis let up, she'd have the runs. The stink of it stuck to me. Piles of diapers were heaped under the kitchen sink, in the bathroom, on the balcony. Why don't you clean up that shit, the smell is soaking into the walls! Pace by night, sing night and day, stare at her bottom, push a suppository smeared with cream into it if she can't shit. Wipe it if she shits too much. Sobs, sobs, sobs … And now I feel a resentment I've no right to. What cows we women are?! We want to catch a man at all costs and when we catch him, at all costs, then the cost is too high?! Fuck it, all this because of a shortage of information. I kept telling Eka, no children, no children, no children. To a child of five or six?! I was constantly by her side. I need to make this clear, I need to say that I was **by her side**. Not with her, not close to her! It's an odd feeling to be so near to someone, eight years we were body-to-body, yet never close. Eight years?! Where did those years go? Why am I not moving through my life in some kind of chronological order? It's all because of this crazy cloud! My life is a series of images that flash before my mind's eye?! Weird! A

person, dead, is supposed to spur a billowy horse at the gateway
to the heavenly court in order to understand which pictures in
the album are the ones that matter?! Matter? Images and pictures
reach me, but, somehow, they don't thrill me, I can't retrieve the
passion, trembling, chills, fear, panic, fury ... All that's behind
me, except my fear of the judgment. If I were to be born again
... Ah, how many times do people say that, if I could only be
born again everything would be different. Yes, it would, I'd look
my daughter in the eye. At school she was often given a frowny
face instead of a smiley one. A frowny face is one of those round
heads with the line that curves down at the tips in a frown, while
a smiley face has the line with its tips curving up in the shape
of happiness. "Stop whining," I'd say, "you'll get the smiley face
tomorrow!" "Mama, my forest monster was the best!" What's a
forest monster? Why were they making creatures out of grass,
wool, leaves, and trash? The children got a smile or a frown for
their monsters?! According to what criteria? The teacher knew
that only my daughter made her monster all by herself, all the
other damn forest monsters were the work of the fathers and
mothers. One mother, the art teacher, made seven forest monsters for her daughter?! My daughter was right to be angry, yet I
didn't take her side. Get used to defeat, don't whine for no reason
and the teacher has the right to make mistakes! I listen to myself,
I seemed to have been talking to her to show her how stupid
and insecure and unhappy she was. I experienced my daughter
as an opponent whom I had to show at the very start of her life
that she couldn't count on me when she was in trouble?! When
she cried I wanted to scream, "Enough! Your trouble is nothing
compared to mine! Now it's my turn to cry!" Her father loved
her the way fathers love pretty little girls whose breasts haven't
yet budded and who don't look at young and old men. He drove
her to her guitar lessons and English classes, in the evening he'd

tuck her in, give her a goodnight kiss, take her to the woods on the weekends. When she grows up she, too, will be a hunter. I knew, I felt, this love wouldn't last forever, the day would come when he, too, would smash her head into the wall. Where would I be then? Would I stand between her and him? How would I answer her questions? She'd hit him back and leave us? When? I'd be left with him? Alone? Or I'll end up in a madhouse with the two of them stopping in to visit? Separately? Together? He never beat me when she was at home. And never, in her presence, did he comment on my bruises, black eyes, broken arm or leg. He'd bring me tea in bed if I couldn't get up. He'd take her to school, to English classes, guitar lessons. Once she said to me, "Mama, be careful getting off the bus." I hated the fact that one of these days she'd become a scared little bitch who'd go looking for and find a man who'd break her bones. I didn't know how to hit back, I was like her grandmother, a shivering blob in the kitchen.

And then suddenly, instead of me, my body began to rebel. Instead of me? Who was I? Someone who wasn't my body? I began shitting blood, he took me to see specialists. Once a month I was given a rectoscopy, they pushed thicker and thicker metal tubes up my ass. Nothing. This had its good side, after a rectoscopy I didn't have to fuck. As soon as I saw him grinning at me, naked, the blood would start dribbling down my thighs. He took me from one gynecologist to another. And that had its good side, I didn't have to fuck. I took hormone pills that turned my breasts into melons. This excited him. I gave him head five times a week. I coughed. A dry, painful, wracking cough! Lung cancer? Bronchitis? Tuberculosis? Allergies? They stuck my arms and back with needles. I'm allergic, I was allergic, that is, to lemon, orange, peanuts, walnuts, hazelnuts, pollen, cat hair, honey, sheep's wool, feathers, sun, cold, smoked meat, chocolate … I hated him. I calculated how long he might last, he was about thirty-eight at the time. In *Household Health* it says that Croatian men live to seventy-five?! Seventy-five minus thirty-eight? Now I can't do the math, I feel like puking, I'm lurching about on this beast, I remember it was too much! Whenever he fell asleep, I'd stare at the slightly swollen lymph node on the left side of his neck and dream that the node had morphed into cancer. Whenever he left the apartment I was sure this was farewell. He'd be run over by a truck.

One Saturday I was in the kitchen drinking coffee. The whole house shook, there is always someone in apartment buildings remodeling on a Saturday morning. I stared at the wall of the neighboring building. The neighbors rested their chins on the sheets they had hanging over the window ledge. The buzz of the doorbell startled me. I peered through the peephole. The police. Three policemen came in. I knew this was it, that my prayers had been answered. But let's take this calmly, slowly. Sloooowly! My whole body relaxed, my heart began pounding at a gallop, my mouth began to twitch like a person who's trying to choke back laughter at a funeral. Oh! I froze and looked the policemen in the eye, my lower lip trembled, my hands shook, perhaps I should throw myself on one of their chests? I threw myself at him. A mistake. I smelled the smell of sour sweat, dirty armpits, unwashed shirt. Through my lowered eyelids I stared at the two men behind him, and screamed, "Nooooooo, nooooooo," the way wives of policemen scream in films at the cop who brings news of his colleague's death. Her late husband, everyone knows he's dead—she and the viewers who sip Coca-Cola and nibble popcorn—her dead husband was a great guy and a fighter against drug dealers. But the movie would be a piece of shit if the police were to go and kill the dealers flat out. They needed a motive. That's why the lovely young policeman is killed, that's why the young wife, mother of a little baby, weeps, aaaaaaaa. I loved movies about policemen killed in the line of duty, I watched them hundreds of times, I had to keen like a real widow, so I keened, while my nose was plunged in the smelly policeman's shirt. Aaaaaa, I sobbed, aaaaaaaaa. He grabbed me firmly, I felt his steely grip, yes, the grip was steely, he lifted me into the air and plunked me onto a chair. "Hush," he said, "hush!" I sniffled and looked at them out of the corner of my eye. "Tell me, is he alive?" I said softly. I knew, three of them wouldn't have come if he were alive. It was a little odd that they came with no policewoman. When the police come into the apartment of a widow who doesn't know yet that she's a widow, they bring a female colleague along, women are better at offering solace. But, I thought, this is Croatia, no one cares about feelings here, this isn't America, that's why there's no policewoman. "Ma'am," said the shorter, broad-shouldered, narrow-eyed one, "were you chopping wood this morning?" "Wood?" I said. "Wood?" "Someone was chopping wood, that's why we're here. Ma'am," I felt he was getting nervous, "your neighbor complained." "No," I said, "our heat is electric. Forgive me," I said, "I thought my husband had been killed, people are always dying on the roads." They left. I'll kill him! I'll kill him! The whole house shook again. I went out on the balcony. The neighbor was chopping wood on his balcony. "Stop," I said, "I'll call the police and say you're a drug dealer!" This wasn't far from the truth. He drove a truck and had bought a new Audi. How? "Don't be angry," he said, "would you like a drink?" "I don't drink," I said.

My husband's swollen lymph gland stubbornly refused to morph into terrible, ravaging cancer whose onslaught would be brief yet deadly. I didn't want him lingering for months at home. In vain. I spoke with Vesna, we weren't particularly close friends, we worked together, she was a music editor. A petite, red-haired woman with small, turquoise eyes. I don't like making the rounds with the story of my life, I don't like people who can hardly wait to bare their soul to someone. From Vesna I wanted advice, not comfort. She'd left her husband and was living with her second husband. "Don't," she told me in the café by the radio station, seagulls had come down onto the waterfront and were gorging themselves on sardines and garbage left by the vegetable merchants, the marketplace was near the waterfront. "How long have you wanted to kill him?" "About a year," I said, "maybe three." "You see," she said, "he's alive and well, and you're shaking like a boozer who's puking her liver out yet can't stop drinking. Drink or death, death or drink, calm down," said Vesna. The seagulls squawked, squawk, squawk, vile creatures, revolting, bullies. I could've inserted a big hook into the fish lying half rotten on the quay and watched how the white vermin fly off blithely toting death in their snow-white bellies. They'd croak out there on the open seas, the big rats! I wouldn't see their death, but I'd know that their yellow beaks were gasping in vain for air, and this squawkless gasping of beaks would warm me, a person needs so little to be happy!

"Listen," she said, "I'll describe one of my days." "Don't," I said, "I've heard about plenty of days, don't tell me about big rats and a small apartment, crying children and pangs of guilt, I know it all," I said. Vesna squinted and flashed her teeth at me between orange lips. "Every story is different," she said. "Women seldom murder. You won't murder him, but before you go, you should know what awaits you, what you'll get." The seagulls were greedily scarfing down the rotten sardines, their beaks red, vile, vile, vile creatures. Their shrieks shattered the windowpanes on the manor by the side of the road. "We get up," said Vesna, "we have coffee, I wake my son. He picks up the phone and wakes his daughter, although she lives with her mother who isn't working. Her mother doesn't work but she also doesn't wake up. The phone rings there, no one picks up, the mother sleeps soundly and the little daughter—even more soundly. 'Should you go over there to roust them?' I say to my second husband. He looks at me and punches in the number though he could just hit redial. The son who's mine—but not ours—gets up. He goes to the bathroom. A half-hour later I bang on the door. 'We don't have much time, eat this,' I shout. **This** is the breakfast waiting for him on the table, corn flakes in warm milk, crunchy. My second husband holds the receiver, I can sense it shaking. With both fists I bang on the door of the bathroom, your corn flakes are getting cold! My son who's not ours comes out. He has beautiful green eyes, which he gets from me." Vesna looks at me, smiles. "'What's up,' says my son.' 'Eat this ...' 'Mama, I'm at school in the afternoon today.' He crawls back into bed. My husband, my second husband, slams down the receiver. His daughter's also in the afternoon shift. My husband, my second husband, smiles at me, we go out, we have a coffee in peace and quiet somewhere out of the house ... The phone rings. 'Yes,' he says, 'I did call, I know you can see the number on the display, I was the one who bought the phone and the display, I forgot, of course I know I have a daughter, I forgot ...' He hangs up and looks at me as if he were the one who hung up on her and not she on him. Is this the same man I fucked at every possible opportunity and for whom I was ready to wage war with his wife to the last gasp? I'm in a war. Who has the last gasp?" "I'm not planning to re-marry," I said, "I just want my husband to vanish from the face of the earth, to keel over, is this too much to ask?" "Wishing won't kill your husband. If that were possible, this waterfront would be littered with the corpses of our past and future hus-bands, the seagulls would be squawking over their bloated bellies instead of winging away with sardines in their beaks. But as it is, my dear, wishes don't kill. And how could you murder, think well, think well! Future husbands aren't so very different than your future formers. Each has a father and mother, a former wife, and children who'll never be former. What you and I and all women need are orphaned husbands, adults who grew up in children's homes. But with our luck, the dolts would be attached to some caregiver who was kind to them at the home. The old lady would turn up sure as you're born on Sundays at our door, and I'd have to fix her mashed potatoes with hot milk. My dear, this world is designed for men." I stared at the birds of prey and felt somehow unhappy. I couldn't accept the likelihood that I'd stay with him to the end of my days. And what if I were the one to swallow the big hook and float off onto the open sea to die, far from the rotting sardines, the squawking seagulls, and vile Vesna who was saying, "And then, that afternoon, we go home," the orange lips parted, "and either the landline or the cell phone rings. She or her daughter recite a list of all they need. Until I married a second time, I thought of myself as a warm human being who loved people and wished no one harm." I listened to Vesna's edgy tone. "I often wish his wife would be swept away by a big truck ..." Jesus! So Vesna, too, is waiting for the truck?! Millions of women are waiting for the truck that never comes?! She squinted. "The truck is no solution! As soon as they wash the street of her blood their daughter will be mine! Oh, how terribly I don't love that little girl!! A skinny, gangly, disagreeable creature who never looks me in the eye! Whenever I think of the child, I wish his former wife a long life, a long, long life. We'll be supporting her for the next fifty years, apparently this is the cost of my blunder. His daughter will marry, we'll go to the wedding. We'll take out a mortgage to buy an apartment for his fatherless daughter who spends more time with him than she does with her, the mother who's by her side. When the daughter has a child, his little grandchildren will remind me until my dying day of his wife, the bitch I'm supporting because this is how I wanted it. Was it worth it?" Vesna looked at me as if expecting an answer. The seagulls were squawking, the waitress was saying, "May I bring you your check? My shift's up." "So maybe you were just anxious," I said. "I wasn't," she said. "Each new prick is interesting for a few months, then the novelty wears off and what's left behind is the child from the first marriage and the former wife who has no job, yet still has expenses. I'm not saying you shouldn't leave your husband, I can't even remember mine, but you should never go on the prowl for a new one! Not in your wildest dreams! What good will a husband do you, woman!?" "Fine," I said, and paid.

Hey, your honors, I'd like the gray stuff under the gray hooves of my gray steed to part so I can see my lover one more time, so he can smile for me, flash me his small, crooked, healthy teeth! Hey, judges! Do the dead have the right to a wish? I can't see anyone or anything, I feel like puking, I'm nauseous, nauseous! Heeeellllllp!

If I were made of sterner stuff I'd have left him. I thought about it for years, this is no lie, generally I don't lie often, and this is no lie, I thought, if I'm good, if I'm better, if I'm the best, if I'm the way I really ought to be, he'll be better. I'll show him! I can be what I'm not! I'm not what he thinks. I'm a decent mother, I know how to cook and iron and obey and shut up and fuck without the wrong sighs and wrong movements. My breasts sagged after nursing, there are lotions, I'm skinny, I'll eat a lot, I'll gobble up corn flakes, smother them in honey, I'll eat cookies and chocolate with no hazelnuts—I'm allergic to hazelnuts—and I'll eat peaches in syrup, the kind that come in cans. I am, I think, essentially, a slut. All women are, essentially, sluts and good actresses, but I'll change, I'll extract my sluttiness and instead insert a right-thinking, normal woman. Oh, how stunned and surprised you'll be, darling, when one fine day you see a me that's not me at all! Oh, how you'll gasp when you catch sight of me, a Real Woman! Different, better, smarter, more poised. I won't cry, I won't go to the doctor, or get sick, or yell, or claw at my allergy-plagued chest until I bleed, I won't shit blood, or fling the phone at the wall after talking with you, I won't kneel down before you and beg, "What can I do, what can I do, help me!" I'll be good, darling! People don't understand this, they think life is simple, he hits you, you leave. But why does he hit you? In his eyes I saw pure, boundless, icy hatred. Am I as I should be?! Can anyone hate this much and be so fiercely angry for no reason at all?! I wanted an answer to the question of my life, what must I change for you to love me, darling? I retraced every wrong move and stared at the chessboard? Days. Nights. I smoked, yet I swore I'd stop? I drank cold coffee, and cold coffee was bad for me?! I told his mother he bit me on my left calf after we'd agreed I wouldn't say anything about it?! I spoke up during dinner?! I let a cat into the apartment though I'm allergic to cat hair?! I went out for dinner on Radio Day and stayed out all night?! Am I a slut—the mother of a little girl who stayed at home with a bad strep throat and with her grandmother, his mother?! I laughed in the City Café with the music editor?! The kid could be my son?! Did I stop to think about this?! He's stressed out because of work? That's why it took him hours to orgasm? I wasn't supposed to get up off the floor, spit out his limp prick and say, "My knees hurt?" What no man likes to hear. That's why he went berserk.

And yet, hand on heart, your honors, to be fair, if I have to speak the truth and nothing but the truth, I was no saint. The child was growing up right next to me, yet I didn't see her, I fucked someone else's husband … We broke it off. I couldn't handle the pressure. When I was fucking with my lover, I quaked with fear that my husband would break down the door to the room or car, when I fucked with my husband I was thinking of my lover. "Divorce, divorce, divorce, divorce," chanted my lover. "You get divorced," I said. "After you, sir," said I. We were in the café of the municipal council where my husband never set foot. The people seated around us were all pencil pushers and journalists. The coffee there was the cheapest and best in town, you could watch people walking along the main street through the low window. The street was right there as if on the palm of your hand, you could see everything, no one could see you, a swell feeling. Once I saw my husband, head high, cruising along, his Burberry draped over his arm, tap, tap, tap, staring into the distance, a good-looking man, tall, big, a dramatically handsome creature. It pleased me, somehow, that this male specimen was mine. I loved attractive people, I couldn't help it.

"Leave your three girls, rent a studio apartment and wait for me, I'll get there when I get there," I told my lover at the municipal council café. "And what if you don't?" he said. "If I don't, then you've lost nothing, you'll have shed a wife you don't get it on with anyway and you'll start your new life." "I don't have the balls for that," he said, "I can't live alone, don't count on me that way, I'm not a hero who does things on principle. I'll only leave my wife for you, your cunt will be my alibi and permanent inspiration. Alone, never." I didn't say, "I'm no cunt, I'm a human being, why do you see only the cunt in me?" I wasn't that sensitive. I liked it, I actually liked it that my little cunt could wreck lives, drape another cunt in black, send two innocent little cuntlets into sobs, burn bridges. Ha! What a glorious feeling! "I can't," I said, "he'd kill me." "Relax," he said, "I, too, am a man." He took off his suit jacket, rolled up the sleeve of his light-blue shirt and showed me the pitiful muscle on his right arm. I laughed, "You don't have a chance," I said, "your arm in comparison to his is like a chicken bone to a pig's knuckle, with the emphasis on **pig's**." "Ha, ha, ha," laughed my lover and flashed his teeth, "Hahahaha." I didn't like myself when I was talking with another man and referring to my husband as a pig. He's a pig, I thought, but I don't have what it takes to leave this pig, take Chicken Bone by the hand, and ignore the people who'll howl after me down the street, to the end of my days, "Slut, slut!" "I can't," I said, "I can't." Off we went, first he, then I, to the bathroom of Madame mayor. The lady who brewed the coffee at the café kept the key. We fucked in the pink bathroom—would it have been blue if the mayor had been a man?—on our heads we sported her clear-plastic shower caps. What would the journalists have done if they'd known?! The poor taxpayers. I'd always, after screwing, daub on her perfume. Dior ... Sometimes I watched her on the News. I'd sit by my husband and watch the lady mayor cut the ribbon on a highway. "What's so funny," my husband would ask, "you always grin when that bitch shows up on the screen." "She's fat," I'd say, "she really ought to lose a little weight."

I didn't have the balls, I didn't have the balls to speak frankly with my husband. Should I have? And to be something I wasn't so I could do something I couldn't do? Have the balls? Have the balls?! Women with a prick aren't women. Yet that's exactly what we were criticized or commended for. We're brave, we have the balls, we're cowards, we don't. Having no balls is the essence of womanliness! Men hold our essence against us. The greatest fault of us women is our femininity? I find that untenable. If my very essence is wrong, if I have no value being what I am, how can I be worth anything? Why am I worth something if I'm what I'm not? If I'm worth nothing when I'm what I am, and I can't become what I'm not, am I worth anything at all? Or am I nothing? If I'm nothing, why do they press to change me? Can nothing be changed to something? Is this a question for physics? Chemistry? If I'm a cunt but am only valued as a prick, why don't men say it loud and clear, hey, to be happy each of us needs yet another prick! Prick plus prick? If there were no cunts there'd be no world! The need for pricks, that constant worldwide cry, only pricks count?! Howling prick, prick, prick, we're, in fact, howling, devil take them! Human beings are obsessed with self-destruction! Is this our essence?! The need for us to vanish, to fuck to death everything around ourselves, and then our very selves?! Are we all merely suicides striding with big steps toward the only appealing thing, plunging a knife into our own throat? Are we not that? Indeed that's precisely what we're **doing**! With the needle, axe, atomic bomb, the destruction of Muslims, the slaughter of gypsies, the beating down of Jews, the blowing up of Palestinians, the raping of Serbian mothers, the smothering of Croatian babies, the slipping of AIDS to blacks, severe pneumonia to the Chinese. The entire world, every person, the history of humankind, all this tells us that people are creatures obsessed with the longing to self-destruct! Vanishing is our destiny! Man and woman, the only beings that can, by fucking, do something to keep the world going, aren't candid with one another. They prevaricate, lie. Who prevaricates? Who lies? Who manipulates? Who is scared? Who is scared?! Now that's the real question. Who is scared? Men? Is that why they hit? Women? Is that why they fail to defend themselves? What are men scared of? Of women's superiority? But women aren't powerful!? Or they are, but they don't realize it. We women, we don't know the secret! We don't know we have power. We think our power is in our cunt. This story was sold to us by men. But men never speak frankly with us. We're the enemy. What's our power? What's my power? If I'd been able to recognize my power, I'd have discovered the secret of life! Then he wouldn't have beaten me. But I haven't the faintest notion of my own power. Nor my essence. It's most definitely not my cunt. Women, all women, including me, feel insecure when they realize their cunt isn't their most powerful weapon. This truth of ours, this truth made me powerless, insecure, a being who's asking questions but finding no answers. Men know but they keep their mouth shut? When we set our cunt aside we'll recognize our essence. Without our cunt—which is not our essence—we'll be left without the men who are after only that. Will we feel better only when we do what's in keeping with our essence? To give birth and be alone. To use a man. Maybe that's our only chance at happiness? To live without men?! Maybe that would keep the world moving ahead and make it better? We women would raise our kids ourselves, far from the male specimen's obsessive self-destruction, and these children would be different people. With no aggressive father around they'd grow up better, more open-minded, warmer. Humans face extinction along with the white tiger. A zoo should be built to help preserve humankind. Man and woman are, indeed, nothing more than animals. They engage with each other ruthlessly when they're compelled to mate. The Church and State have turned the human compulsion to mate into a need for love in order to keep us under control by imbuing us with pangs of guilt. Do not desire your neighbor's partner! A life spent waiting for and seeking the love of your life is a manipulation by Church and State. If we don't find our prince, our life is wasted?! But there's no prince! He's not there! The princes—the ones they tell us about—should be tried and rejected! The charm of life lies in knowing there are no princes! The searching is fun but not the finding. If we women were told the truth—there's no prince, one prince isn't enough for a life, one naturally feels the need to change princes—who'd control the world? Women, freed of the feeling of guilt, would fuck for the hell of it, they wouldn't be meeting the needs of the State, Church, multi-national corporations for whom they toil like slaves, and the one man in their one and only life. Chaos would erupt! Happy women and happy men would surely ask other sorts of questions of the Church and State and Corporations. Hence the stories about Cinderella, Sleeping Beauty, the white horse, the wedding, the oath "until death do us part!" They sold me the hunt for the prince as the meaning of life and fear of loneliness as the horse on which I'll ride until I snare my one true happiness. Marry, you won't be alone! Marriage is a prison sentence that's best if it's for life! They sold me the bill of goods that non-freedom is the only true freedom?! Give birth, when you get old your children will bring you tea! No one tells you that your children will only bring you tea if you can pay them for it. If people have the money to pay a waiter, this waiter needn't be their offspring! The imposition on all women of guilt, the tale of the prince on the white horse, isn't spun at random for little girls. The Church, State, Men, Power, Authority, they all want to squelch our joy of life. When they steal our joy of life, we women go after men who are obsessed by a single desire, to destroy the world we live in. Men! Ruiners! Burners! Warriors! Suicides! Gentlemen, Your Horrors, living was tough. There are so many questions we never got answers for, we the so-called people, we the under-est of underdogs in Earth, we women! Fine, I allow for the possibility that he who seeks an answer may get his answer. But we give birth, coddle, toil, slave . . . Between two risings, three blows, several births, fucking, which you don't want? Who can scream: answer, answer! Hey, Church, answer! Hey, State, answer! Eh, Corporation, answer! Fucked from the start! The Church, the State and the Corporation, all these are men. They're the Power! And Power responds to Powerlessness even when Powerlessness asks no questions. By whip, by fists, by digging out eyes and spinning fairy tales about the prickhead prince. All the unasked questions have been answered in advance once and for all. What are the chances—for us women—that we can squirm out from under the nasty bodies of our husbands and take a deep breath? None whatsoever! So, Your Horrors, when you're choosing guilty or not guilty, keep all this in mind! I killed him because I knew the answers to all my unasked questions.

I didn't know I was going to kill him while, there, that morning, on the edge of that meadow, we waited and waited. I see, I see us so clearly, both of us. We're lying on our bellies, our guns still in our hands, we're at the ready, we wait, we wait, we peer through the sights, we wait. Oh, how well I see us! The three of them come. A mother and two of her fawns. A roe deer? A red deer? I didn't dare ask. The roe or red deer raised her head and sniffed. In vain. The wind was blowing in the right direction. So is this it or are we waiting for a wild boar? Maybe we were waiting for deer, they were valued more than boars I'd say. When one of the hunters killed a deer, it was seldom reduced to a hunk of meat. They'd put it in the freezer and take it out on the day when the hunters' festivities were held. That was a great day in the life of every hunter. The Annual Hunt Ball! The hunters' wives had their hair done, donned their loveliest silk suit, slipped into new shoes. The hunters, of course, wore thick, green hunting garb and green shirts. Even their ties were green. On them was embroidered the head of a deer. A deer's head? How should one word it properly, that you sport a deer's head on your tie? On your tie you sport a ... No matter. Hunters have hunters' hats, on some hunters' hats there's a jay feather. Hats aren't worn to the balls. Game is served on the menu at the hunt ball. The appetizer, smoked venison, the main dish, venison stew with gnocchi. The hotel allows cakes baked by the hunters' wives to be served. The mayor of the town where the hotel is, a hunter, always attends the hunt ball. At his table sits a representative of the Slovenian hunters' society, because the Croatian and Slovenian hunting grounds abut. Musicians on the stage play *Rosamunda* every half hour. When they play *Rosamunda* the whole hall rises to its feet, couples spin around the floor, singing "Rosamunda, prettiest girl in the world, Rosamunda, prettiest girl in the world ..." Then some of the musicians bang pot lids together and everyone sings again, "Rosamunda ..." At the break, little girls, hunters' daughters, sell raffle tickets. All sorts of things are raffled off, from mixers to a weekend stay at the very hotel where the hunters are dancing. The prizes are set out on stage, television sets, CD players, cakes, sets of plastic chairs, hunters' knives with a handle carved from the bone of an animal, cakes, bottles of champagne ... The main prize is displayed at midnight. The lights dim, only the candles on each table are burning. A musical flourish strikes up. A beautiful girl steps into the hall, a wreath of pine boughs in her hair, she pushes a hotel cart, the kind maids use to deliver clean towels and toilet paper. A doe is laid out on the cart. Its eyes are open, its arranged on green pine boughs, it looks alive, candles are burning on the cart so the prize can be clearly seen. The girl steers the cart slowly through the hall, aaaaaaaah, the sighs of the admiring hunters and the whispers of their wives. How beautiful! The girl sweeps slowly along, the music plays softly, something by Kleiderman, the candles flicker, and when everyone, every last person, has seen it, when all of them, every last one, have had a good look at the dead eyes, the girl turns and slowly wheels the dead doe into the hotel kitchen. The lights go up, everyone claps, "Rosamunda, prettiest girl in the world" strikes up again ... After an hour or two the raffle is held. The mayor always wins the deer and he always gives it to the Slovene, and the mayor's always surprised when he wins the deer and so is the Slovene when the mayor gives it to him. The tradition is boring but it must be upheld. No one likes surprises. This, this'll work well as a segue. I told you, no one likes surprises.

And now I'll tell you how I was on my way home one day, walking along the main street. I saw them. There, all four, in the café by the train station. The daughters and the mother all wore glasses. The little girls were sucking a dark-red beverage up through straws, my lover was lighting his wife's cigarette. It flashed before my eyes how small my chances were of destroying this nest of eyeglass wearers. Two little snakes and one bigger one were firmly wound around his neck. My boyfriend, Laocoön. I remember the tale from high school. Two serpents crushed the priest and his sons to death, my Laocoön—the three of them were coiled around his neck! I snapped, I made the decision then and there. Despite the best of intentions I couldn't imagine a weekend with those two little girls poking around my living room in search of their glasses, spitting in my sink, leaving their dirty undies at my place, I'd fix them breakfast, lunch, dinner, all our weekends would be weekends with someone else's kids, little girls whom I didn't like even at a distance, I'd hide the fact that I didn't like them up close either. We'd spend our vacations together, I'd take them to Gardaland, they'd cling to my lover and curse the day their papa left them for this pale, white lady. I stepped onto the crowded, smelly bus, totally shattered. I came home, Eka was at school. In the bathroom I cried, cried, cried, wailed and wailed. Then I splashed my eyes and lay in our darkened room. "You aren't feeling well again," he said when he came in. "I'm not feeling well again," I said, snapping, for a moment I forgot who I was talking to.

The next day we got together again at the municipal council café. I didn't look out at the crowds that streamed by our table. I told him, "I'm horrified by your children, I don't want to see them weekends or for vacations, to toss their little undies into the wash and fold them in a separate pile until the next weekend. I don't care and I won't learn what they eat in the morning, at noon, in the evening, what they're allergic to. I cringe at the thought that they'll lose their glasses in my apartment, and the kids and glasses will remind me of the wife with whom, for now, I share a prick, and, soon, her children ..." He ordered a strong coffee, a glass of water, and a Linzer cookie, I ordered a fruit tea and a Linzer cookie. "I'm not interested in this story, I'm appalled at the very idea, I won't introduce my daughter to little sisters who are her sisters because their father's fucking her mother! No! No! No!" I was too loud, the pencil pushers stared, I lowered my voice. "And the grandmothers and grandfathers? Overnight I'd suddenly become a member of somebody else's family?! I've hardly adjusted to my own gypsy caravan! No," I said, "No, no, and no!" He was startled by my vehemence. "What's all the fuss?" he said, trying to cover my hand with his, I jerked mine back. "If you want, I'll sign on the dotted line right now that my daughters won't come to stay with us on weekends. I'll spend time with them somewhere, alone, between them and you I chose you, it'll be as you say, I'll do nothing without your blessing." "No," I said, "I don't want to pull you away from your kids, turn you into something you're not, take responsibility for the future of your girls. I don't love them, don't like them, they scare me!" "You've never met them," he said and took my hand again. I withdrew it slowly, I didn't care to seem hysterical. "I don't want to meet them and hear the voice of your wife on my phone, pay for tutors for the children who missed days of school because their papa left them, listen to gossip and nasty words on your and my account. Who'll prove to them that you're not leaving them for the slut who stole their father and who doesn't cook drumsticks the way their mama does! I don't want to fix food for children I don't know and suffer through yet another entrance exam! The exams I passed already, I've passed!" "You're wrong," he said, "you're overreacting, you're euphoric, children grow, they leave home, we'll be alone soon enough." "When?" I said, "in twenty years? Today's children stay with their parents till forty, I don't love you enough to tie my life to your children who'll spend their sunset years with us. How can you not understand?" "I don't understand your fury, why are you so angry?" "I'm jealous, your children will always remind me that you fucked their mother." "Easy now," he said, "you, too, have a daughter, and when I look at her, I'm not thinking of her father fucking you. We're adults, each of us has our own past, why wouldn't we start something new? Children are selfish, let's keep them properly contained, we won't be living because of them and for them, we'll live as we please, for ourselves, for the children we'll do what we must with no passion or raised voices. Children don't need crazy love, tears, shrieks, histrionics, we'll be a service to support them as they grow. They won't be the reason for our existence nor the measure of our happiness, let the children be." "So speaks a man," I said, "only a man can talk about children that way." "Unfortunately," he said, "I can only speak as a man. You're with me, I trust, because I'm a man," and he laughed. "What's so funny?" "It's funny," he said, sinking his little teeth into the Linzer cookie, mine was still on the plate, untouched, "how much passion and imagination you're pouring into these future catastrophes. What if none of it happens? Maybe the mother of my daughters will keep her children on a short leash? She'll hate me and never let me near the kids? We'll see them once every three years?" He looked at me with his little eyes, they twinkled. He's mocking me, I thought, my anxiety is foolish to him. "At last we'll be alone, the two of us," he looked me in the eye. "We'll sleep in the same bed, go to the movies, hold hands, I'll read to you in bed every evening, I'll buy you corn at the marketplace and Jaffa cookies, I'll roast you a veal shank under a special clay lid, we'll order the Turkish clay lid from Herzegovina for three hundred kunas, it looks like a flying saucer, red. I'll buy you a Burberry coat, our friends will visit, on weekends, for dinner, I'll buy a stereo set for the bedroom and we'll listen, before we fall asleep together, to the Star Dust radio show with that whiz of a DJ," he looked at me. "In short," I said, "everything you do now with your wife you'll do with me." "You're such a bitch," he said and wiped the traces of sugar from the edges of his lips, "I don't do any of that with my wife, why are you so anxious, jealous and mean, jump in why don't you, swim!" "I'm not in the mood for jumping," I said, I grabbed him by the hand, clutched his hand in mine, the waitress stopped rinsing glasses behind the bar and watched us. "I won't jump," I said, "I'm scared, I'm scared, I'm scared to jump, I won't, I won't jump, don't ask me to anymore!" "Fine," he said. He got up, I watched the short man stride to the sliding door, his feet curved in when he walked, when he was little he'd worn orthopedic shoes, they hadn't help much. He didn't call again.

10

MY BACK HURT, my eyes stung. My arms were stiff. I needed to pee!!! I'm talking about lying on my belly on the edge of that meadow, I'm talking about the hunt. Oof! But. Fine. The roe or red deer won't be out forever on the meadow with its two under-age fawns. It'll leave. This was the crack of dawn. Real day would soon come. And when it came, I'd pee! Quick, quick, quick! I'd pee for such a long time, shshshshshshshshsh! In the woods, by day, I'm free to pee to my heart's content. Then the animals worth shooting, the good catches, go into hiding. Birds can be killed all day long. When they hear you peeing they fly off and then they fly back. The air was crackling with birds' calls. He was breathing lightly, I felt it, I didn't hear it, the doe was grazing, the little ones romped. Every once in a while she'd raise her slender head, sniff the air, she sensed no danger, lowered her head to the grass. We waited. For the buck? The roebuck? A wild boar? An elephant?!! I had to pee! Misery! Torment!!! My whole body was screaming, I'll pee, I'll pee, I can't hold it in, I'll peeeeeeee! Your honors, I really had to pee. Look, even the story about my unbearable urge to pee isn't a proper segue into what I wanted to relate. And I'd like to tell you how it felt when I broke things off with my lover. I felt strange. I stared straight through my daugh-ter, through my colleagues, through my husband. Once he said,

"You're not listening to me." We were sitting at the kitchen table, it was early afternoon, there were women's heads at the windows of the neighboring buildings, they were always there. He got up from the table, came over and yanked out a lock of my hair. My eyes filled with tears, tears of pain, not of fear or grief. Oprah said that bald women look older. If he yanks out two more locks of my hair he'll turn me into an old lady, I won't have to live, I'll die soon, I laughed and got up from the table. The women's heads were looking at me, or maybe they just seemed to? "What are you laughing at, slut?" I laughed and laughed and laughed. I pranced around our kitchen, the part with the cabinets. I yanked out my hair, flung the light hairs about, laughed at the women's heads that might have been looking at me, happy that my death and old age were nigh. "You're mad," he said and walked out. I'd hoped, I was really hoping, he'd grab me by the hair and smash my head against the wall until it burst like a squash. Maybe he, too, had had enough of our life? He needed a better wife, someone who'd aggravate him less, who'd be more sane? I'd tell him I'd had a lover. I'd tell him I'd had a lover! I'd tell him!

I didn't. While I was alive I wasn't stupid. I played the faithful wife, we all must be what we're not if people are to trust us. Those are the words of my later mother-in-law. How did she die? A normal death, she collapsed, they took her to the hospital, one son rushed off to Trieste while she was comatose and cleared out the account for which he held power-of-attorney. Was that son my husband? No. My mother-in-law, my late mother-in-law, lived for some seventy years and then was gone. The only mention of her was each year on the Day of the Dead. Her husband beat her and screwed other women. When I became the wife of her son, she lifted her skirt and showed me her purple-bluish thigh. "You see," she said. She was an odd, and, in a way, dear woman. If she had two kunas in her pocket she'd go off to her neighbor's, borrow another five from her, then purchase something at the store for ten and say, "I'll pay you back in three days' time." She'd always return the money. She loved many people. She was very attached to the nieces of her neighbor's late cousin two doors down and she was also fond of the daughter of a gentleman who was a sailor on foreign ships, these people lived five blocks away. Their daughter, her name was Lidija, was supposed to be married on a Saturday. It wasn't the custom for others to give gifts, only the closest neighbors. Nevertheless my mother-in-law, my late mother-in-law, brought five kilos of sugar, two kilos of flour, a bottle of rum, baking rum, and a half-kilo of coffee. Such was the custom in her village that she was always reminiscing about, although she'd been living in town for forty years. My late father-in-law and my late mother-in-law went off to visit the house, five blocks away. He's the one who told me the story.

They entered and an unknown woman, meaning a woman he hadn't met, leaped out at him, she was the mother of the bride. He handed her the bag, she put it into the corner, and said, "You shouldn't have, good lord, this is far too much." My father-in-law said, "A modest gift, but it's from the heart." My late mother-in-law stood to the side. "Listen," he said to me, "the woman's eyes were full of tears, brimming, as if we'd come to a funeral. 'Right this way,' she took me by the arm, 'No, no, not there, that's the kitchen, come into the room where the gifts are.' She confused me," said my father-in-law, "took me by the arm and steered me into the living room. She was crying. The tables were covered with gifts, it was a rich house. There were boxes holding mixers, television sets, vacuum cleaners. By the legs of the vast table were propped paintings wrapped in dark paper, countless pieces of porcelain gleamed upon it. 'We set them out so that everyone can see that it's a service for twenty-four,' she told me. I looked at the heap of plates and saucers, bowls, and dishes, there were several big, huge bowls. 'Yes, ma'am,' I said, 'very, very lovely.'

'You shouldn't have,' said the woman and squeezed my arm, she looked at me, her eyes wet, 'you shouldn't have, it's much too much, your wife loves my daughter, but this is too much, dear …' She stopped, then she said, 'sir …' She would have used my first or last name had she known one or the other. Then it hit me, Good god, I paid for all of this, I bought all this, the rubbish came from me, and on top of it the sugar and rum and coffee, I paid for it all, we're owing for our electricity and rent, but I paid for it all!! She," he was referring to my late mother-in-law, he told me this story in front of the building where they lived, our feet were in parched, brown grass, "She had stayed out in the hallway. We went into the kitchen together. There were people I didn't know in the kitchen, in that kitchen I made up my mind, when we go out, right there on the street, I'll kill her! I'll choke the bitch to death, I'll throw her under a truck! Never again will people I don't know take me by the hand and thank me for gifts! Never again!" My mother-in-law, my late mother-in-law, wasn't a stupid woman. My father-in-law, my late father-in-law got drunk with the people he didn't know in the unfamiliar kitchen. While the gift-givers were singing songs about the love that binds us all and how love is an ache deep in my heart, my late mother-in-law slipped out the door. The old man came home, he wasn't so drunk that he couldn't wake her up, grab her by the neck, drag her out of bed and plant his foot, shod in a heavy boot, on one of her thighs, the right one I think. I saw the thigh. A huge, dark-blue blood-soaked splotch, dark-red, burst capillaries, a million of them, terrible cellulite, veins running down her shin as thick as rope! Veins? Arteries? Oof, what if my legs look like that one day, who'll fuck me then! Look, look, the old bitch, how dare she spend the money of others, cheat and lie, she got what she deserved. My poor husband, what a mother he has, I'll be a better woman, I won't buy expensive services for twenty-four, or cheap ones for that matter, nor will I buy gifts for people I know, he'll value that, he'll see, this woman is nothing like my mother, that spendthrift. Old lady, if you hadn't bought that pricey set of porcelain from the wife of a sailor who brought the set from China having paid a pittance for it there and then sold it to you for a fortune, you'd never have been stomped on! Old lady, your husband doesn't love you, your son doesn't love you, I won't have any trouble with you. My husband won't waste his time on phone conversations with his dear little mother. This was a consolation.

I cast a glance ... Yes, again I'm in that woods that wasn't a woods, we're lying belly-down by a bush on the edge of a large meadow ... I cast a glance while I was dying with the urge to pee, at the son of my late mother-in-law. He was lying there near me, not right next to me but a little farther off. Still I saw, I felt how tense he was, he held the gun tightly, his wrists were white. I squeezed my legs together, tried to get something compelling rolling in my mind, something to distract me from the aching need to leap into the air and pee mid-flight. White wrists, white wrists ... I watched his hands on the trigger, I've already said that, and remembered the gas station, the one at the east end of town. He got out of the car and told the little girl who washed car windows for a tip that she needn't wash ours. But, sponge in hand, she moved toward the car. When he'd paid for the gas he took his seat at the steering wheel and grabbed it tight, the knuckles on his fingers were white then, too. The little girl soaped up the windshield, and I pulled a ten-kuna note from the glove compartment. With his right foot he stomped on my bare, left foot, it was summer. I held the ten-kuna bill in my hand, the girl looked at us, I pressed the button and lowered the window. He ground down on my left foot. Whimpering, I gave the little girl the money. We left the gas station and pulled over a short way farther on by a bus stop. He grabbed me by the hair and bashed the dashboard with my head. "Slut, slut, slut! Those little bitches don't wash the glass, they just smear the dirt, let her use her cunt to earn her her smack!" It did occur to me now and then to leave him. Kick him out, the prickhead, and go back to Mama! And then just as I would say, "I'll leave my husband," I'd say "I won't leave my husband. I won't leave this husband! I won't leave this husband!" Sometimes I'd scream this to myself.

But, talking to myself, I might have said these same words softly, without hysteria. My dear honors, had I been a quiet, self-controlled woman would I have killed my husband? Had I been a proper little lady I wouldn't have waited for you to summon me nor would I have ridden this heavenly nag and lurched, lurched, lurched. I'd have stridden right into your court! So be it, I deserve this. I'll spell out some of my thinking for you, you'll see what dilemmas were eating at me, what troubled me, you'll learn something about me. It's tough for me to stick to topic because you aren't saying anything, my words have no echo, to whom am I speaking? This is seriously vexing. You do this on purpose so the culprits are exposed, bared to the bone. Foxes! Oh, what foxes you are, you celestial judges! We're building a house, I howled the better to hear myself! We have debts and overdrafts! He's under stress! I'll be better, I'll mend my ways, I won't aggravate him, I'll be good, I'll prove to him that all women aren't sluts, if I'm good, if I'm better, if I'm not crazy, everything will be different! I'll forget my lover! All lovers are the same! They fuck around and they always go back to their wives! They, too, have overdrafts and debts! What can a lover give a woman that she hasn't already had?! All sperm are the same, same taste, same smell, as long as the lover washes himself. Some are a little yellower, others paler. Is the yellow the opposite of the white? No it's not! Some orgasm in a spurt, others with a dribble, sometimes your mouth is full, other times you barely muss your teeth! There's no difference! They all moan, I'm coming, hold me, squeeze, a little, here I am, then they fall asleep, they breathe softly or snore out loud, they're on their side or on their back, they have a belly or they don't, their muscles bulge or their arms are as skinny as a chicken bone, they're tall, medium-height or short, hairy or smooth, they hit or they don't hit, they're all the same, the same, the same!

Life is tough, we made it through the war, it's tough on men, we're the stronger sex, we live longer, just a little patience is all, their life expectancy is shrinking, if they make it to forty-five they're lucky, what's the rush, hey, time to chill! Natasha! Don't, don't tell me, you're repeating yourself, ma'am! Don't say that to me! I know I'm repeating myself, but this isn't easy! Don't forget! And besides repetition is a legitimate defense! I'm repeating myself, fine, I know, I'm repeating myself, but I'm telling you about my life, no one's life is a constantly titillating story with no boring repetitions, life is about repeats, boring repeats. So I'll repeat, what can you do to me, nothing?! Natasha!

She's secretary to our editor-in-chief. I told her, I'm leaving my husband! She had a lover. When the two of them screwed, the musical editor slipped Aretha Franklin into the player. I can't abide Aretha. "Your head's not screwed on right," Natasha told me. "Do you know, do you have any idea what it means to leave your husband and move into a sublet with your lover who has a wife and two kids? Did anyone tell you what abandoned bitches do?" "Vesna did," I said. "Do your homework," said Natasha. "She'll call him day and night. His daughters will suddenly take up French, English, Spanish, tennis, math, snorkeling, skiing, she'll enroll them in a private school. At midnight, at 3:00 a.m., the abandoned kids will constantly be in a panic. They'll come over to your place for lunch and ask, 'Why did you leave us,

Papa?' And if they had no papa they'd have no underwear for their fat asses! Their dear sweet mummies never earn enough. Do you know how much dentists, orthodontics, braces for crooked teeth—the visible ones, the invisible ones—how much they cost? Abandoned bitches have a hundred ways of making your life a misery. Their children will become your concern. How to arrange a weekend so they won't be bored? Your second husband will be buying his former wife birthday presents for years to come to absolve himself of his guilt before his kids. You'll have to choose the perfume and silk scarf for the lady you could have done without. You'll work overtime to pay for the kids' tutors even though even dear god himself couldn't help them earn a passing grade. Each time they flunk, even though you paid for fifty private tutors, they'll celebrate by cheerfully yelling into the phone, 'We flunked, we flunked!' Do you know what it means to live with a divorced man who drags along two screaming brats? To foist his former wife and two kids on your life?! My dear, you're faced with a terrible quandary, staying with a husband who hits you or leaving with a fucker who's great in bed and 'who'll stop fucking you because his life will become so difficult?! Yes, it matters that he won't hit you!" We were in the boss's office, it was quiet there, the air-conditioning was working, we were sipping chilled Pinot Gris, Natasha was doing her long, firm nails. She was painting them a pale pink. "So why," she looked at me with those big, light-brown eyes, "do you have to leave your husband? Go on fucking both him and your lover. You can always claim an inflammation of the ovaries with your husband and sneak off with the lover somewhere two or three times a month. All of us at the office will stand behind you! Goddamn! Forty people will be constantly furnishing alibis! Don't go changing one holy mess for another. But if you want to leave your husband, do it on your own, find a place and live alone, pull yourself together, alone!"

"He'd find me," I said, "he'd break the door down, he'd kill me. If I end up with someone else he'll respect that." "Jesus," said Natasha, "you're looking for a man to protect your back? Is there such a man? Surely not the father of two little kids! There are no men who protect a woman's back, remember that! All those men we're after so that we can rely on them, it's them relying on us. Open your eyes! Calm down, find someone with no kids, or, better yet, have your husband murdered, and before that take out a life-insurance policy on him. I sell Austrian life insurance." Natasha grinned and held the little brush in the air.

"This isn't funny," I said. "Men saunter through life without a care in the world for their children, they leave their wives, change lovers, marry ten times, can't remember their children's names, all of you are just alarming me. Why do you constantly repeat how my lover will care more about his kids than about his prick, how my lover will be forever pampering his children, cosseting his former missus, how our shared life will be nothing but worries about the kids he made with his ex? All of you are divorced, all of you have lovers, you live with the fathers of someone else's children, you don't leave them, you read those other children bedtime stories but you scare me?! All of you! No matter whom I talk to all of you speak of the horror of leaving one's husband, yet all of you did! You're lying, you're jealous of my happiness!" "No, no," said Natasha. "We want to help you. You're obsessed with guilt, justice, injustice, faith in eternal love. Life is something else, fucking with lots of sighs and sweat. Life is acrobatics. As much strength as you invest, real strength, in a real project, that's how much you'll get back. You must never put all your faith in love. Love, or what you think love is, giving one-self totally to someone who has between his legs what you don't have, that's not love. That's a fuck-over. Men are creatures who give us orgasms and cash, not always together, and that's what we should expect from them, the rest is all lies and propaganda. We're not twenty, old lady, forget the lover with a prick full of hungry mouths. Change! The less you expect, the more you'll get!" "I have to do something," I said, "I can't bear it anymore. I'm shitting blood, short of breath, I'm losing my hair, my skin is cracking, my head is all scabs, and as soon as I see him naked I get my period! Look at the rash on my breasts," I undid my blouse, "this itches terribly here," I said and scratched my chest until droplets of blood appeared. "Oh," said Natasha, "you're in big trouble."

11

HEY, A BIG WIND starts blowing, the white laundry ripples, those wings flap. Jesus! What does this wind mean! This heavenly tempest! I'm scared! I'm restless! A storm might bring a cloud! My husband on it? On another cloud my father? Our clouds could merge into one? Your honors! Don't do this to me! Noooooooooo! Up, down, right, left! Can anybody hear me? Heeeeeeeeeeeeeelllllp!

That animal, I mean the doe, the mother of those fawns, grazed and grazed. The young ones romped around her, skipped into the air, four little hooves, then they tumbled into the grass. The baby fawns touched me, little stiff-legged Bambis with skinny bodies. My daughter Eka was a baby once, this is a low blow, I'm trying to sell you a story about myself as a tender-hearted mother. And I am one, in a way, I was, in a way, a mother with a tender heart.

He said, "I'll be home at twelve." Eka didn't like spinach. I put it in her milk bottle and wrapped the bottle in a white rag, let her think it's milk. She sucked and sucked, then stopped and spit it all out. We were covered in green, we giggled. He came home at eleven-thirty. "Where are my shirts?" "They're damp, on the sofa, you said you'd be back at twelve, look what Eka did to me, look how green we are, I'll pull out the ironing board and the iron, just a minute, just a minute." Eka was in her playpen and she flashed her four teeth for us. "Come on, what the fuck do you do all day long, you can't even iron two shirts, is that so difficult, am I asking too much?" "You came home a half-hour earlier, that's all." "You're an ordinary lazy cow," he was white in the face. I have nothing against cows if they're not an insult. That, the thing with the cow, caught me short. "What do you mean, cow?" From the heap of fresh laundry I pulled out his shirts. "You skanky cow," he said after a brief pause. I plunged my nose into his shirts. I felt we disgusted him, both of us, he looked at me as if our daughter had spit up on me, no, as if a drunken hobo had jerked off all over me. I felt that we, both of us, disgusted him. "Listen, if you're in a big hurry to leave for a trip, take the ironing board, take the iron, and iron them yourself!" While I talked I was setting it up. "Your mother deserves to be fucked by a dog! **Me**? It's **me** who has to iron here?! **Me**?! And what the fuck are you doing, what's **your** work?" I was always the one who did the ironing, never he, but I'd thought this to be my choice, not my assignment. And his comment, his reference to … her, I mean my mother, didn't sit well with me. I … never loved her, she meant nothing to me. And besides, that curse, "Your mother deserves to be fucked by a dog!," isn't something that should make a person freeze, breathe in, breathe in, breathe out. I got the message, he wanted to force me to see an image! She, on all fours, a big dog, its bright red prick bared, poised behind her. Who's he to link my mother to a German Shepherd with no master to walk it down the road?! The feral dog was supposed to jump me, I saw that in his light eyes. An unpleasant feeling. My eyes were full of water. I didn't offer his prick to the cunt of a feral bitch. I was angry, yes, angry, I drew the tears back into my ducts. It would've been better had I let the water flow downstream. He loved me tearstained. If I'd cried, he would have hugged me and said, "You're my sweet little boy ..." "Your father deserves to be fucked by a dog," said I. That's what I said. "Yes! Your father deserves to be fucked by a dog," I said. That's what I said! His father had been dead ten days, or maybe a day more. He loved his father. He really loved him. His father's death had hit him full force, because the death was so unexpected, if a death can ever be so or not so unexpected? While we're alive we think death has nothing to do with us, it's other people who end up buried. The ones who are shitheads or too good for this world. We don't think, I'm dead, I see things better, death is as banal as your morning shit or an evening's scratch of your hairy ass. It's clear to us that death is a natural phenomenon but we find it unacceptable. Totally. No one prepares us for death. They always talk to us about life, all our plans are prepared as if there is no death. If we were to live ten lives we wouldn't check off all the obligations on our agendas, that's what I'm talking about. That's why, when you leave for a hunt at dawn, you don't expect you won't come back from the hunt alive. Hunting isn't a high-risk adventure. In your hands is a legal gun, wild boars have tusks, deer have horns, roe deer—slender legs, birds—small beaks, a badger—a shallow den, everything's on your side. And when there's ... A haze, a slender moon in the sky, you, you skulk, you gauge where the wind is blowing from, you think how you'll kill a wild boar and plant your boot on the dead head ... Boom! Who knows what the last thoughts were, how the last sigh sounds of the hunter killed by his fellow hunter, mistaken for a wild boar? Who can anticipate such a death? The hunter? The fellow hunter? Certainly not! The hunter's family? The hunter's son, the hunter??!! My father-in-law was a passionate hunter. My husband told me how they went hunting together. "Eyes open, be quiet, don't make noise, take care, watch, just watch, learn, listen, stop, don't speak, hush, whisper, pee quietly, why are you peeing, the leaves are rustling, not on the leaves, no, not on the leaves, walk, turn, this is the woods, the woods, move, stop, listen, attention, learn, softly, hush, stop!" That's how his papa spoke to the boy. Then he'd pull him up into a big tree. And in the treetop, papa and son, hidden, would wait for the plump jays.

When I was little we had two jays in a cage. Mrs. Meri had a house at the top of the steps, ours was at the bottom. Mrs. Meri's husband, Barba Toni, never climbed the stairs. When he needed something he'd shout, "Meri, Meri, bring me my fish spear, Meri, Meri, bring me my fish trap, Meri, Meri, bring me the net!" Auntie Meri would hurry down the stairs and bring them. A short, fat woman, she huffed up the stairs, puff, puff! Our jays learned to caw, "Meri, Meri, Meri, Meri!" Auntie Meri jumped up and down on the terrace and called back, "Toni, Toni, answer me, Toni!" The jays cawed, "Meri, Meri …" … I hid behind the half-open shutters and laughed so hard I peed in my little white undies. Auntie Meri shushed our jays, she stopped coming out of the house, Barba Toni called for her in vain and then he had to climb the steps himself. A short fat man, up the steps, puff, puff! Pančo lay in front of the house, our two cats lay on his belly. For hours at a time. When unfamiliar cats went by, Pančo would go crazy, he'd shake Risi and Sweet Grapes off his belly and chase them. They'd scamper up the mulberry tree, Pančo would bark at them, bowowowowowow … And then the jays would bark, bow, bow, bow, bow. The Jays, bow, bow, bow, bow, Pančo … Nonna would cover the cage with a brown blanket that had two gray stripes or with a white cloth with AZUCAR printed on it in capital letters. The cloth was from ripped open sacks in which the Americans, once long ago, had sent us sugar. They were used to make sheets. The more you washed them, the softer and whiter they became. Nonna would cover the cage, the jays would stop cawing. This was no final solution. Nonna made a stew of the jays, they raised too much of a ruckus, they irritated the tourists who were coming to visit our little town more often and slept in the morning and afternoon and evening. I ate the jay stew, with polenta on the side, I licked and sucked on the thin little bones, savored them, and all the while I had no clue I was eating jays. When had I eaten bird meat? Never. Mama told me, "Ha, you ate our jays!" My eyes were full of tears. My little heart was bruised, my soul ached. I never forgave Nonna for that. The old bitch, she broke their slender necks.

His father shot at jays from the treetops, they sat together on the fat branch. Papa would stop shooting, the son would climb down, pick up the corpses, pile them into his father's knapsack. They were all big and fat, with feathers the color of sky and indigo shimmering on the dead bodies. They didn't eat the jays, his mother didn't stew them. They'd come and empty the knapsack into the garbage can. I never told him, your old man's a murderer, jays are my favorite creature! Donkeys I was fond of too, I was very fond of them, donkeys, I think, but that has nothing to do with this story from his childhood. He and his father killed dozens of birds, two roe deer, one stag, two boars, a little badger, a boar piglet. Some of the animals I'd forget, perhaps I'd forget all these deceased animals if their glass eyes weren't looking at me from the walls of our apartment. The head of a huge wild boar hung for years over our double bed. I called Mr. Nikola, we didn't have a drill. I told my husband, "I called Mr. Nikola, I'm scared that the boar's head will fall on mine, while I'm asleep." "You're really stupid if you think that four thick dowels like these will give way." He showed me with his thumb and index finger how thick the dowels were. Mr. Nikola came, took down the huge head, I helped him, I vacuumed up the dust from the old bristles, Mr. Nikola inspected the dowels that had been in the wall, from a big, brown leather bag he took out new ones, drilled four deep holes in the wall in the hallway, and now the wild boar's head is mounted there. My father-in-law took pictures of this boar, the owner of the big head, I mean, from when it was just a little thing. He took pictures of it rooting for acorns with its mama, he took picture after picture until the boar grew big. We have a film at home that records the boar's whole life. I've never watched it.

He killed it, so they said, on his seventh birthday. His father was killed by a hunter, an elderly gentleman with fat glasses on his fat nose. This happened in the same woods where my late father-in-law killed the wild boar, many songbirds, a few deer and a little badger ... Was the badger killed by my husband? Yes, the little badger was killed by my husband. He, my husband thought, had the right, he was a judge, to listen personally to what the murderer would say. We went in an official car. The driver, the investigative judge, the pathologist, he and I. I wanted to be with him, I knew how difficult it would be, how much he loved his father. It was a hellishly hot day, August. His father's corpse was laid out on a stone slab in the village chapel. The pathologist had to extract the bullet from the corpse. There were people waiting who were supposed to dress the deceased and place him in the coffin. Two women and two men, dressed in black, stood by the chapel door, to the side, and waited. The men crossed their arms across their chests, the women were kneading white cloth handkerchiefs. They weren't crying. It was hellishly hot. There was no water near the chapel. The villagers brought the pathologist clear water in buckets, from the chapel they toted away pink liquid. The pathologist was young, nearly a boy, clumsy. He kept leaving the chapel and taking from the car larger and larger knives. I thought my husband would keel over. He clenched his lovely lips and big hands. He looked into the woods behind the chapel, the day was scorching. Finally the pathologist said, I can't find the bullet. The investigative judge, a large, tall man, nervous because of the heat and because this was supposed to be the first day of his vacation, snapped. "Listen," he said to the young pathologist, "if the bullet entered the body," he paused, "did the bullet enter the body?" "Yes," said the young pathologist. "And it didn't exit the body," said the judge and paused. "Did the bullet exit the body?" asked the large, sweaty judge. "No," said the pathologist. "That can only mean," said the judge, he paused, "that the bullet's still in the body, doctor!" He was shaking, so the pathologist took a new knife from the car, or was it an axe, it didn't take long, he came over and cheerfully brandished the bloody bullet. He was holding it between his index finger and his thumb. "Good, doctor," said the judge and paused. "Hallelujah," said the judge. I thought he'd keel over, my husband, I mean.

He examined the murderer. The old hunter sat on one side of a long, wooden table, in a dark-blue suit and white shirt, no tie, in sweltering heat. We across from him. In the corner of the large room stood a drum, on the wall hung folk costumes. Red dresses, black vests, black, men's pants, several caps, they looked like little bowls, some sort of a culture center. "I couldn't see well," said the hunter murderer, we couldn't see his eyes through the thick lenses of his glasses. "A boar appeared on the hill, I shot, I brought one down, the others shouted, don't shoot, don't shoot." I smiled, I regret that. We were on our way back. In the car I sat next to the driver, with the pathologist, my husband, and the judge squeezed into the back seat. The car had no AC. I asked the young pathologist, "How can you do this kind of work, does it sometimes make you sick?" "It always makes me sick," said the young pathologist, "on the curves. Stop!" The driver pulled over. The pathologist retched by the side of the road, it was terribly hot. We waited for the doctor to finish spewing, then, slowly, he wiped his mouth, straightened up and breathed deeply several times. He got into the car and sat on the front seat. I sat on the back seat, by him. In the car you could smell the stink of vomit. His thigh by mine was as hard as a rock. I wanted to have sex with him then, I was scared we wouldn't screw because of the death, his grief, for months. I thought how difficult this must be for him, the day was hot, we were driving, skimming across the waves, birds were singing, the pathologist was puking, the judge was sweating, the driver switched on the radio, one of the bleached-hair, popular singers, I was never able to tell them or their voices apart, she sang how he left her but she still loved him. Life was drumming in our car, while on the stone slab, in the bloody chapel—who knows whether they'd wash the floor properly before tomorrow—his father was lying, hacked to pieces with an axe, the being he loved most in the world. He fucked me that evening after all, I breathed a sigh of relief.

When he'd come home that day, when he said, "Your mother deserves to be fucked by a dog" to me and I said to him, "Your father deserves to be fucked by a dog," the story about his dead father was fresh and raw. I told him, "I love my mother," this was a lie, "just as you love your father," this was a lie, bullshit. "My mother's cunt is as sacred to me as your father's corpse is to you." Of course, of course this had nothing to do with the truth. He shuddered when I said the word **corpse**, he looked at me, appalled, I realized, uh oh, he doesn't get it, uh oh uh oh, that his old man's a corpse, that he's rotting in that grave in their village. He thinks the old guy went off on an excursion. It was late, oh so late. He slammed me with his big, fat, right fist in the temple, and with the same fist in the nose. His eyes were white, pure white. Two little egg whites staring at me. Then he swung again. I froze with fear, with horror. I thought, he'll kill me, blood spurted from my nose, he grabbed me across the chest or shoulders, swung me up into the air, and carried me to the balcony. I screamed, "Help! Help!" Our daughter howled in her playpen, she showed us her four little teeth, she shook the railing and stared at us, her eyes were wide, I looked into her eyes while he carried me out to the balcony. The glass door, the balcony, the edge of the railing. He set me down by the railing and said, "Cow, this is ridiculous, find someone to do the ironing!"

I ran myself ragged. To find a woman who came well recommended. The good ones had more work than they could handle. Their weekends were more open, no one wanted them around on a weekend. To our apartment came women who didn't steal, but they did talk. We didn't allow them to be in the house alone, I had to listen to them. "Ma'am, these are bad times now, it's never been like this, blah blah. All my friends are working abroad, in Italy, lately in Germany as well. The women from Ukraine, Poland, Romania, work for ten euros a day, twenty-four hours straight, and they offer, if you want it, their cunt in the bargain, before the war I was boss of a supermarket, I can use a computer, these sleeves, ma'am, do you want them with a crease or without? I'd be much obliged if you'd make me coffee, I have low blood pressure, I'd really like a smoke, if you don't mind, if you do mind I'll go out on the balcony, you have a nice place, there are five of us living in one room, my folks have come here from Benkovac, their house was torched, here they're subletting, papa has cancer." "Where's Benkovac?" that was me asking. "In the Zadar area." "Really?" that was me speaking, "Close to Zadar or farther away?" "About thirty kilometers from Zadar." "That's near," I said, "I was in Zadar, why don't they rebuild your torched house near Zadar?" "Who?" asked the lady doing the ironing. "The government," I said. "Oh sure, sure," the lady doing the ironing pressed a towel, "sure they will, they will. Do you have any slippers, my feet swell, I'm always on my feet, every day of the week I'm ironing, I clean on weekends, you have no idea how dirty some apartments are." "Yes," I said, "our apartment's dirty, it's an endless job, a little child, I never have the time, I emptied the dishwasher and stacked dishes in the hanging cupboards. "God help us, ma'am, how many T-shirts and shirts your husband has, I was just telling my husband the other day, 'listen, you have no idea how many shirts that gentleman has,' and my husband he said to me, 'Fuck the shirts, these two are all I need, he's a judge, I'm broke, but even if I had the money I'd never spend it on shirts, I'd buy a dog, fuck the shirts and clothes, a man needs a dog, I'd go off into the woods, run, live, life is short, a dog is man's best friend.'" "Your husband's a hunter?" I asked and loaded the dirty dishes into the dishwasher. "No, he's not." "I see," I said and wedged a saucer in between two larger plates, it didn't go, the dishwasher was crammed full. "What size shoes do you wear, ma'am, these slippers are too big." "Forty-one." "Too bad, you have so many shoes, I'm out of luck, not a single one of my ladies wears thirty-six, if it weren't for the women I work for, I'd be bare naked, like I told my husband, 'You men are always complaining and wanting a dog for going into the woods, life is no stroll in the park, why's it just us women who have to deal with it, in these tough times, the times are terrible, oh so terrible, we're working out of the house, us women, we toil like this in houses, and what do you men do, you complain that you have no dog and you go fucking other women while we iron.' He wants to send me off to Italy, I'd earn more there, I don't want to fare like the others, here their husbands are fucking the neighbors, buying a car with their wife's money and dressing in Gore-Tex, and the women toil. 'In your dreams,' I told my husband, 'I may be dense but I'm not that dense.' For my birthday I'll buy him a Dalmatian, he doesn't know that yet, he said, 'I want a

Dalmatian,' it's silly that they call those dogs Dalmatians, don't you think?" "Right," I said, I was standing by the dishwasher and staring at her back. "No distilled water?" "Nope." "That'll ruin your iron, one of my ladies, she had an iron, a professional model, the iron had this little container for water, you pour a few ounces of water in there, the ironing goes much more easily, one hundred fifty euros, you get distilled water, regular water has all those minerals, just cleaning the minerals, today, at the dentist, costs twenty-five euros, add in the fillings, resection, crowns, a person would have to work like a horse to fix his teeth. Oh, my lady, oh I'm so unhappy, unhappy when I sit for a bit and have myself a think." "We're all unhappy," that's me speaking, "Sorry, I'm off to clean the bathroom, you iron away." I looked at how I could squeeze by her without bumping up against her, the ironing board was blocking my way to the bathroom. "Yes, those tiles are light, oh so light, you see every hair, such a shame, and about the distilled water, a person thinks to be saving money by not buying it but you aren't saving, like I always say, money buys everything but good sense, am I right?" "Right," I said and wondered whether I could get to the bathroom through the glass door that separated the living room from the kitchen. "Your husband's a judge, you get around, maybe you know, is there any chance for my daughter? She has a university degree, economics, I can't bear to see her like this, she's at home, no work, she had an almost perfect grade point average, imagine, what good are all those years of school, she said to me this morning, 'Mama, I'm going to go ironing today,' she wanted to come here. I told her, 'no, people like older women, no one trusts the younger ones.' 'That lady isn't like that,' said my daughter, 'ask her.' Can my daughter come here instead of me sometimes, ma'am?" "I don't know," I said, "I'm going to clean the bathroom," I stood there. From my sleeveless dress poked my skinny arms with my flabby upper arms, I should be lifting weights, I should get rid of these bats' wings, that's what I was thinking about. In the bathroom I shaved my legs, plucked my eyebrows and the mustache I didn't have. I should tell the woman I didn't want her daughter, that I hadn't wanted her either, but her daughter—no way! Girls were forever on the phone, if they were left, even for a second, alone. There were boys always calling them at every hour of the day and night. They couldn't believe the girls didn't live here with us, our home phone number was saved on thousands of cell phones. The dimwits would call us and yell, "Put her on, I'll come and get her!" "Suck my cock, you ape, do you know what time it is, you ape," that was the voice of my husband. "Your cunt only did the ironing here, did you hear, the ironing, listen to me, the **ironing**, nothing more! And you, too, I fuck you, too, in the mouth!" He'd slam down the phone and say, "You're crazy. You're nuts! Do you even know who's hanging around our house?!" I was silent, it was always about midnight. I didn't say, I don't want women to do the ironing, I don't want to see them anymore, I've had it with them!

Your honors, your horrors, my life is chaos! Will you make sense of it? You will. You'll follow all the threads? What matters, what doesn't, you'll judge? So maybe I manipulate, the images I chose aren't ones you'd have chosen? I'm only a human being after all, a prevaricating creature who, even in death, paints herself—with earthly cunning—as a victim. It's difficult to stop being a person. It gets under your skin, I have no more skin but the impulse is still there, you can see what trouble it is! I feel it's a burden. You must understand me, my gut is in my throat, if I still have a throat, I'm waiting for you to summon me, so I can finally step onto something solid. Do I even have feet? And besides, every court, probably yours as well, asks questions. You'll ask me many questions. I'll answer, I won't defend myself with silence.

I told you how people experience death as something that happens only to others, a death in their home or their own death always comes as a surprise. I'll tell you something about my nonna. When she died, no one was surprised. She was eighty-seven, she'd stopped eating and drinking, we took her to the hospital, they gave her infusions, her body said enough already, she died. My nonna was born to a girl who, one day or one morning, was grazing sheep here in Lika. Some landowner happened by, came over to her, lifted her skirt, she probably fell, scrambled up, he knocked her down and took her from behind. Nonna was born. My great-grandmother's name was Matija, and in their stories they called her Tilda. This is madness, incredible, but the living truth. She sued the landowner, he acknowledged Nonna, and my great-nonna was granted alimony, there were papers. Lika burned in this war, the papers burned. How strange, war kills the living and the dead. It used to happen to me, while I was alive, that I'd be sitting there with my husband and I'd remember my great-grandmother. She was a brave woman, yet I have the puny heart of a cuckoo bird?! I'm not brave, I'm scared of beatings. I'm scared of beatings! Why was I so terribly scared of beatings? Why was I so terribly scared of beatings? I was horribly scared of beatings. If I'd resembled Nonna Tilda at least a little, everything would've been different. I didn't.

Riiiing, riiiing, an ugly sound, who's ringing? I set down the big knife, I was chopping parsley. I always put parsley in my tomato sauce. Riiiiing. And we said we'd take that bell out and replace it with a gentler ding-dong. The hallway is narrow, along the wall, a yellow-green cupboard with a mirror, on the cupboard, under the mirror, the keys. That's why he's ringing, he forgot his keys. On the wall, the boar's head, its beady, brown, glass eyes. I look through the peephole. My husband is hand-some. In a white T-shirt, tall, jeans, a flat belly, broad shoulders, I can't see any of this through the peephole. His eyes are gray. Riiiiing … I won't open the door! Not yet. When I open it, and I'll have to, I'll have an alibi. I'm at the police, across the table is the good cop, "Have some tea, ma'am." The bad cop paces fiercely from window to wall, window to wall, "Where were you when the doorbell rang, ma'am?!" "I was peeing, in the bath-room, sir. I have an alibi." I look at my husband. Where my neck joins my back I feel ice. I'm afraid of him, my husband, it's him I mean. I scratch myself, melt the ice, I want my blood to flow more smoothly through the link between neck and back. The blood is circulating normally, there's no ice, I know this, the doc-tor told me, ma'am, everything's fine. Riiinng … I have an alibi! When I open the door I'll say, "I was taking a shit." "What were you doing, ma'am, when it rang?" "Taking a shit." The policeman will turn off the bright lamp, release me. There's no more reason-able doubt. I know plenty of expressions. Reasonable doubt, unreasonable doubt, a validated judgment, summons, appeal, response, time limit for appeal, default judgment, negligence … My husband's a judge. It rings, rings. Tralalala! I'm beyond all reasonable doubt! Riiiinnng … I won't open it! Later I'll open it! I'll say, "I've got my period, I'm bleeding, I couldn't pull my panties on quickly, I couldn't find a pad, in my hand I'll hold my **evidence**." I switch eyes. I peer through the peephole with my left eye. No, I won't now, I won't yet open the door! I go to the bathroom, I pee, I don't wipe, I pull my panties onto my wet cunt. "Where were you, ma'am, when it was ringing?" "I was peeing, my undies are still damp, look, sir!" And now I run to the door! Slap, slap, slap slap, I slap my flip-flops on the tiles, let him hear me run. There! I wipe the grin off my face, he doesn't like it when I grin, he thinks I'm with someone, in his thoughts, he thinks I'm cheating on him. "Where were you, why didn't you open the door right away?" "I was peeing," I say and look him in the eye. I won't say the thing about my period, first day. I'll keep that in reserve. Later I can add it, I was fiddling with the pad, taking a long time to wash, something like that. If I have to show the pad as evidence, that won't be much in the way of evidence, a little pink stain, I've already been through that, better something than nothing. I go into the kitchen, he comes in after me. "You seemed to be looking at me through the peephole, laughing at me," I feel his gaze on my scabby nape. "You're paranoid," that's me talking. I chop parsley, the pile is big, I'll freeze a heap of the parsley. "Look at me when we're talking." I shift my gaze, I look at the pretty mouth. "Happy? I was taking a shit, I have diarrhea, I have to make lunch for her, she'll be home any minute, I'll dump this parsley into the tomato sauce, I'm not feeling great." "You were taking a shit?" "Yes," I say, my voice is firm. "Come on, let's go!" I don't ask where we're going. My criminal mind strains, in vain! We're in the hallway, we turn right, we step into the smaller hallway, he's gripping me by the shoulder, opens the bathroom door, pushes me in. "Sniff," he said, "sniff, you cow!" I sniff, sniff, sniff, sniff! "Does anything smell bad?" his paw on my neck. "Did anyone take a shit in here five minutes ago?!" My alibi shatters into one thousand three hundred bits. Never confess, never confess, that's the position of all ambitious criminals. "I turned on the fan," I squirm under his fingers, I twist it, I look into his light-gray eyes. "Why are you lying," he squeezes my cold neck, "why are you always lying? Grow up, you're less mature than your own daughter, celebrate your fifteenth birthday, blow out the fifteen candles, puff, puff, we'll all clap, we'll buy you a present, we'll snap your picture, you'll get a kiss!" "What's the truth," I ask. We're in the hallway, I look sideways at my head in the mirror. Short, salt-and-pepper hair, blue eyes, tall cheekbones. There are highlights in my hair. "Do something with your hair, you look mousy!" "Mousy?" "Yes, mousy, that's the word, like a rat." I went to Flora and had her give me highlights, from the mirror a streaked rat looks back at me. "What's so funny?" I was in a good mood, my voice was brighter, my neck was free. "You're always in a good mood when you think you got my goat. You didn't get my goat, you're sick." "Listen, you rang, I didn't hear because I was taking a shit. Shitting." I made a point of this. "A person can shit in such a way that he doesn't stink up the whole neighborhood, I don't eat much, I shit a little, mainly I drink water, Coke or coffee, I don't shit like a bloated cow. I'm skinny, oh so skinny, when people like me shit you don't need to empty the septic tank, dump bleach down the toilet, shove the shit down the slope with a special pole." "You're talking too much," he looked at me. "I took a little shit," I tell my story, "there's a difference between taking a shit and taking a shitlet, I should have said, I was taking a shitlet." I breathe. "I claim I was taking a shit, you claim I wasn't, your word against mine. Why would they believe you in court more than me, why would a jury, on the basis of your statement, decide I'm 'guilty?' Who are you?" I don't raise my voice. "When you talk like this, I wonder if you can hear yourself" He looks at me with his gray eyes. "The court, your word against mine, a jury, when all we're talking about is that I rang at the front door of the apartment we share, you looked at me through the peephole, you laughed at me, mocked me, to be precise. When you, I don't know how long it took, finally opened the door, you lied that you were taking a shit instead of answering my question, why you looked at me for so long through the peephole?" "Do you have a single piece of evidence, do you have **evidence** that I wasn't taking a shit, aside from your nose, which perhaps is inadequately sensitive?" With my index and middle fingers I massage my temple. "Not everybody shits like your uncle, so amply and generously. He approaches shitting as if it's his life's work. Not all people do. You don't have a single piece of **evidence**, judge!" "This is wearing me down," he says. I scoot under his arm, which he's resting on the doorframe. I'm in the kitchen. All the windows on the building next door are wide open. The women's heads are on their bedding that's hanging over the sill. They're staring at the façade of our building. Parsley again, the sun is shining, the kitchen is light, red, a wooden clock on the wall, it's eleven ten, maybe. "Listen," he says, "we can sit down like people and talk about this." "Talk about what?" I ask politely, interested. The knife and my eyes all are on the shrinking heap of parsley. "We'll talk about how you looked at me through the peephole, laughed at me and mocked me, you didn't open the door, you made a fool of me. We'll talk about your sickness for which there may well be treatment. Go to a doctor why don't you?" "Go to a doctor why don't you?" my voice is bright. The knife bounces through the parsley. "How do you know you're healthy?" "I'm healthy," his voice sounds a little worried. He opens a kitchen cabinet, takes out the coffee pot ... Oh, nooooo! Noooo! I'll admit everything! I'll admit everything! I'll admit everythiiiiiing! Everything, everything, everything, everything! I didn't pee! I didn't shit! I'm only on the first day of my period, I couldn't have been on the toilet for ages! I didn't, I didn't, I howl to myself! I was lying, I was lying, I scream to myself! He pours three cups worth of water into the black, enameled Turkish coffee pot, two for himself, one for me. When he makes the coffee we'll sit in the living room, me on the sofa, him in the armchair, he'll put the ashtray on the glass tabletop of the bamboo table, he'll pinch the cigarette between his index finger and his thumb, he'll lick it. Nooooooooo, I scream inside! Hey! Am I not screaming inside? Am I screaming outside? "What's wrong," he asks me, interested. "Nothing." The researcher in my head digs, burrows. What was wrong with me? Why did I scream? There can't be … nothing? I stab my left index finger with the tip of the knife. That's what's wrong! I show him my bloody finger, stick it in my mouth. He looks at me, then he turns to the gas burner. The water boils, he stirs three teaspoonfuls of coffee into it and two spoonfuls of sugar. We're in the living room, me on the sofa, him in the armchair. I look at his dark-gray eyes and pink hairless face. I wait. When he finishes pinching the cigarette, when he licks it and lights it, he'll say something. The cigarette burns between his fingers, he has beautiful, big hands. He opens his mouth, speaks, "Look at yourself." His eyes are on mine. "Look at you, your shirt's dirty, you haven't changed your jeans in weeks, your hair sticks out every which way, why don't you wash your hair?" "I washed my hair," I say, "that's why it's sticking out." He sets his cigarette on the porcelain ashtray, yellow porcelain, on the ashtray—violet and dark-blue flowers, green leaves. His gray eyes ride my blue eyes. His eyes are a stud horse, mine— a mare. If the mare submits, the stud will shove it in. The mare isn't in the mood for sex, she has a big ass and fat legs, she doesn't budge. I don't look away. "OK," he holds the cigarette between his teeth, "Go to the hairdresser's do something, if you won't do it for your own sake, do it for the girl, kids like an orderly, sane mother." "No way! The effort's pointless, you animal!" The mare has become a bronze monument. The mare is made of bronze that's too thick. The horse prances. "No way!" I look him straight in the gray eye. "My daughter likes me disheveled," my voice is bright, I smile, hold on, mare! "Drink your coffee," he says, "it'll get cold." I drink, I wait. On the wall Stojni's *Black Cavalry*, a vast oil painting on canvas, black horses gallop, on their backs they carry black riders. It'd be so perfect to tie my husband to the tail of a black horse, let it drag him off into the distant steppe where they'd be building a hundred-story skyscraper. All that's there now is this pit for the foundations and these Mafia guys, grim men dressed in black wearing gold chains, cigars clamped in their teeth. They untie him from the horse's tail, he's alive, he shouts, "Wait a minute, you've got this all wrong . . ." Two of the gangsters grab him, they tip him back and forth on the edge of the deep oh so deep pit, one, two, three! He plummets, plummets, howls, no one can hear him, this is the bleak, oh so bleak steppe. A giant truck arrives, a cement mixer. It pulls up to the edge of the pit. The concrete mixes loudly, krrrkrrrkrrr, krakkrakkrak, the truck driver pushes buttons, the mixer rises up and spews out a broad, noisy cascade of concrete into the abyss. "Aaaaaaa" he shouts because it's deep and he can see the concrete gushing down onto him, then he's silent. The truck leaves, the two gangsters who tossed him into the pit wipe their hands on the trousers of their Brioni suits, the other two flick away their fat cigars and stomp on them with their Paciotti shoes, they climb into a long black car with dark glass windows, they drive away. Is there, in fact, a hundred-story skyscraper anywhere under construction on the steppe? I guess he ducked that one. I'm glad that, at the very last moment, the father of my child was saved. I look away from the Black Cavalry.

Then I look at Đurić's *The Dog that Ate the Sun*. The dog is grinning, the sun is in its jaws. Will the rabid dog break it to bits? "Why are you smirking," that's his voice. "I'm not smirking," I say, "I'm smiling, this is a smirk." I smirk. "So why are you smiling," the cigarette is between his teeth, "What's so funny?" "You were tied to the tail of a black horse, it dragged you and dragged you, it was looking for this construction site, a skyscraper and a cement mixer, it didn't find one, the gangsters were wearing Paciotti shoes, the concrete didn't bury you, you were saved, the steppe saved your life. If the black horse had headed to New

York City you'd be walled into the foundations of the new twin towers." He looked at me as if he were seeing me. "Listen, honey, tell me what's bothering you," this is my bright voice. His legs in his jeans are twitching, his Magli loafers are restless. "What's up with you, what's up with you," the cigarette is burning on the edge of the ashtray. "What's up with you, what's up with you?" I repeat his question. "I rang the doorbell and again found my crazy wife at home, that's what's up with me." I slurp my coffee. "You're slurping," says my husband. He stubs out the cigarette. "I'm slurping," I say. "You're aggravating me," says my husband. "How?" I ask. "You want me to snap, that's what you want, and when I hit you then it'll be my fault. You're in luck," he smiles, "today I'm in a good mood, I'm listening, tell me, what's going on?" "Why do you think I'm aggravating you?" I smile, "why wouldn't I dare to aggravate you?" I smile. "But why would you aggravate me?" his lips are still stretched. "And why wouldn't I?" and my lips are stretched. "You aren't sane today," I no longer see his teeth. Oh pa, I show my teeth to him, my eyes are squeezed tight because I'm smiling, "You said that **today** I'm not sane, does that mean that otherwise I'm sane?" He says nothing, looks at me. His eyes are the beast again that wants to pounce on the roly-poly bronze mare. Don't give in, mare, hold your own, my beast! I look him straight in the eye. He takes a new cigarette, pinches it, licks it, lights it. "I wonder," I say, "whether I'd be fast on the trigger if I were six feet tall and weighed 200 kilos?" "Please be clearer, if you can," my husband says and looks at me with interest. "Would I aggravate you if I were a sumo wrestler?" "I don't fuck sumo wrestlers," his lips are stretched again, I see his nice teeth.

A movie scrolls by before my eyes. A sumo wrestler as tall as a mountain bows to the audience, stands in the center of the ring. He's just beaten a mountain much like himself who's lying in the corner. In his black hair-do he has a yellow bone and a red bow, his ass is the size of a bread oven, he's wearing a black, silken thong size six hundred and fifty, he bows and bows. The audience howls, he bow, bows, and bows. The audience howls and howls. The sumo shows some his ass, others his belly. The ones looking at his ass see my husband enter the ring, his little prick is tense but minuscule, only the ones standing right by the edge of the ring can see it and they shout to the winner. The ones sitting a little farther off can't see it, the little prick, I mean, my husband they can see. My husband tries to shove his little prick into the sumo's ass. The sumo bows, he feels something tickle, he reaches back to scratch, feels my husband, lifts him into the air and heaves him into the audience. The audience howls. My husband vanishes in the stampede of the raging crowd. End of film. Oh! I smiled. "Why are you smiling?" "You're witty. This, 'I don't fuck sumo wrestlers,' this was great, it was terrific!" "Be clearer," he wants me to describe to him the movie. "OK, so would you hit me and fuck me in the head if you knew I could fight back?" "I don't hit you often, you're exaggerating. Control yourself and everything'll be fine." "Oh," I sigh, I stand up and for the first time since we've been together, I fart loudly. "I need to take a shit," those were my words, "if you can believe me." He looks at me, his eyes grow lighter. I go into the bathroom, sit on the toilet, flush the toilet, let him think I'm shitting. Then I get up from the toilet and start running the water in the bathtub, let it splash and sound and roar. I know I'll have to fuck with him, it's a foregone conclusion. Enough fucking with him! Enough! I've had it with fucking with him! From the woven-twig basket that stands on the washing machine I pull out a pen and on a piece of toilet paper I calculate how many times he and I have fucked. I've fucked, let it be a round number, for fifteen years, on average three times a week. I say on "average" because for the first six or seven years, don't hold me to the numbers, this isn't my strong point, we fucked three times a day. So three times weekly times fifty-two, that's one hundred fifty-six times yearly, one hundred fifty-six times fifteen, that's 2340 times! I wrote the figure 2340 in large numbers, circled it and added three exclamation points. So I've fucked my fill! Today I'll take a break! I'll give him a blow job, a quickie, terrific, and besides I've got my period, the first day, that'll be today's argument. Back in the day that wouldn't have saved me, back in the day, when I was still running under a thousand. Blow jobs don't count, Clinton said, oral sex isn't really sex. It's not a particularly intimate act, I blow him more often now because it takes less time, is less tiring, you can suck away while thinking about the right stuff. I don't want to put the blow jobs on paper. If I were to count up all the blow jobs and all the fucks I'd get a number that'd be worthy of a pension for the sluts in Holland and other civilized countries. Fucking is fuss. It's all more imaginative, candles, sticks of incense that I'm allergic to, my eyes tear up, the vanilla smell makes me sick. Those incense sticks have the same vanilla smell as the spray that we use in the bathroom after someone takes a shit. That's prob-ably how it has to be, vanilla is vanilla, but because of it I can no longer eat vanilla ice cream—for years my favorite food!

He's pounding the door. "Open up, open up," his voice sounds nervous. "I'm not feeling well," I groan, "I'm throwing up," I say with a shaky voice. I can vomit on demand. I'll retch up something before I leave. If I puke a lot I'll be a white, sick little bunny, messy, with bloodshot eyes, I won't have to give him head. Oh, oh! All my life I've done all sorts of things to keep his prick up! Pluck my hairs, wax my legs, exercise, jog, the hairdresser, highlights, short hair, long hair, pedicures, dentists, I wore braces, what haven't I done so he'd fuck me?! The effort was often both painful and futile. And now, this minute, it's killing me, how to get his prick to go limp?! Oh, us poor women! When will our desires and theirs conicide? I want a prick, just not his. That other prick tells me, see how big I am, I'm not like his, we're all different, why did you get hooked on that little nubbin? There are, my lady, a hundred pricks that are jiggling in this world and waiting for you to handle them, many heads will leap to your touch, take me, touch me, see my big head! I'm looking at my face in the mirror, my eyes are surprised, looking at me. You're talking with the prick of a stranger, are you in your right mind? This is what my blue eyes are saying.

"OK," I call, "I'm coming out. Don't bang on the door, I'm coming, I'm not feeling great, just let me throw up one more time." I shove two fingers down my throat, my index and middle fingers, up from my gorge come bile, coffee, Coke, I don't wipe off my mouth, I leave a slimy rim around my lips the color of green coffee. He doesn't bang. He's probably lying there naked on the bed in our bedroom. Yes, I'll give him head there, even if I end up throwing up afterwards, a real quickie, better there than here in the bathroom. This bathroom is filled with sad, oh such sad memories, here I had to put up with his thousands of ideas. Light sticks of incense, light candles from Ikea, arrange them on the toilet seat, turn off the light, scatter dried violet flowers on the water, sit in a tub of warm water facing each other, the violet flowers float, float, then sink. It gets colder and colder in the bubbles, there are too many of us, you can't budge, add more warm water, more, more, the hot-water heater empties, it would've been better to have a heater on natural gas, or one of those instantaneous water-heaters, everything smells of vanilla, of candles. The fragrant dry flowers strewn about on the bottom of the bathtub, it gets as hot as in hell because the fan is blowing, our butts are ice, our heads hot, I get arrhythmia … He, finally, caves. We get up from the icy foam that's no longer foam, pick the violet shit off our wet bottoms. I don't gripe, I don't say, "What the fuck are we doing in icy water in a bathtub that's too cramped, what good will these violets that aren't violets do us, they're five times the size of violets, who gets off on that, on vanilla that makes my head ache, on a fan that gives me midlife flashes, why all the candles, who died, and where am I headed with this?! Darling, at this very moment, right now, I feel like bashing you, not fucking you, I want to **bash** you! Do something for me, for us! Don't fuck me with that Indian shit, if the incense sticks are Indian?! Maybe they're Chinese? Macedonian?! You ape, you ape, you ape!" Never, never did I say any of this to him. I'd pored over too many textbooks and women's magazines. One mustn't talk with men as if they're normal human beings. In every manual for how to live with him and at his side, it says, men are morons and you're supposed to keep smiling when the fan is fucking you over and when you know your ovaries will be inflamed by the icy foam and the burning vanilla is making your eyes tear! Smile, caress him, suck him, shut up, stick out your ass, wiggle, don't wiggle, scream when he thinks you should, say ah, and oh, grab the towel rack on the bathroom door and push your ass toward him so he can push his against the washing machine. Why the washing machine behind his ass, why the towel rack on the bathroom door, why vanilla and not lemon, why the purple flowers, why, why?! Because, we oh the stupid cows that we are, we weigh less, we're shorter, quieter, lighter, because he'll tear our head off if we ask why! We don't dare ask questions of the heroes of our lives. Didn't we desire them, want them, snare them, get them? We did! Okay, we relished the pleasure of the hunt!

"Come out, come out!" The door is rattling again. "What the fuck, what are you scared of, come out!" His voice doesn't sound nervous. I'm not scared, it's clear to me that I must proceed to the feast. Pound away, this is great, being safe. "Just a minute," I groan with a tired little voice. I stick my two fingers deep down my throat, vomit noisily, burp, retch, loudly, like a lion. He walks away, I hear him walking but I'm not sure where. To the living room? Cigarette, pinch, pinch. Lick, lick, lick. He's waiting for me. Dear, dear, oh so dear god, if I were in a horror movie, something would happen! The murderer would sink the knife into my neck or the police siren would wail, eeeeeee, eeeeeeeee. It's just in life that nothing happens! Life is what goes on quietly between two pukes! Fuck! Fuck! Bang … baaaang … baaaaaang!!! He'll break down the door!

Oh how he fucked me after his father's funeral! We took a shower, I wasn't expecting sex, not while his father was lying in his freshly dug grave. If they'd lowered my father into a slimy pit, I thought, I'd hardly be celebrating with a romp. I lay on the bed, it was hot, my husband came in, he flipped me over on my belly, shoved his little prick into me, we were silent, he jabbed me with it as if it were big. When he came, I turned over onto my back thinking we were done. We weren't. "Get up," he said. I got up. He grabbed me by the neck and steered me to the mirror in the hall. In the mirror I saw myself, naked, skinny and whatever and him, a blond giant with his Cupido cock between his legs. "Look at yourself," he said, "your tits are hanging there like little tents, your tits are like crumpled Kleenex!" I said nothing. Because his father was in his grave. He was lying there instead of sitting perched on a fat branch waiting for songbirds and a hefty wild boar. If my papa were lying in a cold grave I could've pulled him over in front of the mirror, and pinched his little cock between my thumb and finger and said, "Look, look, a nubbin of chewing gum." But, my father wasn't a corpse dressed in hunting garb in a dark grave, whose head a gentleman had mistaken for a boar's head. These are the thoughts that were crumpling in my mind. I looked at my little sacks, and said, "That's from nursing." "Don't put the responsibility on the child," he was angry, "that's not fair, do something about yourself." He patted me on the neck, "You'll feel better," then he let me go. I went into the bathroom to wash off the sperm that was oozing down my legs, in the bathroom I threw up bile and Coke, I spent a significant portion of my life in the bathroom retching, and then I … Bang … baaaaaaaang!!

Jesus, he'll break the door down. "OK," I say in a normal voice. "I'm coming out," I say in an even more normal voice. I dry off my body, wrap it in a thick bathrobe. I retch one last time, sop up around my mouth with a sheet of toilet paper, I don't brush my teeth. He's in the hallway, his eyes are lighter. "Why were you banging on the door?" I ask in the voice of an intelligent, mature, adult woman. I'm pleased at the smell coming from my mouth, around my lips there are traces of bile and coffee. I start moving toward the kitchen, he's quicker. I turn into the living room. I sink onto the sofa, he into the armchair. A cigarette, hands, pinch, pinch, lick, lick, flame, burn. On the glass tabletop his cup is full, mine's empty. I say nothing, look out the window. The neighbor's out on her balcony hanging her black coat on the line, airing it out. This winter her husband died. Deep snow, night, the hearse came, she went out to greet them in front of the entrance to her building, she was alone on the white street, they came in, walked out carrying a stretcher and on it a corpse in a black body bag, they covered it with a red blanket. I felt sorry for the woman. Some people love each other, for some people death is a loss, I thought while I watched her through the living-room window, it was about 3:00 a.m. I wasn't sleepy, I never feel like sleeping. A few days later I saw her in town. She was shouting in the middle of the square, baring her white teeth, and in her hands, clothed in black gloves, she held a paper bag, from it she was plucking little pastries and stuffing them between her bright red lips. Ugh! When I saw her,

I felt, I mean I really felt a sharp tug of jealousy! When will I walk around in widow's weeds on the big squares in town and laugh like a crazy lady?! When will I pull a red blanket up over a black body bag! I must go out and buy a red blanket! I have no red blanket! All my blankets are pitiful and pale brown! Am I the only one who wants to cover her husband with a red blanket? Did this merry widow's husband die because she so hotly wanted him to or was the man seriously ill? How many women the world over want to see their husbands in the state of rigor mortis? This is a delicate question. I'm a journalist and still I wouldn't dare stop women on the street and ask them, "Excuse me, just a moment, ma'am, we're running a survey, would you like your husband to stiffen once and for all, this is an anonymous survey, you may answer with no fear . . ."

I look at the moist cigarette and big hands and Adam's apple, up, down, up down. What a handsome corpse he'd make! Handsome, yes, handsome. He'd lie there in his oaken coffin with a white satin lining and would look healthier and younger, strapping, in a dark suit, anthracite-gray perhaps. Canali. I know how it goes, my nonna died. You wait in the anteroom, then the lady comes out and you give her the clothing for the deceased. Beyond the door through which she goes out there's another door, and in there is another lady. She dresses the deceased and then he's laid in the coffin, probably by men. So I'd hand the first lady a big bag with my husband's new Magli shoes, without the shoebox. The words "Bruno Magli" would be on the big paper bag. It'd hold a suit, underwear, shirt, socks, a tie. Socks, undershirt, boxers by Calvin Klein, all that's unnecessary, heaven only knows, will the lady use them when she dresses him? It'd be better to take it all home to her husband. Who's going to check and see what one's late husband is wearing under his suit? Only the widow has the right to do that, the widow, that's me, and I don't care whether he's naked under the suit or his little prick's being warmed by his CK boxers. But no, no, no way, you can't tell the lady who opens the door, right there in front of everybody, there are other people waiting, you can't say to her, "Use the suit and the shoes, keep the rest for yourself, ma'am."

I look at him, we're sitting in the living room. His legs are crossed, his legs twitch slightly. I'd buy him shoes three sizes smaller. Instead of forty-five, forty-two. There's no lady who'd accept the Bruno Magli bag and then, after an hour, call the widow, "Ma'am, my condolences, forgive me for bothering, but the shoes are too small for the gentleman." No one would ever do that! People today in Croatia are dropping like flies, it's all the war and the stress, the corpses are being dressed in their suits on an assembly line. The ladies who receive the sacks and bags know these are trying moments, the widow is disoriented, the family friend in Trieste made a mistake. The lady couldn't know that I personally selected shoes in Trieste for my husband's corpse. This isn't done. If it were done there'd be many a late husband wearing shoes three sizes too small. The lady would simply say to the men arranging the corpse in the coffin, let's go, gents, it is what it is, break his toes! Yes!

Again he lights a cigarette, there's a purple cyclamen in a green vase on the balcony. The church. You can hear the bells. Ding, dong, ding, dong, dong, ding, dong sadly toll the bells. I don't go to church, I have no idea what a church looks like when somebody dies, but what does that have to do with anything? My husband inhales the smoke and doesn't realize the bell tolls for him. I'm in church. White flowers hang in oh such large clusters. No, that's when there's a wedding. White is innocence, this is death. Dark purple flowers cascade down in big clusters from the high walls. A wisteria bough hangs down over the wooden benches ... No! Wisteria is a tree, you can't pull up a hundred-year old tree for the needs of **one single** funeral. I'm pulling it up! The wisteria hangs like a thick, dolorous, purple willow. A sad, oh so sad girl in a thin white dress, skinny, plays Beethoven at the organ. I adore Beethoven and Franci Blašković. No, at a funeral Blašković's *Mens sana, mens sana in malvazija istrijana* wouldn't do. In one of the Beethoven symphonies you can hear the melody that's also in the children's song, "The Bunny and the Stream." "Deep in a winter's evening, there where a steep hill rose, a little stream froze over all covered by the snow, an itty bitty bunny searched everywhere for the stream, where had it gone away to now his little heart beseeched, the little bunny cried and cried so very sad was he … tra la la la la la la …" Me in the first row. On me oh such dark widow's weeds. A hat, dark glasses, black shoes, and black undies. So my cunt mourns, too. He's up on the bier, his toes broken in the too-small shoes. The organ intones sadly, and the little bunny cries and cries so very sad is he … "I'm talking to you," he says. I come back to the living room, I look at him, hastily I strip off my widow's weeds. What did he say, what did he say? He's pinching, licking. Three convulsed cigarettes are lying in the ashtray. "My head hurts, I can't follow you, my head is pounding, that's always how it is, the first day, tomorrow, once it gets going I'll feel much better, the day before I'm always tense, the first day all I need is one pad, today there are only a few drops on the pad, my head is pounding, tomorrow, once it starts I'll stay in bed for the day, I won't go to work, they can do without me, I'll feel better, the second day my head doesn't ache as much, I'll have to change ten pads, the third day is great. I'm worried that my periods are lasting longer and happening more frequently, I should go see my gynecologist, maybe this is some sort of hormonal problem or an early stage of menopause. Oprah said that menopause begins, it can begin as early as thirty-five, I …" "Don't talk shit!" he's angry. He hates it when I talk about my periods, he's disgusted by excretions, I'm careful not to talk of it. I was careful. Today I decided, I won't be careful about what I say, I'll be free, I won't be scared. I feel good, really good, the nape of my neck isn't icy, I'm not scratching myself, I'm not picking the scabs off my scalp, usually I'm bleeding there. I look at him. Who is he? He's just some gentleman who's smoking and sitting, he'll get up and go, he needs a little time, a little more, a little more. The cigarette is burning down. "Goodbye, ma'am." "Goodbye, sir, it was a pleasure, don't come again." I get up. "Where are you going?" "I'm going to the kitchen, I'd like a drink of water." "I'll bring you water." "It's in the kitchen." "Do you want a pill?" he asks. "No," I answer. Mistake! "Your head doesn't ache anymore?" he asks. The fox! I see I've fucked up. I said I had a headache but I don't need a pill?! Why was I so careless? My thoughts were wandering like a riderless horse?! I mustn't dismount from the horse and let it graze in the grass on someone else's meadow! Come over here, you nag! With menstrual pain this is the voice of a woman who often reads *Household Doctor* and *Vita*, this is my voice, the Caffetin isn't helping. I toss a lasso over the nag's slender neck, come here, you wild creature! When I have my period, the first day, this is cunning, so cunning, why didn't I think of this before . . . When I get my period the first day it's best if I lie down. When I relax, when I lie down in a dark room ... Yes! Yes! Just the ticket! Maybe I'll dare drag this body into a cool room, lie down, close my eyes and pretend I'm in painful sleep ... He's at the door of the living room with a glass of water in hand. "Sit, drink the water, you'll lie down later, you'll feel better once you drink the water, sit!" Oh! The helium-filled balloon in the shape of a lovely Father Christmas deflates up in the clear blue sky and tumbles down all over me, covering me with its plastic tatters. Oof, and oof! He's in the armchair again. I'm again on the sofa. I drink

the water, stare at the edge of the glass, I can't see, I feel him rolling the cigarette, licking it, lighting it. But the darkened room,
the cold compresses on my head, darkness, darkness, darkness
… Until he leaves. Then get up, turn on the CD player, listen to
Franci and chop parsley, chop, chop, chop … "What's wrong,
talk to me, you're different somehow." I want to tell him, old
man, I've had it with you, I'd rather you didn't walk down my
street, this isn't the Middle Ages or any other age in which you're
the boss of the galley ship and I pull the long oars and chant,
ever since they've shackled me to the deck … Put down the whip!
Take off the manacles! Ha! Ha! "Why are you smirking, what's
so funny?" he asks. What could be funny? What could be funny?!
What could be funny??!! I drag in our daughter, she's sometimes
funny. I say, "Eka once popped a rock into her mouth …" "You're
lying!!" He's very upset. I'm not looking at him, but I feel him.
I'm looking at the cyclamen. "You're dragging the child into this
as your alibi!" I turn my gaze, his gray eyes are no longer gray,
they're light, they mustn't get even lighter, that might be dangerous! I'm a crazy cow, hysterical, too scrawny, irrational, lazy,
disorganized, insecure, I have skin-thin breasts, my thighs wob-
ble, I don't exercise enough, I don't exercise at all, I read stupid
women's magazines and *Household Doctor* and *Vita*, I didn't weep
at his father's grave, I'm not a good mother, our daughter doesn't
speak English well, she made a mistake at the recital at her music
school, everyone laughed at her, I cuddle my daughter, I drool
over her, I'm always looking for her and calling her, I'm jealous
and crazy, once I called the police when he hit me, as if he weren't
a judge but some drunken dockworker, he wouldn't have hit me
if I hadn't aggravated him, so change and everything will be fine,
go to a shrink, I don't cook well, I don't eat, I don't fuck with
passion, I fake my orgasms, I don't orgasm the way I'm supposed
to, I'm frigid, stupid, I think he doesn't see any of it but he sees

everything, I went off to work as a journalist because I enjoy the spotlight, tell us, sir, for our radio audience, do you have regular bowel movements, sir, tell our radio listeners, he sees everything, he's not stupid like the other morons whose wives turn them into dishrags, I'm a crazy, crazy, crazy, oh so crazy cow! He looks at me. I tell him, "I'm healthy, I'm in a good mood, the day is lovely, why don't you go out for a walk? I'm sitting here, why am I on the bench, in which film are you playing, you're not in court, I'm not accused of anything, I'm not on trial, I'm your wife." I speak with a rising voice. "Why are you sitting, half-dressed, on the sofa, it's noon, it's almost noon, you haven't cooked anything, you're showing me your sagging tits, and you're talking on and on about how, and at what intervals, blood drips from your cunt. If this is healthy, what's sick like?!" "Why does it upset you to talk about periods?" I ask. "This isn't a conversation about menstruation," he says, "don't change the subject, this is a conversation about you." I look into his light eyes, the cigarette is burning. "Why are we talking about me?" "Because you're the mother of my daughter, because you're my wife, because I don't want my child to have to go to visit her mother at a lunatic asylum once a month. I want a healthy wife, a healthy mother, that's why we're talking about you," his voice was under control, the voice of a teacher who's well paid for tutoring the retarded son of rich parents. "So, why are we talking just about me, parsing my mistakes. You're healthy? You're free of sin? You won't end up in a straitjacket? You're not the only father whose child will be visiting him once a month?! The women you're always fucking and who are forever calling me and then hanging up, these are the babes of a healthy man? Your yelling and questioning are sane? That you beat me, that's sane? Just because your father beat your mother his whole life doesn't mean you watched the right movie! Man, you're in the wrong movie, in the wrong role, step off the screen! You're talking to someone else! Today I changed. That's right, today! Today! I've had it up to here, I've had it with your fucking, your little prick, your attendance at seminars, your return home at five in the morning, the ironing of your shirts, the listening to the woman who comes to do the ironing, your revolting Uomo Roma fragrance! Man, you make me retch! I don't feel like letting your little prick into my cunt anymore, or my mouth, or my hand! Can't you see that? Why don't you go off with one of your sluts and leave me in peace?! Fuck off once and for all!" My voice was rising too high, I was talking too fast, I was looking him right in the eye, I was breathless. This wasn't a good performance. I should've spoken slower and softer, smiled now and then, looked out at the cyclamen or those women's heads in the windows of the concrete building across from us. He looked at me, surprised, and with approval. "I love it when you fight," he said, "I love women fighters." "I thought you loved me," my voice was better, more secure, deeper, brighter, this was the first I'd heard about women fighters. "I've never thought that the bond between a woman and a man is combat. If you love **women**, am I allowed to love **men**? Men who aren't analysts, shrinks, investigators, judges, know-it-alls, big fuckers with small pricks?! Might I be allowed to venture out and catch boys like that?! Would that be a sign of health or serious illness?" "There were sluts in your family," he said and grinned. Nasty. One should never tell the hero in one's life stories from one's child-hood. But today I'm not whiny, weepy, snotty-nosed, I who could hardly wait for the curtain to drop, then race to the cloak-room, cover my ears so I wouldn't hear the catcalls of the angry audience! Not me today! Today I'm a great actress, the greatest! The performance is nearly over, it's just the two of us on stage. "List all the sluts in my family," I say icily. You could hear a fly buzz in the theater. "Why should I list them," says my partner, "you know your sluts better than I do." "There are no sluts in my family," I tell my partner, "but, if you insist, I'll mention the slut in your family." He looks at me in a way he's never looked at me before, with huge interest. "Say it," he says cheerily, "say her name." The nape of my neck goes cold, I feel a compulsion to scratch, scratch, to pick at the scabs that have formed over my wounds. I steady one hand with the other. I won't allow my nails to rampage! His sister fucks with as many people as she can manage, the whole city knows that. She fucks with whomever she desires. That certainly doesn't mean she's a slut, I'm fond of her, she sells ferry tickets and beds any traveler who strikes her fancy. The ferry often sets sail for Split missing a gentleman on board who'd paid for a cabin and transport for his car. I love his sister, she has two little girls, a son, and a husband, and it doesn't bother me that the woman fucks around with whomever she can and whenever she can. I'd be lying if I were to say she's a slut. She's no slut. She just doesn't give a fuck for what other people think. A genuine life is marching along, not giving a fuck for what other people think … Still I say, "Your sister's a slut." I watched one of our long-jumpers. She sprinted, pushed off, flew, landed on her feet. How far she jumped, god only knows. Maybe she broke a world record, maybe she didn't. They showed her jump, later, in slow motion. I don't like sports. Athletes are hunks of meat who slide on boards, run after a ball or smash a ball with a racket. Hunks of meat and heaps of muscles that reach their destination a hundredth of a second faster than other hunks of meat and heaps of muscles. But I love the slow-motion shots. Still I didn't see him slowly get up from the armchair, come over to me on the sofa, lean over, whack me on the face with the upper side of his left hand. I feel blood in my mouth. I'd be lying if I were to say I saw stars, I saw not a one. I got up, went into Eka's room, locked the door. On the wall was a mirror in a green frame, she picked it out at an Indian shop. My chin was bloody. I took her black T-shirt, kids today are constantly in mourning, I wipe away the blood. Maybe I bit my tongue, or something broke in my mouth? I move my lips left, right, run my tongue over my teeth, wiggle my tongue and poke it into the wound on the inside of my lower lip. I'm standing by the window. I can pull back the dark-blue linen curtain, there are yellow suns shining all over it, we bought it at Ikea in Vienna. I can pull back the curtain, stick my head out the window and shout, ayoooooooy, people! ayooooooy! Old Irma would certainly hear me, she lives in the little house across from our building. I can shout and say to myself, who gives a fuck what people will think about a battered journalist and a gentleman judge. I don't stick my head out the window. I care what people will say, that's at the core of my being. I feel a terrible need to be the way I think others think I should be. And something else. I'm mulling over the feeling that he's right. He wouldn't have beaten me up if I hadn't said, "Your father deserves to be fucked by a dog." He wouldn't have hit me if I hadn't said, your sister's a slut. He wouldn't have punched me if I'd ironed his shirts, he wouldn't have lashed out if he hadn't been under stress, he wouldn't have battered me to keep me quiet if I'd been better behaved. So whenever he beats me I feel like crying. I feel guilty for having turned him into such an animal. He always says, if you were normal you wouldn't cry. Don't cry, change! Change! I'm not asking much, just change! Always, whenever he beats me, I do look, it's not that I don't, I really look for a way to change, how to be better or at least different. But recently, yes, lately I've been snapping. I'm tired. Bam! Bam! Bam! The door to the child's room and the wall built of porous concrete blocks is rocking. He's forgetting that we sold the apart-ment, we have permission to live here for another six months and then we're moving into our new home. If he knocks down the wall we'll have to pay for the damage. I lean against the wall to prop it up. I feel him kicking with his loafers, the door is flimsy, will it hold? I look at Nela Vlašić's dark-yellow house, she's my favorite painter. Bam! Bam! Bam! I step aside, if he knocks the door down I'll be crushed beneath it. I stand by the window, the door rattles, he's gone mad. I'm not afraid, he'll get over it. I'll unlock the door, I won't laugh or smile, laughter and smiling drive him wild. I pull off my panties and the pad, we'll fuck, then he'll relax. I look at the door, I'm calm, I'm always calm when I have a plan. My greatest problem is that I don't know what I want. Whenever he questions me I want to tell him, you have no right to pound on doors that I, too, paid for, you have no right to beat me, I've had enough of this parsing of my sins, you were away from the house for years, why did you suddenly decide to be home all the time and watch me breathe, go back to your sluts, I hate you, I hate you, I hate you! There, when thoughts like that come bounding into my mind I scream though only on the inside. I feel like crying, I pound my fists on the wall, I wail and weep and sob. Then he pauses, hugs me, "Calm down," he says, he wipes away my tears and the blood around my mouth, "It'll pass, you're my sweet little boy …" he licks my tears, licks my blood, carries me to bed and fucks me. He comes noisily, fast, "Did you come?" he asks. I pause, as if I'm catching my breath, as if I'm returning to myself, or to him, or us, or the room, because—I was somewhere else. I say nothing, hug his neck, nuzzle my head into the dip by his shoulder blade and I think, "Maybe this is someone else. He's not pounding any-more!" I look at the door. There's a splintering sound. He's trying, with some sort of tool, to pop it out of the doorframe. I wipe away the blood. "Leave the door alone," I say. No answer. Jesus, Jesus, how long will I be in this movie?! For another twenty years he'll be going to court, I to the radio, he with his colleagues to a café, me with mine to another, I at the microphone, or at a press conference, or on live broadcasts, I'll go to parent-teacher meetings, together we'll attend her graduation, our daughter's wedding, we'll become a grandfather and grandmother, he'll go off to seminars three times a year. Will I be alive only while he's away at seminars? What if they stop holding them?! If the minister decides, enough jerking off, gentlemen, you have a million unresolved cases, let's get to work! I won't be able to write the minister a letter, "Dear sir, you've got to be kidding, your seminars are my life, don't abolish the seminars!" I've heard that the minister batters his wife, everything's known, this is a small town, this is too small a country. Maybe the old jerk-off wants to abolish the seminars because his wife's wounds are healing too fast? While the old guy jerks off on Hvar or Rab, her wounds scab over. Fuck a wound that's covered by a thick crust, down with the seminars! Men, men, men! Louts, louts, louts! Fucking judges! Fucking fishermen! Fucking ministers! Fucking sincere intellectuals! Fucking anti-war fighters! Fucking warriors! Fucking peacemakers! Fucking publishers! The door is quiet. I breathe deeply and more slowly, then even more slowly, then normally. The door is quiet, I wait. From the wall, above the computer, the brown glass eyes of a badger look at me. He was sure I'd have a son. For him, the future hunter, he'd killed the badger. The badger's head is small, is it a baby badger? It's fitting that the head of a baby be mounted on the wall of a child's room. I've read that taxidermists use powerful poisons to turn the raw head into a charming ornament for the homes of hunters. This poison forever after leeches out, poisoning the hunters, their crazy wives and their young, but slowly, oh so slowly. He opened the door. We look at each other. He grabs me by the neck, pulls me out into the little hallway, I try to get into the bedroom, his sturdy thigh is like a wall, together we swerve into the living room. He pushes me into the middle of the room, locks the door. I sit on the sofa, he in the armchair. He pinches a cigarette, licks it, taps it on the edge of the glass tabletop, lights it, he looks at me, his eyes are very light, very, very light, that place on the nape of my neck goes cold, I scratch the place, scratch, scratch. I'm no longer what I was a minute before. The white T-shirt is still, the jeans are still, the shoes are motionless, he's waiting, he stubs out the cigarette, he only just lit it, why is he stubbing it out, what's happening, he's lighting a new one?! Jesus, Jesus! He licks it, pinches it, this should be the other way around, first the pinching, then the licking, why is he so furious, he lights the cigarette, stubs it out, looks at me, pulls out another one. "Hey," I said, I don't know whose voice is speaking, this is the first time I've heard this voice, I can't recognize it, "if you take out one more cigarette, if you lick, pinch, lick and pinch, I'll throw up, I haven't eaten at all today." "Shut up," he looks at me, snaps the unlit cigarette, pulls out a new one, looks at me. "Puke," he says, "puke!" I feel ice, there, and ice. I scratch myself, my stomach rises, but I already retched, there's no more bile or coffee left inside me. I burp loudly, nearly retch, like a decrepit old lion. "What's going on with you?" his voice is quiet, "you don't love me anymore, you want to leave?" "Yes," I say, "I want to leave, I want to die, I want to disappear," somehow I'm losing control again. "Drop the sob story," he says, "drop the death talk, life is beautiful. Where would you go? With whom? You're hoping a prince will ride by and sweep you upon his fat horseback, you, this puking, anorexic princess who farts, stinks, whimpers and burps? You believe there are any princes like that?" "Why do you think what I need is a prince?" my hands are back in my lap, one hand steadying the other, I tighten my fingers. "I've had it up to here with princes," my voice is stronger. "Why wouldn't I live alone? There's such a thing as a princess with no prince," I unlace my hands and fingers, wiggle my fingers in the air, fake sudden cheer. "You? Alone? You can't live alone, you'd kill yourself alone. You need a master and a whip, you're a creature that can only find your true direction with the whip ..." "You're sick," I yell. Why am I yelling? For the first time in my life I'm talking with him and yelling? What's come over me? "You goddamn mother-fucker, sit right where you are," that's my voice. I jump over to the open window. "If you touch me, you ape, I'll yell until a million people come running! Nothing will help you, the police or your one hundred ten kilos! I'll scream, I'll call the city paper, I'll tell everyone what a sick bastard you are!" "Calm down," he says. He's sitting, smoking, watching me, his eyes are darker now. "Stub out the cigarette or I'll turn on the siren!" He stubs the cigarette out. Ha! Well, well! Brilliant! "Coffee?" he offers me his cup. "I mustn't drink cold coffee, you've said so a hundred times, you mustn't drink cold coffee! Remember how you flung a whole cup of cold coffee all over my new blouse, for my health, you bastard?! You threw my whole dinner in my face once, too, remember that, bastard?! Why am I always so damn meticulous? Why am I so precise when I say you threw my dinner in my face **once**?! So does 'once' mean just this side of 'never?' Could 'once' actually mean the same as 'never once?' Why am I thinking of once as **just** once? How many times have I thrown your dinner in your face? Whom am I telling that you did that **just once**?! Is it me I'm telling? Or am I telling you? I'm always grasping at excuses for you, you bastard! You pompous, stinking, icy creep! I've had it with you! Let me tell you something! Learn how to fuck! And don't believe everything they say in the advice columns!" "What are you talking about?" he looks at me with his gray eyes. I'm standing by the sill to the open window and yelling. "Don't touch the cigarette, leave it!" He puts the cigarette back into the pack. "What are you talking about?" he says, "You aren't well." "I'm telling you, don't go reading those advice columns, they're for **women**! You're a man, a man and a half, why do you read advice columns meant for women? Fucking women?!" He said nothing. He was waiting. "You read this piece about how there's a G-spot in women's cunts! You're constantly rooting around in me, looking for my G-spot! You look for it with the sensitivity of a crewless tank taking aim at a target. Fuck the G-spot, you rotten seeker! Burrow, burrow! 'Where's your G-spot? Am I it?! Is this it?! Is it here?! Did you come?! Did I find it?! Tell me I found it! Tell me, tell me,' I'll tell you," I drop my voice and look him in the eye, "I'll break it to you, you never found it. Never did! Never did find my G-spot! If it was in there somewhere, it eluded you! I don't come! You don't arouse me! Because of you I lost my G-spot! You goddamn motherfucker! You apprentice!" I'm feeling pretty good while I'm yelling like this by the open window. I see heads I haven't seen before on the windowsills of the neighboring buildings. He sees them, too. The amphitheater is slowly filling. "I'll tell you something," I say more softly, "I'm dumping you, I'm done, I'd rather take a bullet to the brain than have to look at your mug for the next twenty years! Beat me up or let me go!" On the windowsills of the neighboring building viewers were clamoring for tickets. "Who's stopping you," his eyes were lighter. He sees the people at the windows. "No one'll beat you up, I'm not your papa, your papa stomped on your mama." Never tell your dream hero stories from your childhood. The window is open, my voice carries, why not take advantage of this here and now? "My papa stomped on my mama **once**, your papa **was always** stomping on yours! Your papa on his wedding night fucked a woman from the wedding party in a stable by the church! Your mama saw her eyes under her husband's back! It's wise to listen to other people's life stories. Your father was an imbecile, an old ape who fucked with your mother's head the way you fuck with me! She was saved from him by poor visibility at dusk and the man's bad eyesight! Why don't you go out at twilight and hunt for boar! Save me, too!" "Let the dead be," he says. "Why?" I ask, "are the dead innocent because they're rotting deep down in pits? The dead disappear, they putrefy, worms eat them, but the bodies of the living remember, wounds are left on the living bodies, marks, scars!" "You got your period," he says, "you're bleeding down your leg." Yes. Fine. So what? I can stand here a little longer. I can jump out the window? I can yell and call for help? I'm bleeding. What's the point of all this? Why am I scared? So upset? He can smack me, smash me, beat me up, kill me. I don't care. I strip off the terrycloth bathrobe, wad it into a big sanitary pad and stuff it between my legs. I'm Lady Godiva without the long hair, on a fat, terrycloth horse. "Now that you've started your period, maybe you'll be able to talk in a normal tone." Vicious. I say nothing. He goes over to the door, unlocks it, opens it, and with a slight bow, shows me that my path is unobstructed. "Aren't you going to the bathroom?" he asks. "No," I say. "I am," that's his voice. I see his tight, lofty ass go out into the hallway, then into the small hallway, and then disappear. I'm riding, bowlegged, on my white horse. I'm feeling pretty good, relaxed, hungry. I don't want to go into the kitchen. I can't hold my sanitary pad with both hands and look for chocolate. I could put down the bathrobe, and stuff fifty paper napkins between my legs, I'd be more ambulatory that way, the ones that are white with the little red checks, or are they red with white checks? Ha! The Croatian national colors! Sick. Stuff the Croatian national colors between my legs?! I mustn't clothe my cunt in the national coat-of-arms! This is against the law! There's a Law about the Coat-of-Arms, Anthem and the Presidential Sash. If you buck up against all that you can get into big trouble. Might you be sent to jail?! Ha! The

courtroom! Everyone rises. The judge reads. A judgment in the
name of the Republic of Croatia. The judge's wife, guilty because
on such and such a day at such and such a time in apartment
number five, fourth floor, Homeland War St., with the intent of
defacing the coat-of-arms of the Republic of Croatia, has committed a crime as defined by Article such and such. She's hereby
sentenced to a prison term of … This silly short film has bright-
ened my spirits. I feel great. Am I an animal after all? Physiology,
biology, nothing else going on inside me? Blood and water? Why
am I vicious before I get my period? Is it PMS? If I were constantly menstruating I'd be more relaxed, my life wouldn't be
divided into before, after, and during. What time is it? I was
mean. There are many, so many women in the world better than
I am. Women who are better than I am get up at 4:00 a.m., they
go to market centers, sit at a cash register or go to a clothing factory. All day long they sew the same sleeve, the bathrooms at the
plant are flooded, they work Sundays and Saturdays and at night.
They never see Italians, though they know they're out there,
somewhere far away. Salaries minuscule. These good women have
small children, they have no vacations, no weekends. Good
women, better than I, have a university degree yet work for two
thousand kunas, under the table, while garbage men are paid
three thousand. Some of them come into classrooms every day
and in just one day see one hundred fifty nasty, foul monkeys.
They carry their children off to day-care centers, these children
are greeted by poorly paid teachers, if they can be called teachers,
they don't have enough diapers for all the bare bottoms, the
children go home with sores between their legs, the mothers salve
the sores with expensive creams. Many women don't dare use
their sick leave, they cook in the evening for the next morning,
iron, console their husbands who can't find any work anywhere.
They tell them everything'll be fine, all that matters is we're alive

and well. These women, better than I am, climb into bed at 3:00 a.m., their husbands aren't sleeping, Croatian men are generally well rested, and then, these women who are better than I am, fuck quickly. Some men don't like a quick fuck, they're in no rush, they're on a permanent vacation and they fuck their weary wives slowly. I'm a happy, ungrateful woman. My husband's a judge, judges are well paid, it'll be no problem for us to pay off the mortgage on the new house, I work on the radio, radio staff don't kill themselves with work. A little music, an ad, a little blah blah blah blah, on the air, how are you, can you hear me, hello, hello. A judge isn't a well-rested man, he doesn't burrow much, he'll be burrowing less and less, he's under stress, he's tormented at work by various worries. Why is that young judge always drunk? How did the journalists find out that the lady youth judge took a bribe from parents whose kid killed an old codger on a crosswalk? That very skinny judge has hundreds of unfinished cases in her drawers! The journalists praise to the stars one of the young judges, but his decisions aren't **his**, they're the decisions of the **chamber**?! Fucking reporters, dunderheads, if you were to draw it on paper for them they still wouldn't get it! Who told them that the new misdemeanors judge is gay? Why is that news? This is a democratic country, if gays have the right to marry they have the right to adjudicate! During a break from a hearing, rape of a juvenile girl, the tall, burly judge said, "That tasty little piece should be licked!" Who's telling tales?! Fucking, fucking reporters! I ought to be happy. I'm sitting on this terrycloth horse, bowlegged, my thighs ache, I'm bleeding, I look around me brightly. We're moving from this concrete hole, we'll no longer live in an apartment that looks exactly like every other apartment in the building and all the neighboring buildings. Tell me where you live, I'll tell you who you are. When we move into the house we'll be different than we were. We'll live as we deserve to live. My husband will advance, the country court, and then higher and further, maybe he'll become a government minister. It's all the fault of the concrete, the two bedrooms and the living room, a seventy-square-meter trap. It's the concrete that makes him aggressive. He's a hunter, he loves wide open spaces, the woods, meadows, fresh air, the sky, birds, thick branches, tree-tops. In the new house we'll have three terraces, a cat, a dog, a garden, a fig tree, two cedars, a grill, a camelia, a magnolia, we'll have guests over, we'll throw parties, they'll take pictures of our house for women's magazines. "And now if you'd show us the bathroom, ma'am. Take a picture of that toilet, Patrick, it's wild. Do you have any eccentric lamps in the house, maybe, we could take a pictrue of a lamp, that'd be enough detail for your house to look fantastic on our pages. Here's the lamp! Brilliant! Gorgeous!" "Tiffany's, from Split," that's my voice explaining to the photographer and journalist what sort of lamp it is. My life will no longer mean elbowing through the row of unemployed men in their undershirts, drinking beer at the entrance to our building from bottles they bought at the kiosk. I'm not the masses, I'm not just anybody, I'm me, unique in the world, unique in the universe, I'm me! He slinked out with his tail between his legs! He realized that I'm me, from today, **me**! He's still not calling me by name, he still speaks down to me, this won't last long. He'll use my name! Elated, I sit perched on the bathrobe-sanitary pad, behind me is my first victory, ahead of me is the war I'll win! Life is for the bold! Never, never, never until today did my husband tuck his tail between his legs in his war with me! Today, for the first time! Now I've learned. Yell! Keep the window open! Fight for my life, it's life or death! A person has to know what he wants! Fiercely with my husband, my folks, the editor, my daughter, the women who do the iron-ing, the workers who are building the house! Fiercely, fiercely!

People are animals like any other. They need a blow to the ribs, a knee to the balls, a whip to the neck! Yes, yes, and yes again! I'm hungry, my legs ache, I pull them together, put my feet on the terrycloth horse's white head, giddy-up, giddy-up, I'm feeling brilliant! What's he doing in that bathroom? If I don't have to give him head after all this, today will be pure joy, not a cloud in the blue sky. There's a book with that title. Are the workers at the building site? They should be. They should make use of every sunny day, the lazy stinkers!

It's aggravating, once a week, to go to the building site of one's own house. He didn't go, buying the house was my idea. We have a supervisor whom we pay to oversee the creeps at work. I'm not satisfied with him, I'm certain that the people who are doing the contracting pay him not to supervise. Who can believe anyone, these days, in Croatia? One thief after another! He's invariably courteous. "Hello, ma'am, what a pleasure to see you." As if he's surprised, as if it isn't Tuesday, the day I always come. He greets me full of fake reverence, extends his hand, watch your step, ma'am, the boards are full of nails. He behaves as if he's afraid of me, not I of him. I'm scared of workers, I know nothing about construction. Someone said to me, be careful, the terrace must be laid at a slant! If they don't lay the gradient properly, whenever it rains the water will pool on the terrace. You'll have a lake at your living-room door. The test is simple, when they lay the tiles, pour water on them, if the water drains away, fine, if it stays, then screw their Bosnian or Albanian or whatever mother. I poured water onto the tiles. It turned into a big, shallow puddle. Forty light-brown Italian ceramic square meters glistened. The supervisor praised him. Ma'am, Milorad is top notch, in Germany he installed tiles for twenty years. I stood in front of the puddle on Liberation Day or Establishment Day or whatever day it was. I deliberately tried this out at the construction site when there was nobody around. I didn't want to insult their downtrodden pride. When I saw the water shimmering and pooling, I flew into a rage. I called the supervisor. He'd turned off his cell phone, he was celebrating the great defeat or great victory. Milorad, who, he told me, had been a physics teacher … Wait, wait! How could he teach physics, lose his job ten years back, and then install tiles for **twenty** years in Germany?! Pigs! Liars! What could I do? Talk to the supervisor, have the supervisor talk to the owner of the company that was contracting the work, have the owner of the company talk with every subcontractor individually. To cut this sad story short. Only the subcontractor could fuck the mother of the unregistered Serbs, Albanians, Bosnians, and Milorad, the fucking schoolteacher who hadn't, in fact, been laying tiles for twenty years in Germany. The former teachers, former marine engineers, former judges and prosecutors and police chiefs, Serbs, former chairs of the Board of Revenue and future doctors, dentists, archeologists, businessmen, all former and future stroll around Croatian building sites and wreak havoc. Finally the day was over, which commemorated what happened ten years ago, when we were established, or won, or lost, or the Pope sent us a letter, we're a Catholic country, the Pope is our god. I came to the construction site the next morning, with no warning, it wasn't a Tuesday. I'd taken two Valiums, two mgs each. Milorad, the tall, skinny creep, watched me rudely as I came over, bucket in hand. I poured out the water onto the terrace and splashed his feet. "Look," I said. "I see," he said, "I didn't glue down the tiles permanently, I can unglue them, I'll fix it." "Sir," I said, "I'm not paying you to pull up tiles." They watched us, they stood around us instead of building the dividing walls, roofing, whatever. There was the smell of rain in the air. "I'm paying you to put down tiles," I said. My voice didn't quaver, it was neither too high nor too low, I made an effort to appear to be a civilized, controlled person who's beside herself with anger. "Why are you so pompous," I said, "you stand there like some government minister." "If I were a government minister I'd live in a house like this, I wouldn't be on my hands and knees slaving on terraces." Well well, the creep had the mouth of a politician, and the attitude of a tile-layer. "What do you mean, 'I'd live in a house like this,' this is a modest house," I said. Why did the little shit think our house was a palace? Hey, I'm from a working man's family! My father was a fisherman, a creature at the dregs of society. He toiled all the livelong day, he **worked**. He has probably fifty years of active working life. He shoveled, hoed, trawled heavy nets! Slaved! He earned like any slave, enough not to croak, too little for a decent life. I've been watching workers for years. I despise workers from the bottom of my heart, their silence, their resignation, their weakness when something needs to be changed in their lives but their great strength when they knock the heads off their wives or daughters. Workers disgust me, they disgust, oh so disgust me, I don't pity them! They watch their boss out of the corner of their eye, spry like an animal, from one day to the next, and they think it has to be that way. I ban this creep from laying the tiles I paid for at the wrong angle! He tells me he can unglue the tiles at any time?! And still he has the balls to look me in the eye?! What is this, what the fuck is this?! I was furious. My father looked only me and my mother in the eye! In front of everyone else his eyes fled into a mouse hole and there, in the dark, alone, they blinked. This Milorad was looking at me as if I were his **wife**?! My father did whatever his boss said. He was a gardener, not a professional fisherman, the fishing was in his spare time to keep starvation at bay. If need be, and there often was a need, he'd plant and dig up, plant and dig up, ten times a day, fifty times a day, for **a single** cypress! For **one** cypress he'd dig thirty holes and keep his mouth shut! And he'd never look the boss in the eye and ask, "Why so many holes for just one measly cypress?" What is this today?! "Listen," I said, "I'm paying you, obviously in the vain hope that you'll do your job properly. You can't pull up forty square meters of tiles without breaking a single one. Who's going to pay for my trip to Trieste, who'll pay for my time, who'll pay for the tiles I paid one hundred fifty euros a square meter for?!" I was lying, I paid twenty-five euros a square meter for them, but so what? The forlorn, horse-like muzzle looked down at me from above. The six Albanian guys, who'd been paid to roof, weren't roofing, they were sitting up there, watching us. The Bosnian guy, paid to lay the sewage pipes and link the pipes in the house to the waste pipe in the yard, stood and stared, his hands hanging by his scrawny frame, he was barefoot. A kid of fifteen, a snotty-nosed, straw-haired lout, paid to **chisel** shallow drainage canal into the wall, wasn't **chiseling**, he watched us, agape. Bosnian guys, stripped to the waist and soaking wet—the air was oppressively humid—weren't digging at the stone beneath the future living-room floor with their picks. The living room had to be excavated because the ceilings of the old house had been low-hung. They weren't digging, they were resting. They held their picks and watched me with their evil eyes and bare bodies. Oof! That instant I understand the problem of today's world. On one side, me, a lady who bought an old house in the most expensive part of town, a lady whose husband would soon become the minister of justice. On the other, the Albanians, Bosnians, dead-end intellectuals, and juveniles going in a bad direction were united! Oof! Some have a pick in hand, others have bare hands to strangle me, but they won't, the third have only their gaze with which to kill me, but they won't. I gave up. I'm the winner here, the winner should be gracious. I won't fire him. I felt good. I am Power, I am up, they are down. I, almost at the top, they, always at the bottom. They burrow and burrow and burrow and burrow, they'll be rooting about their whole lives yet they'll never unearth anything. My father didn't unearth anything either, if it weren't for his Italian pension he'd have died like a dog by the side of the road, by the cypresses he himself planted in forty-five holes. The three days he spent in the Italian army have helped him more than the fifty years he spent digging holes and trawling nets. My husband saved me. Who knows what would have become of me if I hadn't found a husband like him. If I hadn't found my husband I wouldn't have a house like this, my salary is a pittance but he has a big salary, as a minister he'll have an enormous salary, in this part of the city there are no drug dealers or fixers. "Fine, sir," I said to Horse Head, "I'll have a word with your supervisor." I walked toward the garden. I wanted to vent my fury far from this stricken, nasty crew. It was terribly hot, sickeningly humid. I felt the daggers of their eyes, they didn't budge from the spot, they watched and waited. For what? I smelled a hideous stench. I was walking around the future garden, which was a temporary storage area for construction material. That's what I thought until it hit me that I was stepping on a carpet woven of their feces. I'd sunk into it up to my ankles. This happened because I'd forgotten to keep in mind that the slaves had to shit somewhere. With my shit-caked feet I stepped onto the terrace, which was, fortunately, a puddle, and walked through the future front gate.

He's still in the bathroom. Is he jerking off? Brilliant, terrific, he won't plague my poor little mouth. Maybe he drowned or the hair dryer dropped into the tub? I didn't hear a hair dryer. He'd probably taken a shit, wiped himself, crouched over the bidet and was washing his ass with warm water and soap, drying it and wiping it with my Nivea wipes for sensitive and dry skin, I use them to strip off my make-up. Or he's wiping himself with one of the baby wipes. My husband takes care of his ass the way the municipal authorities care for a world heritage site. He needs hours to preen. Then he offers me his body in bed. Under his arms, Lancôme Bocage, on his face, aftershave, Bulgari, on his body, baby lotion, on his ass, baby oil, I never know who's fucking me, above the waist a man, strong, pungent musk, below the waist, a baby. Sterile, totally. I spread my legs, now I'm perched on the bloody terrycloth pile. I'm in a grand mood. It's all biology after all. He'll come out and plant his sterilized body in our room. I'll go into the bathroom, a tampon up my cunt, panties, and into the bedroom. My husband will stand by the bed. On your knees! On the wall-to-wall carpet! The smell of urine, several years old, will sting. Eka, when she was little, used to wet her bed in her sleep. I'll give him a blow job. It could last several minutes, no longer, he'll climb into the bed, inhale deeply, exhale, within three seconds he'll be sleeping the sleep of a weary horse. His head thrown back, his mouth open wide, his big white teeth showing. The perfect moment! From the mound of parsley I'll take the big knife and plunge it into his neck where that vein thrums. No, I won't! I'll chop the parsley until the mound is tiny. When he wakes we'll go to the restaurant by the market for a pljeskavica with cheese. My husband's always in a good mood when he comes, almost always. We'll come home, I'll blow him again, men can come ten times a day if they don't have to wiggle their prick. I'll take two Valiums, fall asleep. And so it is for days, for months, for years and for weeks. Wait, the weeks should come after the days. Doesn't matter, I'll blow him forever! I'm perched on the bloody pile of terrycloth and I don't want to think about that. If wives who are sick of their husbands spent their lives obsessing only about that, the world would be made of women who are sad, oh so sad. But life isn't just about one's husband. Life is a new house or apartment, occasionally a lover, a slightly better job, a passing grade on your daughter's transcript, a son who plays "Frere Jacques" and "Row, Row, Row Your Boat" on his guitar, a purse, shoes, a new Dior perfume, a blood test that shows the cancer is in remission, the death of rich parents, unexpected, the death from natural causes of a young husband. If you want life to mess with you, if you obsess over analyses and meaning, life will mess with you. If you catch on, at some point you must catch on, that the story about happiness is merely a manipulation by well-paid psychiatrists, psychologists and the authors of manuals like *How to Take Your First Step and Touch the Stars*, everything'll get easier. There's no happiness, least of all for two, so what's the point of the analyses, long conversations, the need to explain things to someone. No one listens to anyone. He'll never understand what I'm saying. It's already huge if I can see that he can't see. I can't leave. I'm scared. Now and then I'll yell to make sure I'm still alive. He'll yell more. I'll get a smack on the head, he'll break my arm or leg, we'll spend our life in a war to the very verge of extinction. I'll have to ward off the self-pity, the nasty thoughts that other people are happier, the false insight that the struggle means something, the need to change him, the hope he'll change on his own, my efforts to prove to him that it's not my fault. I'll have to keep my mouth shut more, shut, shut, shut. He'll never go too far. No point in overstepping, who wants a victim who doesn't move, but lies there, dead and bloody, between the legs of the victor. What a waste. A hero needs a living victim. Even a cat doesn't toy with a dead mouse. The mouse may be savaged, its guts hanging loose, one eye in the middle of the kitchen floor, a tail behind the counter, but, as long as it can still move it's interesting to the cat. When the mouse goes motionless once and for all, the cat pads off, yawning, and bares its sharp little teeth to all and sundry. He's the cat, I, the mouse. This game doesn't always end the same way, who says that every mouse must end up as a motionless, gray, dead little body between bloody, feline claws? Who says?! I must wait. I decide, I'll wait. I'm resilient, I'll wait. I wait for the bathroom door to open, for the showered cat to step out, for us to continue our game. Differently. The mouse has the advantage now, all the pieces on the board are under my control. Ha! He comes out of the bathroom, shuts the door, steps into the little hallway, then the larger one, enters the living room, smiles. The green bathrobe with dark red stripes, wet hair, pink whiskerless cheeks, the belt isn't pulled tight, you can see his bare body, flat, smooth, hairless chest, small prick, long, very hairy legs. I sniff the Uomo Roma, he's pulling out all the stops. He wants to be dashing. I rise with my bloody mound, I hop toward the bathroom. "I'm waiting for you in the bedroom," he says. "Nice," I say. I'm in the bathroom. Hot water is running. Maybe I'll shower, maybe I'll bathe. There are only two little cupboards mounted on the wall. "No shelves," said my husband, "I don't like it that everyone can stare at our intimate things." "No one'll stare at our intimate things," I said quickly, "who comes to visit? Shelves are nice, they break up the monotony, having only cupboards ..." "They break up the monotony," he said. "Why do you think it's stimulating to see your curlers full of hairs of all lengths, packets of sanitary pads of all weights, the grim little towelettes you used to strip your make-up, who knows when, the floss dangling from its little container, toilet wipes in the bidet you use to wipe your ass with a yellow stain in the middle, bloodstained pads next to our toothbrushes? Who'd find that thrilling, how can one break up any sort of monotony with these?" This isn't the whole truth and nothing but the truth. He knew perfectly well that I wipe my ass with toilet paper because I'm allergic to nearly all the cleansing wipes. My husband hides his traces. When you come into the bathroom after him you won't find discarded boxers on the lid of the laundry basket. There are no undershirts on the wet floor that might serve me as foot wipes, nor does he leave behind his socks. His jeans aren't hanging on the towel rack. I get undressed and into the bathtub, blood dribbles down my leg. I check my breasts, I often check my breasts. I don't know whether I want or don't want to find something. I check and check and check. Nothing. My tits are sagging little sacks, so there's nothing to find. Even cancer won't sprout in these sagging little sacks. Yes, I'm no knockout. But there are times when I experience myself as something more than just tits, belly, stretch marks, thighs, wrinkles, dry skin. I'm not always just a bedraggled female, or even a **female**. I do always think of my crotch as my ID, that I'm someone's **sister** and a member of one half of mankind. I'm female, you're female, we're sisters, we're the same. Dear sisters, I'd never attend your summit. I gaze into the foggy mirror. The fact that I have a cunt says nothing about me. Do without me, dear sisters, I'm not one of you! I gaze into the mirror and speak aloud to the vast gathering of woman? Hmmm?! I'd never consent to go under the knife. To stop my tits from sagging, if that's even possible. The fuss about beauty is a fuss manufactured by the media, cosmetics producers, aesthetic butchers, fags who sell women theories of what they should look like even though they fuck only men. And we buy it. Ladies, why are we such fools?! The mirror is fogged with steam so I can't see the hundreds of thousands of women who are listening to me. Why would some old man with trembling hands remove the bags under my eyes with a laser when he doesn't care a whit about the bags under his own watery eyes? Aesthetic surgeons build villas with swimming pools on the mounds of our pumped-up tits, liposuctioned thighs, and eye lifts. And then in their villas they fuck boys and girls who are the same age as our daughters?! Ladies, listen. You can hear a butterfly fluttering in the air of the vast hall. The women gaze at me. You butchers, editors of women's magazines, producers of wonder creams, gay fashion designers, all the creeps are trying to persuade us that it's a disgrace to be forty?! The audience is barely breathing. I don't need to raise my voice, I'm speaking at a normal volume, the microphones are powerful. My tits need to be puffed up to a D-cup size? Who says so? Why are we tits, cunt, ass, eyes, hands, fingernails, thighs, shins, ankles, hair, teeth, lips?! Men aren't the sum of their wobbling double chins, wrinkled necks, sagging asses, flaccid muscles, toothless grins, milky eyes, bad breath, loose teeth, droopy eyelids, balding pates, hairy ears, hairy nostrils, bushy eyebrows, bulging hard stomachs, flabby bellies, wobbly breasts, yellowed toe nails, knobby knees, pimply backs, hairy asses, gray pubic hair, ruptured capillaries on their nose, fungus between the toes, soft little dangling pricks?! They're none of these things! Men are spirit, reason, charm, mind?! Dear sisters, let's wriggle our asses, chase their spirit into their little pricks, then snap them off, spit them out, take a long drink of water and rinse out our mouths! Powerful applause, the spotlights dim, I step down.

"And when, precisely, did you notice, ma'am, that your spouse no longer interested you," the psychologist asked me. He found him. I didn't know what to say. I'd forgotten. "And when did this 'lack of desire' manifest itself? How could you fail to desire your husband?" The psychologist glanced at the clock on the wall above me. The door to the office was lined in pale-yellow leather. We couldn't hear the voices of the patients waiting in the narrow waiting room. They waited, they had appointments for a certain time slot?! This was the most expensive psychotherapist, as he called himself, in town. You had to know someone to sit in his office and answer his questions. My husband leaned on all his connections and secured me a slot on Thursdays. "I never desired my husband, ever," I said. "When he goes on a trip I don't desire him to come home, when he does come home

I desire him to take another trip, when he leaves the house I desire him to be run over by a truck, to be killed in a car crash, to be killed by a stray mafia bullet, to be felled by a stroke in a game of basketball. That's how I don't desire my husband," I said. "I don't desire him by day, by night, in the morning, in the afternoon, when the sun is at its zenith. I'm disgusted by his smell and taste. When I hear his voice, the nape of my neck, at the place where my neck connects to my back, goes all icy. I'm scared of him. I'm horrified when his eyes go all light, horror sweeps me when his eyes go white ..." "Explain that a little to me, **go white, go light**, said the psychotherapist. "His eyes go white," I said. "He has gray eyes but when he's angry at me they go light. Always, before he hits me, they go light, then white ..." "Your husband hits you? Tell me about that." "Sometimes," I said, "sometimes." "Tell me more about that, ma'am." "I no longer like the way he smells." "The way he smells?" said the psychotherapist. "Can you be a little more precise?" "When we met," I said, "he smelled as if he were . . . fresh. For a long time I could recognize him by his smell. Today, in a full bus, if I were on the back seat and he up by the driver ..." "You take the bus?" asked the psychotherapist. "No," I said, "but if we did take the bus, he and I, if we were on a bus at the same time and my eyes were covered with a handkerchief, if all I could do was smell, sniff, sniff, and if someone were to say to me, sniff, come on, sniff, find your husband, I wouldn't be able to. But fifteen years ago I could have." "How does he smell today?" said the psychotherapist. "He has no smell," I said, "he sprays Lancôme Bocage under his arms, a deodorant that kills all smell. Perhaps he does smell when he doesn't use that ... the Lancôme Bocage," I said, "Lancôme Bocage." "Yes," said the psychotherapist. "Then," I said, "without the creme, he smells sort of sour." "Sour," said the psychotherapist, "well that's a smell. If he smells sour at least that means he smells, he smells different, but he does smell, but you said ..." "OK," I said, "he smells different." "You probably meant to say," the psychotherapist struggled, his blue eyes squinted, he was chewing gum, angrily, intently, "ma'am, surely it seems to you that your husband, today, is a different person." "Yes," I said, "yes, he's different, yes, yes, different," I nodded my head quickly up, down. "You're troubled because you no longer know who your husband is? Fresh or sour? Why are you laughing?" "Fresh, sour," I said. I was relaxed, my hands were in my lap. "It's funny the way you talk about my husband." "You're the one who called him that, ma'am. It'd seem to me, perhaps I'm wrong, that you went slightly overboard with all this attention to the sense of smell. We people aren't dogs, our sense of smell is diminishing, for the most part. It may be that when you got to know him he smelled just as he does today. Food, as you know, has an impact on body odor. If a person eats garlic, his sweat will smell different from the sweat of someone who ate an unsprayed apple. Odor changes, no one smells the same all day long, I say, your husband probably smelled as he smells today, before ..." "In other words, I'm wrong?" my voice rose and moving my hands from lap, I gestured. "I'm sick of all this guilt," I raised my voice, "In other words my husband was just as full of shit fifteen years ago," I yelled, "but I didn't care to see it then," I screamed, "and today when I see he's full of shit as he always was," I groaned, "now I'm whining about it, saying things and seeking sympathy," I hissed. "But all this is just my confusion, I'm guilty, guilty, guilllllltyyyy ..." I sobbed and clawed at the nape of my neck, my fingernails had their hands full. "Quiet," said the psychotherapist, "this isn't a courtroom, we're not talking about guilt, calm down." "Maybe I am guilty," I sniffled, my nose was running, I couldn't find a tissue, "but you must be patient. I'm paying you well, my husband's paying you well, you shouldn't be blaming me, everyone blames me," my tone rose, "I want help, I don't want to hear the truth about myself," my tone rose, "I'm blind, I can't distinguish smells, I can't live with my choices, I don't want to hear the truth about myself," my tone rose, I was rooting around on my blood-smeared neck, I can't keep my voice down," I howled, "I raise my voice," I screamed, "I howl," I howled, "instead of speaking in a normal voice, instead of saying things softly, with the voice of a lady who's paying three hundred forty kunas an hour to a psychotherapist who's chewing gum, don't chew gum, sir! Not while you're speaking with me! It's vulgar! Respect my money if you can't respect me!" I took a deep breath, pulled my fingernails out of my skin, steadied my bloody fingers with my other hand and shrank into the armchair. The psychotherapist took out his chewing gum and dropped it into an empty ashtray, "See you on Thursday, ma'am."

I'm still in the bathroom. A strange woman is looking at me from the mirror. The left side of her lower lip is swollen. How will I give him a blow job with a mouth like this? Ugh! My eyes are full of tears. My self-pity has overflowed. One minute you're up, the next you're down?! I looked at the lip hanging fatly to one side. Why is this a tragedy? The swelling will subside, the wound will heal, my teeth are all there, I don't have cancer, we're building a house, my child is healthy, this is how people see me from the side. My greatest problem is that I don't make use of their lateral vantage point. Depression is crushing me. Depression is worst for us people who have both arms and legs and have no cancer. This is a nasty feeling. Sometimes when I'd be sitting in the kitchen and staring through the closed glass balcony door and watching the women's heads in the windows of the neighboring building, Eka would come over, she'd hug my shoulders and sniff my hair. Mmmmm. I felt as if she'd read me. This eight-year-old is more resilient and mature than I am. I'm crying in the bathroom, scared that the other side will swell up, too. I'll look like a white black woman with pinkeye. Why am I always guiltstricken? When I come back from the building site, with the voice of a culprit I tell my husband, "The workers still haven't finished roofing." Or I howl, with the voice of a crazy woman, "I don't give a fuck, I'm not the supervisor, no one's paying me to tell the Albanians what to do, I'm an easy target, it's much easier, so much easier, than going yourself to the building site and manhandling the supervisor, the Albanians and the Bosnians and the intellectuals ..." And then my husband says, "This was your idea, just your idea, darling. Learn to grab life by the horns. Life means dealing with problems, not just howling and bursting into tears." Whenever he says that to me I'm in tears, streams gush from my fat eyes. Then he strokes my hair as if I'm a wounded cat or a dying bitch. "Calm down, you snotty cow, you're a grown woman, don't go acting a helpless chit of a girl, do something to make your life nicer." Then I wish I could disappear, I'd like to plunge a big knife into my little tits. I get out of the tub, towel off, arrange a nighttime sanitary pad, pull up my panties, I found them in the cupboard, I smear lotion over my body, brush my teeth, my wound is still bleeding, it smarts, I jabbed myself right in the cut with my toothbrush, I spit out saliva and water and blood, rub lip salve onto my lips so they're ready. Ha! I can barely open my mouth, my lips are getting fatter by the minute. Could it be some sort of allergy? What if my throat swells, what if I choke to death on his prick? I'll be the first ... I laugh. Hahaha! To myself. My saliva slides down my chin. Liquid the color of coral. He calls me. Ready? He's waiting for me in the little hallway. Through the flimsy door I hear his breath. "Just a minute," I say out loud. I pad my feet around on his wet, white T-shirt after retrieving it from the laundry basket. I use the T-shirt to wipe the floor, it's full of our hairs, I toss it in the laundry basket, open the door, step out into the little hallway. I'm barefoot, I'm standing on tiles in my panties at the door to our bedroom. He's lying on our bed, which is covered by a colorful bedspread that only looks as if it were sewn of many different patches of colorful cloth. The room window is open, the curtains drawn, linen, yellow with blue suns, we bought them in Vienna, at Ikea. "Come," says my husband, "come, my love." I look at him, I didn't take a Valium, not even one, and two would be better, I can't go back to the bathroom, I can't say, "Just a minute while I go take some Valium." Actually why wouldn't I go back? It'll take two seconds, two seconds there, two seconds back? I visibly adjust the pad between my legs, as if it were chafing, although there's no chance, today's pads fit so snugly that you feel better with them than without them. Men don't know that. I tweak at the nighttime pad and say, "Sorry, just a minute, sorry." I take a step back, again I'm in the bathroom.

I look in the mirror, my lips are getting bigger and bigger?! Why?! I take two Valiums, 5 mgs, and a Claritin so I don't choke to death, if this is an allergy, this thing that's happening to my lips. I drink a glass of water. And another. And another. I'm really thirsty. And another. I need to pee, so I pee. I inspect the color of my urine. Dark urine means cancer, mine's clear, I see light-yellow water and a trace of blood, great. I wipe myself off, wash, put on a new pad, wrap the old one in toilet paper, throw it in the tin trash can, pull on my panties, take a paper towel, wipe the floor of the bathroom, let it be clean and dry. The towel is filthy brown and covered in hairs, we're shedding, we really are shedding, I toss the brown wad into the toilet bowl, wipe the mirror with a paper towel, let it gleam … I don't pick up the comb and I don't peel the hairs off the curlers. I should. I'd do that with such pleasure but I can't tell my husband, listen, wait half an hour for me to peel off these hairs. And besides, hand on heart, why wouldn't two people who live together be frank with each other? How great would that be, to be able to come out of the bathroom, go into the bedroom, lie down next to my husband and tell him, "Honey, I'm in the mood right now to peel the hairs off the curlers, this minute that's exactly what I feel like doing, I'm going to peel the hairs off the curlers." "Go ahead, darling," my husband would say. Is there a husband who'd understand a woman who, between his prick and hairy curlers, chooses the curlers? Nevertheless I clean a curler. It's big, green, I use it for my bangs. I peel off the hairs. I drop them into the toilet and the curler into a wire basket. I smear cream on my face. Did I already do this? Yes, the hair on my neck is damp, I dry it with the violet-colored hair dryer. In the mirror I see how crooked my fat lips are. Is this a smile? Old lady, come on, old lady, come on, old lady, come on, old lady, come on, old lady. Come on!!! So out I come.

I step into the small hallway, I look into our bedroom. He's not there. I smell coffee. Coffee??!! I go over to the kitchen door. He's waiting for the water to come to a boil. He won't put his little prick into my bloody mouth?! God almighty, this was all a misunderstanding?! All he wanted was to have a cup of coffee, get dressed and go out into the fresh air?! Why didn't he say so? Men don't talk?! I say nothing. We say nothing. My mouth doesn't want his prick, his prick doesn't want my mouth! Why are we saying nothing?!! Who's fucking with whom here?!! Why don't I ask, hey, husband, who's fucking with whom here? Would he understand the question? Can two people spend their life together fucking without words? What kind of a life is that? How long can it last? A whole life? I'll spend another thirty years looking at a prick that doesn't interest me? Is this my life sentence? Who'll pronounce the verdict? What's the crime? Am I the only woman? Why does no one speak of this if I'm not the only one? Where are books about this? Novels, articles, studies, congresses, round tables?! Is this not a topic the world over? Isn't this a story?! Women keep silent. And I keep silent. I am silent, I watch the coffee brew and I think, I'll be swallowing his sperm till death do us part! This isn't a nice feeling. A person doesn't feel a warm glow around the heart when facing this. But am I a person? Am I a being who has the right to a choice? To swallow or not to swallow till death do us part?

The coffee's done. He pours it into **one** cup?! "Let's sit down in the living room," he says, "we'll talk about everything." Why didn't he pour me coffee too?! Why didn't he pour me coffee?!! We go into the living room. The blinds are down. Why? The windows are closed. Why? The curtains are drawn. Why?! Why??!! "Let's sit," he says. We sit. I on the sofa. He in the armchair. He takes a cigarette out of the pack, licks it, pinches. it. Licks it first?! Then pinches it?! Why? Why?! He lights it. He looks up at me. I see! I see!! His eyes are **white**??!! Two little egg whites staring at me??!! "Oh," I say and jump up onto my feet! He, too, jumps! His fist knocks my head back! I wake up. My head is wet, my hands are bound with white strips. And my feet at the ankles. He tore up a sheet. I'm slung over the arm of the armchair. I see him sideways, my head is pounding. He's naked! He's holding a belt! Brown, leather, broad, long, silver studs! "You cow!" he says, "you'd yell! You won't fuck me! I'm not your radio audience, hello, hello, can you hear me?! I'm not impressed with your charm! You can't pretend with me, I know you!" "Let me go," I whisper, probably with my voice. "You slut," he says, "calm down, slut! I won't become your rag," and with his right hand he caresses the leather belt. He's left-handed. "You won't ruin my life!" "No," I groan. "Don't," I say. "Let me go. I didn't do anything," I whisper. "I'll be good, please. Please," I say. I cry. "Please, I'm praying to you as if you're god, I'll be good, I'll be the best

in the world, I'm not a slut, I'm not a slut, I love …" "Wait," he
says. He slips a CD into the player. Dandandan, dandandandan,
dandandandan. Beethoven's fifth. The whole apartment shakes.
He strikes me on my back. My kidneys! My neck! My shins.
Dandandandan! Dandandandan! On my head, my back, my kid-
neys Dandan dan! Dandandan! I yell. Heeeeelllp. Dandandan!
Dandandan! On my back! My head! The buckle on my neck! The
buckle on my neck! The buckle on my neck! The buckle on my
neck! Dandandandan! My neck! My neck! Danananadan! I yell.
Uuuuuuuuu! My neck! My head! Dananananandan! My head!
Dandandandandan! My head! My neck! Danananadan! I scream!
Noonnaaaa! Nonnaaaaaa! Nonaaaaa! Dandandan! Dandandand!
"Mamaaaaaa!!!" I look, sideways. Eka is standing in the living-
room doorway.

Oof! Your honors! Your horrors! You'll say, OK, ma'am, we
understand. You killed him in a moment of passion, you got
up off the floor, you went into the bedroom, you took a pistol
from a drawer and shot him several times in the head. OK, calm
down, ma'am, let's go over this slowly. Little Eka screamed …"
"Yes, Eka screamed. I was draped limply over the armchair, he
freed my hands and feet, I slipped to the floor, I'd peed myself.
He turned off the CD player, tightened the belt on his bathrobe,
went into the bedroom, got dressed and went out. I was shivering, naked, on the floor and looking at Eka, she was crouching
in the hallway, her eyes like saucers. She was looking somewhere
and nowhere, trembling. I dragged myself to the bathroom,
pulled on his bathrobe, the dark green one with the red stripes,
terrycloth, Svilanit, and went over to Eka, took her by the hand,
we went into the kitchen, I sat on a chair, Eka sat in my lap. We
were quiet and quiet, we were quiet and quiet. Those women's
heads, the ones on the window sills of the building across the

way were still there. Women's heads are always in the windows of concrete buildings. They stared at us, we stared at them.

My husband and I, we're still at the edge of the big meadow. The doe is grazing, the fawns are hopping about and prancing. I need to pee! What a feeling?! It'd be an unheard-of impudence to toss my rifle, drop my pants and panties, spread my legs, and release the yellow stream into the grass! He'd beat me up right then and there! We were waiting for a wild animal. It had to appear! The leaves were rustling, shshshshshsh, shshshshsh. With the edge of my hand I touched the damp grass. **Damp** grass! Everything was russssssssssstling! Around me it was all **damp** and **wet** … The first drop? The second? A stream! A cascade! I was peeing!! I squeezed my legs tight but the torrent swept away the dam! I was peeing … Peeing … Bam! The world collapsed! The gun on my shoulder went off. The animals vanished. I squinted, my pants were soaked, I was peaceful, half-dead, guilty, terrified, horrified, frozen, convulsed, broken, crazy, soaked, damp, my mouth filled with spit, I clenched my teeth, my hands were wet, the nape of my neck was burning, there was drumming in my ears, I steadied my fingers in my other hand, my nails were headed for the dry scabs on my scalp … I made all that noise! All that noise! He'll kill me! He'll kill me! **He'll kill** me! I lay there and lay there, as quiet as a rotting corpse. He got up and went over to the middle of the meadow. "Good job, come here," his voice was full of a strange joy. I stood up. My thighs were wet and my pants. I could say it was from the wet grass, why didn't I think of that before? What a cow! I went over to him, cheerfully, soaked with pee, relaxed, happy. "All done for today!" His voice rang out, my body hopped joyfully. I reached him. He was smiling, patted me on the shoulder, took my hand in his, kissed it, looked me in the eye. My knees buckled. My icy, pee-wet pants chilled my hot thighs. "You're my Amazon," he said. Eek, if he only knew the truth he wouldn't be saying, "You're my Amazon," Amazons don't wet their pants, they slice off their right tit so it doesn't interfere when they draw back their bow, they cripple men, fuck with them once a year so that they can have children ... Me? An Amazon? This was a little much, I looked down. And saw the dead doe. It's brown eye, small, round, the red wound on the slender neck, the half-opened muzzle, the tiny protruding tongue, the little teeth. "Splendid!" he said, "You're a hunter!" I felt no compassion for the dead mother of two fawns. Joy erupted in my mind! True fireworks! I'd discovered how, forever, to capture my man! I found the person in me he needed! I'd be a woman hunter! What did the late doe have to resent me for? Had she had her buck? Yes, otherwise she wouldn't be out grazing with the two fawns! How had she snared him? She'd used cunning, dirty tricks. The decent does were slumbering quietly while she was off in the deep woods, wagging her lusty hindquarters. Some does are sluts about which zoology hasn't had the last word! And I! I needed my male specimen! If the only way I can snare him is over the corpse of a four-legged critter, surely I won't, because of this, weigh myself down with a guilty conscience! The doe would have shot me for the love of her four-legged mate! All of us are the same, us females! "Oh," I said and touched the dead body with the toe of my shoe, "a good feeling! I've been waiting for this moment for fifteen years!" That's what I said. My voice rang out. **My** voice rang out! "We'll put the doe on the roof of the car, we'll drive through the village, let people see what I caught," I pranced around the dearly departed. "No can do," he said, his eyes were dark gray, "this is closed season, you killed it for just us, for you and for me." He turned around, went over to a bush, with his hunting knife he whittled a long, thick stick. Good god, my stomach shrank. He peeled away a little of the green bark, pulled out a big pen, and on the peeled side of the stick wrote, a roe deer, Brdina, the date. He handed me the stick, "Keep it, and next time you kill something we'll peel off a little more, until you fill in the whole stick, and then I'll cut you another …" "Thank you," I said. In our apartment we had his two sticks and his father's six. The death notices for the animals killed were arranged by date, and their heads were mounted on the walls. I'd joined the club. I held the stick, looked at it and looked around. I waited. It was time to go. Between my feet was my knapsack. He leaned over to it, opened it, pulled out a bottle of mineral water … No! No! I wasn't ready! No! He wanted to fuck me! To pull his prick out of his shorts and pants, rinse it off with Radenska and fuck me right next to the dead doe?! Holy shit! No!! He set down the bottle and stepped toward me. "No," I said, louder than necessary, almost shrieked! "What's wrong?" "I'm too excited," I said quickly, somehow I was a little breathless, "this is a big day for me, you don't understand …" "I understand," he smiled with his eyes, "I know you've heard a hundred times how I killed my first deer …" I knew the story by heart. But, go ahead, tell it Scheherazade! Go for it, blah blah blah blah blah blah blah … Papa and I went into the woods, we crept and crept and crept, then stopped, a doe was grazing, I took aim and hit her in the eye, "Bravo!" my papa said to me, "you'll come to something yet," then Papa took his flask out of an inside pocket on his hunting jacket and at the age of fifteen I had my first swig of alcohol …" I looked at his lips moving. The head of the deer on our apartment wall, her brown eyes, glass, she had lashes, you could see her little teeth and tongue. She looked alive, even though she had only a head. "I sipped, Papa laughed, my eyes stung, it was plum brandy …" When he finished I dropped to my knees and opened my mouth. While I was sucking him, I thought back, a person has to have something to think about while sucking a

prick in the middle of a vast meadow, to how much I had enjoyed
reading *Lady Chatterley*. I was a little girl, the fucking in the wet
woods aroused me. I was the lady, but the fucker in my dreams
was never a driver! No! The drivers of my childhood were fat,
vulgar, they smoked while they drove the bus that I took to high
school and they were always shouting, "Step back from the middle door!" In the summer their blue shirts were dank under the
arms and there was always a little salt along the edge of the stain.
Jesus! Wet woods, me, naked, running because I have to run
from the fucker, there's no point in giving in to him right away,
men like a race. So I run, but I can't run forever, so finally he
grabs me, with one hand he lifts me, with the other he tears from
his stocky white body his light-blue shirt with the Jugobus logo,
the salty rings. No, I wasn't a lady of that type! In my girlhood
dreams the fucker had the body of the Lady's chauffeur, but he
was no driver. I never thought much of ordinary laborers, dock-
workers, truck and bus drivers. For me workers weren't kindly
human beings ... No, no, not at all, they weren't the heroes of
my life! If I were a lady I'd never let a lumberjack fuck me! Never!
Maybe young ladies dream they'd fuck a lumberjack when they
grew up, I know nothing about the dreams of young ladies, lumberjacks are my specialty. Yes, the dead doe lies there, he stands,
his legs akimbo, his thick hunter's pants and boxers down around
his ankles, I kneel, dressed in hunters' garb, I haven't taken off
my jacket, I suck, suck, I really suck! When I was young I
thought men were either stinky lumberjacks or lawyers who
washed five times a day, and in the woods they rinsed their prick
each time with a different beverage. Tea. Coca-Cola, Whisky.
Grappa. Chamomile tea. Mineral water. So I sucked away, I held
him in my hand and with sharp movements I slid the foreskin
on his prick up, down, up, down, with my left hand. The birds
shrieked, my knees chafed, my lips hurt, I was hungry, my neck

went stiff, he, probably, groaned, I couldn't hear him. Finally, hallelujah, there was mineral water mixed with sperm, and he screamed … You wouldn't believe it?! He screamed … Can you believe it?! For the first time in his life he, while he came, screamed … Your honors! He screamed, "Tildaaaa …" See? He screamed "Tildaaaaa …" And Tilda? Tilda, that's my name. My name's Tilda. I'm Tilda. Never, never had he ever used my name for me. Never! And then I killed a doe and he screamed Tilda?! Strange are the ways of men! I got up and brushed off my knees. He did up his fly. "I'll carry it to the car," he said. He heaved the dead deer up around his neck, I carried the whittled stick and his knapsack, and had mine on my back. He walked in front of me. I stumbled, the ground was uneven. Morning had come. I didn't have to tiptoe, tiptoe, tiptoe, tiptoe anymore, nor did I have to place my feet where his had stepped a moment before, but nevertheless I did just that. I looked at his broad shoulders and firm back. He was bowed over under the weight of the dead animal. He walked along in front of me with firm step, the man of my life. I realized how I'd become his one, eternal love. I'd walk through the woods, stand, lie down, take aim, shoot, kill a grazing doe! I'll kill, I'll kill, I'll kill! Watch out for me, you slutty does! We got to the car. He lowered the deer to the ground. From the car he took a big nylon tarp. We can't put her into the trunk like this, she's too big, we'll have to break her legs. I stopped. He bent over. His big, tense back swung in front of me. He took one of the slender legs in his hands. Snap, you could hear it! Snap, you could hear it! Snap, you could hear it! I took my hunting knife out of my belt. Every hunter carries a knife, no hunter goes off on a hunt without one. I kneeled. Swung …

12

"Ma'am, ma'am, ma'am!" That's someone speaking to me. Shaking me. I've gotten down off the billowy horse! I'm dizzy, I feel like puking, I'm nauseous, but I'm no longer up there in the sky! I'm not afloat! I'm not lurching in an ad! I'm not waiting for the Terrible Judgment! I open my eyes. In the distance ... Jesus! Now I'm in a cheap movie?! I'm waking up from a coma. There, far away, in a haze, I see a doctor smiling at me the way doctors always smile in the movies at ladies who wake from the dead. Oh! His face?! He has a black mustache, black hair, dark red lips and white teeth?! I'm in a Mexican soap opera?!! "Ma'am, ma'am," he takes my left hand. I shut my eyes. "If you hear me, squeeze my hand." No way. I won't squeeze his hand until I hear what he has to say. I know how it goes in those romance movies. She squeezes his hand, he says something nice. What if this is a horror movie?! I don't move my fingers. First say something, then I'll squeeze your hand. I'm silent. He says. "Ma'am, there's a gentleman here who'd like to say hello, here he is, at the door." Oh! A gentleman? A gentleman?! A gentleman?!!! If I could speak, I can't, but if I could, I'd say to him, "Mr. Doctor, sir, a gentleman? There are three gentlemen in my life who might be coming to say hello. The first is my husband who survived because I'm not much of a hunter. The second is the investigating judge who'll be coming to examine me, 'Tell us what happened.' The third gentleman is my lover, the only man whose stink I can bear. Which of these three gentlemen is here at the door to my room?" But I can't speak. A tube in my mouth is getting in the way. So I open my eyes and look at the door.

Afterword

Do you come away from this novel with the impression that Vedrana Rudan has had personal experience with the sort of abuse she describes? To this question Rudan brings her characteristic candor. In the blurb for the original Croatian edition of *Love at Last Sight* (Croatian title: *Ljubav na posljednji pogled*, 2003), Rudan zeroes in on her motivation for writing the book: "I felt the need to scrub off, to strip from myself the filthy skin in which I had been walking the world for more than fifty years. I was a victim of violence as a little girl, then as a married woman. The feelings of guilt and misery choked me even as I wrote. There were times when I went out on the terrace, took a deep breath, gasped for air, trembled. That horrifying experience is behind me now. I feel much better. Into the book I wove all my tears and sweat and teeth and skin. But *Love at Last Sight* is not just my story. This novel includes the stories of my friends, acquaintances, neighbors, colleagues. Violence is the favorite pastime of Croatian men."

Love at Last Sight is Vedrana Rudan's second novel, following on her first, *Night* (Croatian title: *Uho, grlo, nož*), published by Dalkey Archive in an English translation by Celia Hawkesworth in 2004. Not only has Rudan come out with another eight books, but she also maintains a regular on-line blog in which she critiques the Croatian government and the country's social mores. Her reputation is built on her suffer-no-fools stridency and her candor is appreciated. As this book goes to press, there are more than 150,000 followers on her official Facebook page and another 15,000 friends on her personal Facebook page. She is widely admired throughout Bosnia and Herzegovina, Croatia, Montenegro, and Serbia, where her books are read in the original Croatian. One or more of her titles have also appeared in Albanian, French, Hungarian, Italian, Macedonian, Polish, and Russian translations.

When asked, in an interview with Ana Lučić, about the peppering of her prose with obscenities as uncharacteristic for the writing associated with women authors, Rudan replied: "I have never thought of myself as a 'woman.' I am a human being who lives in a country in an age that allows the poor only one weapon in their duel with life, and that's swearing. Swearing is the scream of a victim, their only normal way of speech. If they don't swear aloud, they swear inside. There are many people out there who, after they read my book, realized what rage was brewing inside them. I am a loser, I don't have lots of money, I don't have power. But, I have an opportunity to express my rage and not many people have this opportunity. I didn't want to break any rules, I didn't even know that there were rules in literature. And this thing about how some people think only men can swear ...Who fucking cares about them! What's important to me is that the book is being read."

Anger is Rudan's favorite expressive tool and it certainly dominates the emotions developed in *Love at Last Sight*, but there is also an underlying wry humor without which her rants would lose their depth and humanity. As the translator I found that the humor was what sustained the narrative voice through the bouts of fury. Bringing that voice into English was not, for the most part, an insurmountable task. We English-speakers are reasonably well equipped with ways to express vulgarity and righteous indignation.

There is one crucial passage, however, that offered a particular challenge. Dogs are notably lacking in English-language carnal imagery. Ducks, for obvious reasons of rhyme, are better represented, but not dogs. The pivotal quarrel when the narrator's abusive husband says a dog should rape her mother turns on a typical Croatian obscenity that is both completely strange to English and profoundly gender-specific. Many native speakers of Croatian (and Serbian, and Bosnian, and Montenegrin) utter this without stopping to consider just how appalling the visual image is which it evokes, much as is the case with the English 'motherfucker', also often uttered without a thought to the real meaning, and similarly offensive. When her husband offends her with this phrase, the narrator first experiences the Croatian image in its full, disturbing viscerality and then snaps back with the inverse curse. Her retort, suggesting that her husband's recently deceased father should be raped by a dog—coming as it does from a woman and referring to a man—is suddenly far more offensive, as 'fatherfucker' might be in English. Because the image of the dog comes up in subsequent paragraphs there was nothing for it but to retain the Croatian image and phrase it in such a way that the reader has the chance of understanding her repartee as a deliberate slap in the face to her already raging spouse. But more important than the particular choice of wording at this key juncture in the story is being sure that the translation conveys the essential asymmetry underlying the entire novel, the fact that a man can get away with the use of a vile, obscene curse, while when a woman utters much the same curse her choice of words is suddenly untenable.

Rudan's defiance of political correctness, her intent to offend, do their job. Her writing does offend. It's her exploration of feelings and experiences we thought we knew that nudges us to see them differently. This is what makes her books worth reading.

VEDRANA RUDAN was born in Opatia, Croatia. Formerly a journalist, Rudan wrote for a number of years for *Nacional*, Croatia's largest newspaper. She has published nearly a dozen books, including *Uho, grlo, nož* (2002), which was translated into English and published by Dalkey Archive as *Night* in 2004.

ELLEN ELIAS-BURSAC translates fiction and non-fiction from Bosnian, Croatian, and Serbian. Her translation of David Albahari's novel *Götz and Meyer* was given the 2006 ALTA National Translation Award. Her book *Translating Evidence and Interpreting Testimony at a War Crimes Tribunal: Working in a Tug-of-War* was given the Mary Zirin Prize in 2015.